# Gently Love Beckons

### JUNE MASTERS BACHER

**HARVEST HOUSE PUBLISHERS**
Eugene, Oregon 97402

Scripture quotations are taken from the King James Version of the Bible.

**GENTLY LOVE BECKONS**

Copyright © 1989 by Harvest House Publishers, Inc.
Eugene, Oregon 97402

Bacher, June Masters.
　　Gently love beckons / June Masters Bacher.
　　　ISBN 0-89081-738-3
　　　I. Title.　　　　　　　　　　　　　　　　　89-31538
　　PS3552.A257G46　　　1989　　　　　　　　CIP
　　813′.54—dc20　　　　　　　　　　　　　　　AC

*To*
*"Miss Mary Belle"*
*(Garrett, Leonberger)*

*My first teacher*
*and still*
*a "driving force" in my life!*

# Contents

*Behold, I stand at the door and knock; if any man hear my voice, and open the door, I will come in....*

—Revelation 3:20

*Blessed be the Lord God of Israel from everlasting, and to everlasting. Amen, and Amen.*

—Psalm 41:13

# CHAPTER 1

# Needed: A Rainbow

It was a strange day. The rain would pelt down for about an hour. The sun would come out for short periods. Then another bank of dark clouds would roll in, and with it another hour of heavy rain...then sun again. Courtney, in preparing advance copy for *The Territorial Gazette*, probably would refer to the weather as "interesting."

But "interesting" was too vague a word for the misgivings churning inside as she packed a single suitcase for the journey back East. In fact, no single word could put together the emotions she herself did not understand. The weather seemed to be saying it better.

Mrs. Rueben had a few choice words in her native tongue for the freak July storm. Served the housekeeper right, Mandy said with just a shade of malice. "Whur wuz it 'rit in de Good Book dat a body had t'wash come Mondays, rain er shine?" Glowering at the rain puddles and the cloud-dodging sun, Mandy, concentrating on the cake she was beating, had avoided Courtney's eyes and changed her tone to pleading again. "Courtney, hon, won' y'all know de Lawd dun might be speakin'? Hit ain't right, y'know, fer a purty young thang like y'all t'go traipsin' off all by yo'self. Could be a sign—ain't neber been nuttin' lack unto dis. Me'n Him, bof uv us is warnin'—"

The honey-toned voice tapered off. Like the rest of the family, Mandy might as well surrender. Nothing much was apt to change her courageous mistress' schedule—

7

not even her precious lambs so in need of their mother (and her firm hand!). Not even Mr. Clint—and him worrying like he was. The child just hadn't been herself since that strange letter came . . . and here was that pesky rain again . . . a sure sign . . .

Upstairs, Courtney Desmond snapped the suitcase shut with more bravado than she felt. It had been easier when, one by one, she used the art of gentle persuasion on the family—answering their questions as to why she must return to her childhood home with such objectivity that she was most convincing. In fact, all of them were excited now. All except her husband. Clint refused to stand in the way of her trip, but telltale lines of concern creased his forehead as he read her brother's letter over and over as if looking for some hidden clue as to why Courtney should make the trip. After all, Efraim and Roberta were in Washington, D.C. It was only a short journey from the nation's capital to New England. The legislature had managed to stay in session when the Representative and Mrs. Efraim Glamora had visited the spot before. Why not again?

"Because, darling, whatever is left there concerns *me*," Courtney had explained patiently. "You read Efraim's letter."

"Which makes nothing clear. I wish I could go with you—if you insist on this. You're sure it's not a whim—I mean, it was my understanding that Waverly Manor was sold, then burned. What is there left that concerns you?"

Courtney invariably overcame Clint's objections by standing on tiptoe to comb her husband's unruly hair with loving fingers. "That is what I must find out. It is no whim, Clint—you know me better than that. It breaks my heart to leave you—"

The little scene always ended the same: Clint putting his strong arms around her . . . stooping to kiss the part in her hair . . . telling her his words were unfair . . . and (if only he knew) weakening her resolve. How could she leave him? And yet, there was the nagging feeling that she must—even though the demands on Clint's time between the pressures of keeping the newspaper alive until Efraim's term was completed, keeping a watchful eye on the bank in which his brother-in-law owned the controlling shares, managing his own one producing silver mine, and maintaining his carefully-thought-out balance of farmland and timber prevented him from accompanying her. So many decisions to make. And Clint, bless him, went back to the Book of Esther in regard to the wisdom of women in making decisions. Where Efraim and Roberta had resorted to verbal arm-twisting before reaching a decision, she and Clint considered first their commitment to one another. That commitment, Clint said with conviction, embraced understanding—something one did not abandon in time of differences but, like faith, clung to with renewed strength in time of small decisions or great calamity. It worked.

So her husband would need her as well as miss her. This was the year that they must decide the matter of harvesting more timber in order to sow more land with wheat. Clint could look at the sky-scraping fir trees, envision the lumber so much in demand, and calculate the cost of blasting out the stumps with kegs of black powder. And he could envision the monetary returns and needs each board foot would meet. He could look beyond the labor and smell freshly turned earth, virgin soil so rich one could toss a fistful of grain in any direction and then—if one had a mind to—simply sit back in a rocker, fanning oneself and sipping Mandy's cold cider in pleasant interlude, until miraculously surrounded by new gold seas of waving grain.

But how much timber did he want to sacrifice? There were generations to follow, and they had a right to the legacy of Washington State as God created it. If God had intended this new land to be all grain, would He have planted trees? Clint was working hard to get the idea of conservation across to other settlers. There were those who thought housing (or the almighty dollar) was more important than futuristic thinking—downright silly, really. And that brought about another matter the Desmonds must decide.

The two settlements, across the river from one another, were still somewhat disgruntled over the merger which should have united them. Scant choice, they grumbled, about unification—sending a representative to petition the federal government to establish regional self-government and the like. Robbed them of freedom unless, of course, they got decent, broad-minded men as local representatives—kind of a city council for this nameless place. Clint's name had headed the list. The others, Brother Jim said, amounted to a flock of bandy-eyed vultures separated from their skulls. Clint Desmond had no political ambitions, but that was one of the other decisions. . . .

"Whatever is the matter with me, Lord?" Courtney whispered, shoving the suitcase toward the bedroom door with the point of her high-buttoned kid shoe. "It is not as if I were going to be gone forever—only it will seem like it. I guess what I need is a rainbow—"

Yes, it was easier when she had to badger her way into convincing others about the wisdom of this journey. The only one who needed convincing now was herself. One word, even at this late date, and her defenses would crumble. It was not too late to change her mind. Surely she could return the train ticket. But no—with a quivering sigh, Courtney squeezed back the tears. If she broke down and cried, Clint would refuse to let her go. The sky did the weeping for her. And then, as if for a sign, a beautiful rainbow arced across the eastern sky and bracketed the entire valley. . . .

# CHAPTER 2

# The Ache of Farewells

❦

Goodbyes to her family were emotional. When Efraim's letter came, Courtney had felt a sense of adventure. Short-lived, of course, because the idea was ridiculous. Sure, her brother's brief note held a certain intrigue— less from what he wrote than what he omitted. It was unlike him, usually so open while so legal-minded, to communicate with little innuendos. Of course, he knew mysteries had fascinated her when as big brother he piqued little sister's interest with made-up stories which stopped short of an ending. Well, why try to understand? Returning East to see what little remained of their birth-place—which held few happy memories of the past and no promises for the future—was out of the question. But her mind behaved like the weather, so here she was ... chasing an invisible rainbow ... leaving her precious family for the first time. . . .

It was agreed that she would tell the children goodbye at home. Clint would take her to the station, but Court-ney made him promise to leave her before departure time. True, she would feel desolate—even frightened— journeying with strangers into a near-forgotten world. But there must be no tears in her husband's presence. None at all. *None!*

Just why she chose to wear the blue dress with its white collar and cuffs, the dress that—although as good as new—had lain folded in the cedar chest since she wore it for arriving at Mansion-in-the-Wild so many years ago, Courtney would have been unable to explain.

11

A woman of more vanity would have preened before the mirror—perhaps even calling the attention of others to the fact that she was only 16 then and still possessed the same petite figure. But Courtney Glamora Desmond had spent little time concentrating on herself or her appearance. Always her thoughts had been on the needs of others—first her demanding mother, and then her husband and children as well as the extended family: twin brothers, Efraim and Donolar; other members of the household; dear Cousin Bella and her beloved doctor-husband (both gone now, leaving the "household staff" of Mrs. Rueben and Mandy to look after Courtney's needs—except that, with her natural love and concern for others, she often reversed the roles); and neighbors near and far. "Near" would translate to Brother Jim and his bride, "Miss Lizzie." The preacher-teacher pair would look after the little Desmonds when they wore the house-keeper and cook to a frazzle—as they were sure to do while Courtney was away.

Courtney smiled in anticipation of the reports of their antics upon her return, unaware of the lamps the smile lighted in her great, often-sober brown eyes. Unaware, too, of the sheen of her dark hair as she adjusted the burnt-straw poke bonnet to cover the center part where Clint usually planted his kisses. The smile faded and then she replaced the bonnet carefully inside the hatbox in preparation for calling the children to her in the parlor one by one. Together, they would set up howls that would qualify for the paid mourners' bench. Anyway, each was as different as the roses in Donolar's garden, and each must have special care.

"You first, Jordan," Courtney summoned. "You are next in line for the throne."

Jordan, without the smile she had tried to coax, marched in with all the dignity of a boy-king. Even though he was at the awkward stage of adolescence, stumbling over other people's feet because his own seemed attached to ever-lengthening stilts, her sister's son retained a certain beauty of childhood. That angelic look was carried in the Bellevue genes and, in Mother and Vanessa's lives, helped cause their downfall. The golden curls, catching every light in the spectrum, the astonishingly blue eyes, and the Dresden-china skin spoke of royalty, Mother had declared as if her husband's heavier features were a hateful reminder of peasantry. Courtney, in explaining family background and history to the children, carefully avoided mention of such talk. Snobbery was unknown to them, and for that Courtney and Clint were thankful.

Jordan shifted self-consciously from the right foot to the left. "May I sit down, please?"

The boy's formality both pleased and surprised Courtney. "Of course," she replied, suppressing a smile. "How thoughtless of me not to invite you. Are you wondering why I wanted to see you first?"

Jordan studied the toes of his shoes. "So I can take care of Jonda just in case, well, you don't come back—like when *she* went away?"

Courtney was too taken aback to speak for a moment. When words came, they were not at all what she had planned. Gone was her resolve to be stoic. Here was a child who had carried a burden all these years, a child who needed her love and reassurance. How could she be objective? And how could she have missed the signals that he was troubled?

Quickly, she moved over and patted a place on the love seat beside her. "Come here, darling, and let's talk. Surely you know how much I love you. How could you think I would leave you for long?"

"*She* did—" Jordan gulped, his voice breaking like Courtney's heart.

Courtney's arms were around him instantly and all intentions melted into their combined tears. "*She* was your mother, Jordan," Courtney said softly, smoothing the tousled curls and pulling his head against her shoulder. There was no audience so Jordan made no objection.

What *this* mother and he talked about would never go beyond this room, so it was safe to behave like a girl and cry!

"It is best that you remember my sister as a mother who died—"

"She—my mother, my *other* mother—didn't love us!"

"Your mother loved you in her way, Jordan—of that I am sure. But we love you in a very, very different way—a way that will hold us together forever and ever the way God wants families to be. You believe that, don't you? You must tell me that you believe it, else I will cancel the trip. You are far more important—"

"I believe it!" Jordan straightened, wiped his nose with both cuffs, and struggled to regain his dignity. "I want you to go."

"Then you will reassure Jonda if she asks questions or has bad dreams? You see, you are the man of the house when Daddy is away—"

"I know."

The talk was over. Courtney could tell. She must let the emerging man in the child direct him even though she longed to reach out as he bolted toward the door. There he paused and, in answer to Courtney's unspoken prayer, bolted back just as fast to throw his arms about her neck and squeeze hard. "Thank you," he mumbled—either to her or to God. Courtney's heart soared. Whom he was addressing made no difference.

Jonda, a feminine-gender carbon copy of her twin brother, fluttered in like one of Donolar's butterflies. She kissed Courtney affectionately, then twirled about the room to bolster her courage, her cascade of golden curls fanning outward like the full skirt of her blue-checked guimpe. Pausing to adjust the taffeta-ribbon bow which drew back just enough hair at the temples to reveal the achingly beautiful planes of her face that was so like Vanessa's. Jonda's blue eyes met Courtney's brown ones in the mirror. Both of them smiled.

"You look lovely," Courtney said, wondering just how many prayers she had sent up asking God's help in letting the fairy-like creature know that she was beautiful without her becoming vain, immodest, and intoxicated by outward appearance as Mother and Vanessa had done.

Jonda stopped, rosy lips pursed in concentration. "I do? Then why does Uncle Donny say beauty is just a 'summer fruit' and won't last? He calls it a curse."

Again, Courtney was astounded. Covering her confusion, she said quickly, "Uncle Donny reads a lot. I suspect that he is quoting someone. There is nothing wrong with a pretty face, darling. It is a gift God gave—"

"But Uncle Donny says that Satan uses it. Is that true?"

My word! Oh, why had she tried this without Clint?

"Mother?" Jonda prompted, always impatient, needing to know now.

"Well," Courtney said slowly, fumbling for words, "I suppose it could be his tool if we allow it to be by forgetting it belongs to God. But there is a way, I believe, to hold onto beauty—"

"How?" Jonda, in her eagerness, knelt beside Courtney, placing her hands in Courtney's lap as she used to at prayer time.

The words came then—surely as an answer to prayer. Courtney was certain she never would have thought up such an answer alone. "A woman who loves will never grow old—the way I love Daddy and we love you children; the way we love our neighbors and our friends; and most of all, the way we love God! There is a shine in the heart which reflects in the face. Shall we call it an 'after-summer' beauty?"

Jonda raised a radiant face and Courtney, through unshed tears, fancied a halo about the upturned face. "Oh Mommy, you say beautiful things! I want to be exactly like *you*. Hey, look at our dresses! We match."

Match? She, the "dark throwback" (Mother's words) to the Glamora side, could never be a match for Vanessa's child. The twins, like their natural mother, were

Bellevues as were Efraim, Donolar, and even Kenney in some ways (although he grew more like Clint every day). No, she and Jonda did not "match" (even the blues of their dresses clashed), but today they had begun a new relationship. Theirs was one in which a more mature love and understanding could flourish and, with patience and prayer, their *values* could "match." And that, indeed, was the more important.

"You have paid me a high compliment, darling," Courtney said with a catch in her throat. "I hope I can live up to it."

"You are already the most wonderful mother in the world—and I love you. Oh, I *love* you!"

They stood, clinging to one another briefly. Then the beautiful butterfly was gone.

Kennedy Desmond, first of the two children born to Courtney and Clint, was seven. At Miss Lizzie's insistence, the Desmonds had allowed him to enter school at age five. It seemed so young to Courtney. Of course, he did have the advantage of the twins' constant chatter about school and Donolar's tutelage on science, history, and literature, she had said in hesitation. But the teacher, who had every opportunity to observe the child since she and Brother Jim occupied the Glamora cabin (constructed before the decision to build another large house to replace the Mansion), said it went far deeper than exposure to learning—although that helped. "Spraying it on can only enrich," Miss Lizzie said with conviction. "First, there has to be healthy root stock, native intelligence. Why, it would be unfair to society to hold that child back. He could do square root while others struggle with the alphabet."

The Kennedy namesake of whom Arabella Kennedy Lovelace—grandame, in rank, of the clan—had been so proud, entered, slamming the door behind him. A signal of his distress? Courtney waited until he went back, opened the door, and closed it politely. When he turned to greet her, the pink face—still round with baby fat—was adorned with his usual roguish grin. Pushing at the waving hair that fell over his forehead so like Clint's—a constant source of irritation to Kenney and Clint but so endearing to Courtney—Kenney said he had been helping Donolar take honey from the hives.

"Oh sweetheart!" Courtney gasped, trying to do an overlay of the two personalities within her son: the dedicated student, and the little imp who went along with every prank the twins could contrive—and they were capable of contriving plenty. Jonda and Jordan reported with pride that Miss Lizzie had moved them up front to "seats of honor." Kenney did not tattle, but the way he tucked the corners of his mouth in to hold it still told Clint and Courtney what they needed to know. "Kenney, are you holding something back? The truth now," Clint had said. To which Kenney said soberly, "Well Daddy, I guess Miss Lizzie had them move so they could use their fine minds." Which meant, of course, so teacher could watch them. They were to put those "fine minds" to work then, and their father would consider that they occupied "seats of honor" when Miss Lizzie moved them to the *back* of the room. Kenney, fearing that he would be labeled the "good boy" or "teacher's pet," pinched everybody within reach in an effort to be moved beside them right in front of the chalkboard. His scheme worked only in part. Miss Lizzie moved him up front at the same time she moved Jonda and Jordan back to their original seats. All three learned from it.

Courtney's mind came back to the bee hive. "Were the bees home?"

"Bees are always home," Kenney told her with a faint air of superiority. "Well, the workers go out in search of pollen after the 'bee dance' shows where clover, alfalfa, and sage are. But the queen bee stays home—you know, 'The queen was in the parlour eating bread and honey,' " Kenney giggled. "I know lots about bees—"

Undoubtedly, Courtney smiled proudly. "And you must

tell me sometime, but right now, I want to give you a bear hug—"

"Bears love honey. They rob the hives. I make pictures—"

"The hug?" Courtney glanced at the small enameled watch pinned to the pleated top of her blue dress. There was a closer train station now, but one could never be sure of the schedule.

Little Kenney's mood changed. No longer the dispenser of invaluable information, he was a child again, running to his mother as if wounded. "Do you have to go? We need you—but (straightening and jutting out the round chin) I will save you some honey—we—we need our queen bee."

"And I need my workers, my darling. Mother will be back. Soon!"

"And we will talk?"

"And talk and talk. There will be so much for us to tell each other. I just want you to know how proud I am of you—how special you are—and how much I love you."

"Me, too—I mean, I love you, too. Our whole apiary does—that's a colony of bees. I will bring you our Blessing."

*Our Blessing.* How appropriate for the baby. Baby? Blessing was five! She was special to the entire family because she was the baby that doctors said could not happen, a miracle child—and the last. And she was special to Courtney because she was the only "Glamora" among them. Dark of coloring, sober and shy, Blessing gave the appearance of seeing beyond her immediate surroundings. Blessing did not fill the house with laughter like the other children, but when she smiled, her face lit up as if she knew some secret that someday she would share.

"I adore my baby girl," Clint said to Courtney over and over. "It is as if she is revealing to me what my sweet madonna was once like."

Courtney agreed—even she could see the resemblance and *feel* it. "I must be very, very careful to see that Blessing is never lonely."

"Fat chance around this mob. Set your mind at rest, sweetheart."

"Lonely children do not talk about loneliness, Clint. On the surface, they appear adjusted and make no demands—loving deeply but vulnerable to every hurt. Eventually, something dies—unless someone cares. Had it not been for you, Cousin Bella, and—"

Blessing was crawling into her lap, sitting very still with a pensive look in the wide-open eyes that looked too large for her face. Tenderly, Courtney pulled her youngest to her breast, noting with a sort of sadness that a front tooth was missing. She, too, was growing up—growing up, but retaining her baby needs.

"Are you gonna wock me, Mommy?" Courtney moved to the cricket chair and began rocking. "Daddy will wock me w'en you go—and he says God will wook after us all. How big is God, Mommy? Show me."

Courtney wondered if she were meeting her children for the first time. "Let's see—God is bigger than the world, dear one. Big like this." She stopped rocking and made a wide arc with her arms. "And yes, He can look after His family no matter where they are because—well, His love goes with us in our hearts."

"Wike you leave some in our hearts?"

"Exactly," Courtney whispered against the soft, dark head of the sleepy child.

At the station, Clint held her close, hungrily storing up kisses for their time apart. *Oh Clint!*

A few stragglers slouched about the platform. One of the men told Clint that the train was right on time, according to the station agent's "clickin' machine that knowed all that stuff." Clint placed her suitcase beneath an empty bench inside the station just as the distant wail of a train whistle pierced the air.

"There are no women," Clint said, glancing about uneasily. "I should stay—"

"No, please, darling—*please*. I will be all right—"

*And I don't want you to see me cry*, she might as well have added.

Clint came close to glimpsing her tears. "I'll miss you—I love you—"

The station agent was shoving luggage about matter-of-factly. "Better get your belongings together," he said from beneath his sunshade.

"Go—" Courtney gulped, giving Clint a little shove. He started for the door, paused to raise his hand, and waved uncertainly. She waved back, biting her lip until it bled, and turned away. When she looked over her shoulder, Clint was nearing the buggy. At a distance, and almost lost in billows of smoke from the approaching train, he looked more boy than man...sad...uncertain...and utterly lost.

As was she. It occurred to her suddenly how much they both needed Cousin Bella (*her* paternal cousin, Clint's paternal aunt) to guide them. *Grownups need reassuring, too, Lord,* her heart whispered as she put the suitcase beneath an empty seat and her bag in the overhead rack. Then, almost as if the Lord had addressed her, Courtney realized that indeed Arabella Lovelace *was* with her or at least looking down upon her—certainly her spirit was not encased in the little plot in the churchyard. Like Brother Jim said, Christ had taken care of that. And so Courtney was not journeying alone. Cousin Bella's love would not allow her to be frightened. Courtney found that comforting. And then she frowned. What had Cousin Bella to do with this trip? Something, she was sure.

And she was equally sure that the trip would change things. She wondered how....

# CHAPTER 3

# "Home" Revisited

❦

Dead-weary, Courtney leaned back and closed her eyes as the train jerked warningly, sending a shiver down its long spine of cars, and lurched forward. It was all so long ago, but it seemed only yesterday that she had made the trip West, seeing its beauty in wide-eyed wonder when Clint met her and the governess at the Great Divide and became her guide through his beloved "Dream Country." She had been too excited then to sleep. Now she was too exhausted to stay awake—even long enough to reread her brother's letter.

Toward dawn, the train, straining to climb the mountains separating east and west, came to a near-halt. Courtney knew a moment's fear then, wondering desperately what would happen if two trains met on these winding mountain roads. Teams, responding to a "Whoa back!" from their drivers, pulled aside—sometimes reversing their course until they reached a wide enough space for two wagons or buggies to pass. But trains? She relaxed when word traveled through the coach that the engineer had slowed down to allow a herd of antelope to cross the track. Now, if the train could start again under such conditions—

It did, and with such a determined thrust that baggage flew all directions from the overhead racks. Courtney reached to recover her oversized paisley bag and felt for Efraim's letter. Dawn was painting the eastern sky in its pink promise, but she was barely able to discern the brief message:

Precious Courtney: How long it seems since we talked. Perhaps when this term of office ends—but that comes later. For now, there is something you must know. Land on which Waverly Manor once stood is up for business bids. One building remains. It seems imperative that you see what is stored there. I am writing this during a filibuster and really can say no more. Please come AT ONCE—and will you be able to spend some time with us? Roberta and Yada will expect you—recess! E.

*Yada.* Carefully refolding Efraim's letter and returning it to her bag, Courtney closed her eyes again while before her floated a vision of the son who had entered their world in such a strange manner. Would he still be beautiful like his mother, the innocent maiden they had thought to be Indian only to discover that she was of Jewish birth and reared by a tribe sworn to secrecy? Would Roberta and Efraim honor the young mother Rose Wind's dying request about his upbringing? The childish plea would linger forever in Courtney's memory:

"I go—leaving gift. Roberta—take gift. Man needs male child—carry name. . . . His name shall be called—Yada, Hebrew for 'to know'—he must know—God—and His Son—carry on—teach ways of my people—ways of Indians, too—but teach him love of Jesus. . . ."

Rose Wind never saw her gift, the miraculous gift which saved Roberta and Efraim's marriage. With a small sigh of contentment and a faint angelic smile, the child-mother was ready to meet her Savior—and Yada's father, the young Hebrew student, cruelly robbed of his life.

Courtney shuddered, trying to rub out the ugly, godless horror of that chapter. The train rounded a curve and she fancied that, like the beauty of the Northwestern Territory, that part of the past was history, nothing more—gone, erased from man's view. Little Yada was a Glamora.

But no, she would not detour by way of the Capitol. When business—whatever it possibly could be—was finished, she would take the most direct route home, no matter how much she longed to see Roberta, so happy in her unexpected role of motherhood—a blessing nature had denied—and the precious Yada whom Courtney herself had helped into the world. And Efraim, of course. She *needed* to see Efraim to discover what the mystery was all about . . . have him guide her . . . give her confidence she did not have in herself. What would she do all alone? Only she wasn't alone, she reminded herself, allowing herself to drift into sleep again while the train gathered speed and hurried east.

———————

"Pennsylvania Station!" the round-faced conductor singsonged. Her getting-off place! Courtney gathered her belongings and in minutes found herself standing alone on the wooden platform that had been worn smooth by hordes of hurrying feet. For the first time in her life, she hailed a carriage and, ignoring the driver's inquisitive eyes, directed him toward the once-exclusive neighborhood where the wealthier dwelt.

"Ain't nobody there now, miss—er, ma'am—save the old feller who ain't hearin' no more. Folks hereabouts say there's somethin' mighty queer 'bout the place 'n them what used to live there." He removed a stiff-brimmed hat, scratched his head, and replaced it. "Seems to me like you'd best be findin' a hotel—ever'thing's business here now."

Courtney, assuming an air of self-assurance she did not feel, reassured the man that she would be able to identify her destination—and she was. Waverly Manor was gone, of course, but she recognized the old carriage house which must be the "one remaining building" Efraim spoke of. There was the hedge through which she and Lance, her childhood sweetheart, used to crawl, hiding from imaginary enemies. Sadly, she noted that Sterling House, too, was in the process of demolition. She paid the driver, refused his offer of further help, and stumbled forward.

A sudden hand reached out from nowhere and took her bag. Old Mr. Ashbury—the sober-faced mute of her childhood! What had kept the caretaker here?

# CHAPTER 4

# Old Things Made New

❦

"Old Alfie," as Courtney and Lance had called him, deposited the bag at the sagging door of the old carriage house without giving any indication of recognizing her. Still, Courtney had the distinct feeling that the gentlemanly caretaker expected her. Turning so abruptly that he almost bumped into her, Mr. Ashbury motioned for her to follow and ambled toward Sterling House. Noise of the wrecking crew was deafening, but above it, memory called out every childhood scene between her and Lance—even their tender goodbye. She wondered fleetingly where Lance was. Still in Europe undoubtedly, perhaps studying under the masters yet, although his own artworks had become famous in their own right—rare combinations of old castles discovered there, nostalgic glimpses of childhood memories, and always tinted with soft greens and blues of the Pacific Northwest where they had last met.

Mr. Ashbury stopped. This time it was Courtney who almost bumped into him. He pointed a gnarled finger at the sign swinging boldly in front of the rambling one-time mansion beyond Sterling House: BOARD AND ROOM. When she turned, he was gone. Quickly, she made arrangements for lodging with a powerfully built woman whose every move caused the foyer to look as if it were flirting with collapse. The woman had an eye for business, sharp eyes looking her guest up and down before naming her fee. Courtney was glad she had worn the ancient blue dress when the landlady lost interest and named a reasonable charge. Courtney paid and hurried to retrace her footsteps to the carriage house where she was sure she would find Mr. Ashbury. She was right, at least in part. The caretaker had been there, left the door open, and disappeared—probably taking the back way to return to the boardinghouse with her bag.

The inside of the old carriage house smelled musty with age. When her eyes adjusted to the darkness, Courtney made out ghost-like shapes which could only be furniture grouped together like tombstones, waiting for sale.

In that split second, she knew. Not from memory, because she had never known the owner. It was more *a priori*—something preceding the order of time. Something of which she had no memory, but a knowledge. There flashed before her a setting which was dearly familiar yet, uncannily, one she had never seen. Sunny windows revealed hand-carved chairs clustered around a harpsichord—so real Courtney strained her ears to hear the music. The vision did a slow fade-out and in its place came oversized canopy-topped beds at rest on hand-loomed rugs. In *that* corner stood a broad frame on which a partially finished punchwork design—it's beauty perfuming the stale air of the carriage house like a slowly opening rose—stretched, patiently awaiting completion. *That* corner? What corner? The place had her completely mesmerized. A current of relief went through her body when Old Alfie, unnerving as his soundless appearances and disappearances were, entered to stand beside her and hand her a note he had scribbled. "Glamora—yours," was all it said.

And again she had the sense of knowing. Something her father had told her, perhaps—or could one be born with a memory? Courtney only knew that nothing to her here was a stranger, and neither was its owner, Grandmother Glamora. This man, Old Alfie, somehow had managed to preserve these precious possessions which her own mother, Gabriel Glamora's beautiful but haughty bride, had ordered removed from the Manor as "worth-less junk and cheap trinkets." Grandmother Glamora had not been alive to see it happen, and Courtney, sad-dened now, was glad.

Incredibly it was to belong to Courtney! This she knew, too. Oh yes, she remembered that part now ... some-thing Mrs. Thorpe had told her. The Glamora children's governess had made no secret of her dislike for "the Lady Ana" and—under the guise of teaching family history— had divulged that all their father's heirlooms were to be reserved for the youngest daughter. Not that Vanessa would have wanted the ancient treasures, Efraim knew, and that explained how he had come to contact her.

Fingers trembling with eagerness, Courtney stripped the furniture free of its shrouds. Oh, how beautiful, beautiful, *beautiful*! This, of course, was what the new house back home needed—furniture mellowed by age, having echoed a baby's laugh, known sorrow with all its tears, but which offered security, love, and a certain foreverness which, blessed by faith, bridged the way from earth to heaven.

Twilight, clad in soft purple robes, danced across the pearly ripples of the great Atlantic. Courtney wished for more time. Even in the dimming light she could see that the furniture in the crating was well-preserved. Quaint. Old. Of rare workmanship that only a caring hand could carve. Some of the needlepoint cushions would need replacing. Cara Laughten had done that kind of work at the Mansion when Cousin Bella declared Courtney its mistress. Cara would do it again, and gladly. The scrolls of rugs and carpets whispered of happier days, the thick pile unfaded and the designs—though muted with age— were still pleasing to the eye, homey and unpretentious. It seemed important to study the ancestral paintings in hopes of finding a resemblance to her beloved father in one of the great golden frames. Courtney still felt a sense of loss when memory took her back to the all-consuming fire which took from her the ancestral lineup that used to adorn the library wall of Mansion-in-the-Wild. These paintings, however, went back even farther—back to days of knighthood, periwigs, and farthingales. Days, she supposed, when her Glamora ancestors, too, could trace their bloodline back to castles and suits of armor. But they were strangers, and their identity had died with Grandmother Glamora. Would Mother have felt herself so superior to her husband had she known? "Chickens come home t'roost," Mandy was fond of saying darkly of those who misused others. Only, Mother never knew. It was just as well, Courtney mused, all bitterness gone.

Darkness was settling down. In vain, she groped for a lamp but found none. Further searching and planning must wait until tomorrow. She turned to the rectangle of light made by the doorway, struck suddenly by a strange feeling of *déjà vu*. It was all so familiar, and yet unfamiliar. She was homesick for her loved ones but at home in her surroundings.

And then she knew! Of course—Cousin Bella. Dear Cousin Bella had known. It was as if she stood beside Courtney now, guiding, directing. "Someday, my dear," the winds whispered, "my beloved mansion will be restored to its former glory—a home for the multitudes."

"I understand," Courtney whispered reverently— whether to Cousin Bella or to the Lord. Then she stepped out into the shifting shadows, pausing only long enough to feel the refreshing salt air against her face and admire the deep bowl of blue-black sky, now fringed with stars, before retracing her steps quickly to the boardinghouse.

A clock chimed the hour solemnly as the landlady, layers of cheap beads adding girth to the ropes of fat of her neck, opened the door before Courtney pulled the bell cord. With eyes piercing Courtney's the woman asked, "Did ya find what y'er lookin' for? This maybe?" And, dying of curiosity, the landlady handed Courtney a letter. Courtney recognized Efraim's handwriting immediately.

# CHAPTER 5

# Sealed with a Promise

❧

With unsteady but determined fingers, Courtney lettered the last packing crate: CLINT DESMOND—DESTINATION: "GREAT CIRCLE ROUTE," WASHINGTON. The waterway, she thought as she stood to ease the tension of her back, circled the globe by way of the Orient. And she must travel across the country to get back to her family. The west-to-east journey she had dreaded, but returning would be easier. Oh, the joy of reunion! Anticipation tingled up and down her spine.

How it would have pleased Grandmother Glamora to see all the fragile century-old china and the quilts she had pieced from worn clothing back in the "auld country" during those lean years when Grandfather was trying to coax enough coal from the earth to feed his family, loosened from cobweb tetherings and given the welcome they deserved. Were she and Cousin Bella reunited in heaven? Courtney hoped so, for surely they would be rejoicing with her, Clint, and the children. It was a lovely thought, as lovely as the reassurance that the Creator Himself was everywhere at once. Hadn't He hung His sun in the sky as one of the million signs of His presence? The same golden beams which lighted this brilliant morning would be parting the mists above the sky-touching peaks at home to unlock the fragrance of the pines and highlight their fluted cones before dipping into the iridescent depths of the white-plumed Columbia as it rolled toward the Pacific. *Home!*

Perhaps it was during those few moments of communing with God through nature that Old Alfie entered. Old Alfie was harmless, his intentions good. But there was something unnerving about his gauntly gait that took him so noiselessly from one spot to another, his ill-fitting old clothes, blank stare, and inability to communicate. Maybe that is why Courtney found his simple act of handing her a small tarnished key disturbing.

"For me?" Her voice trembled a bit as she pointed to herself.

Mr. Ashbury nodded vaguely, without a change of expression.

"But what—?" Courtney began and then stopped.

The matter was closed, a pair of hands—knitted with gnarled sinews, calloused palms turned upward—told her. Whatever Old Alfie knew, if anything, he would keep to himself. What good was a key if—

Courtney's thoughts were interrupted by excited voices. Efraim! Roberta! And oh, they had brought Yada! With a little squeal of delight, she dropped the mysterious key into the pocket of her apron and rushed to meet her brother.

Again, the caretaker had seen. He had tethered the horse at the hitching post by the watering trough before Efraim could lift his beautiful five-year-old son from the carriage. Roberta in her excitement backed down the step, caught a heel in her crinoline petticoat, and would have fallen had it not been for her husband's steadying hand. All were laughing and talking at once. A million questions asked and answered, while one small boy stood formally waiting to be recognized.

Quickly Courtney knelt beside him. "Oh darling, I am sorry! Let me look at you," she said, pushing the raven-dark hair back from the smooth ebony of his round forehead.

"I have grown," Yada said with manly pride. "Would you have known me?"

"Anywhere in the world I would have known you, but I might have wondered with whom you changed legs and arms."

Yada smiled shyly, still standing erect. The childish pleasure at his aunt's gentle teasing showed in the enormous ripe-olive eyes. Courtney assessed him guardedly, something telling her that he formed relationships with care. Here, she thought, is as nearly a perfect human being as one will ever see, more like a picture than a flesh-and-blood child. And yet, there was something that went far deeper, a feeling of love and tenderness beneath that mature exterior that won her heart. Oh, how God had smiled on the family by adding Rose Wind's "gift."

"This is your Aunt Courtney, sweetheart," Roberta was saying as she adjusted his round collar.

"I know," Yada said soberly. "Blessing's mother."

"Blessing is all he talks about," Roberta said aloud, then in a little aside to Courtney, "so I hope she remembers him."

"Remembers? That one never forgot a thing in her young life!"

And then they were all embracing, laughing, and talking again, with Yada asking questions about Blessing when there was a lull in adult conversation. "We will be back home soon. Is this not true, Father?"

"Well, yes—we do plan to return, son, but it will be a while. Daddy has work to do in *this* Washington before going to that one."

"It is confusing for you, but my father understands," Yada told Courtney. "He is very smart."

Efraim's fair skin colored, but there was no mistaking the pleasure in his Bellevue-blue eyes. "That kind of talk is what makes a man stand ten feet tall," he told Courtney with pride.

"As well it should," she said with a lump in her throat. "I am so happy for you all—but oh, how we miss you."

"Efraim will not seek reelection," Roberta said, her amber eyes shining. "He feels there is work for us back there with all of you. Pioneers at heart, we have become like the land—ready to start over. And oh, Courtney, our children can grow up together!"

"Tell about the other school, please, Mother, not the synagogue or the Christian—so many schools," Yada said with an exaggerated sigh for Courtney's benefit. "Now I want to go to the other in the woods where the first Americans lived. May Blessing come along?"

"We will see, darling. I do believe I hear the moving wagon. Do you want to give your father a hand with some of these things?"

As Yada happily joined Efraim, Courtney burst into laughter. "You are as transparent as ever, dear Ro. Yada knew he was being dismissed."

Roberta raised both hands in mock despair. "Perhaps it is just as well that we are unable to have children. I doubt if I could handle another—and I wonder if I am bringing this one up properly. Everything has been so correct, so proper, so—well, scholarly and stiff. I promised, but after all, he *is* a child."

"A very bright one, but he will go native when he gets back to our brood, believe me. It will be good for them all—and for *us*."

The two women chatted and planned ahead as the movers grunted and groaned, shouldering the heavy crates up an improvised ramp—with Yada's help. Periodically, he paused to look back, obviously for Courtney's approval. Roberta, too, seemed anxious that she take note. Fleetingly, Courtney wondered if Roberta took motherhood *too* seriously.

"An absolute darling," Courtney said of Yada, letting go of her concerns. "I will have so much to report—and so much to do refurbishing our home, which needs a name now. How good that Efraim was here to know of the changes. Otherwise, I would never have known of these treasures. But I am not ready for a farewell, even with bags set out—"

Roberta's eyes clouded with disappointment. "You mean you are leaving without a visit?"

This was the time Courtney had anticipated so much, yet dreaded. Part of her—the part with wings—longed to soar forth happily on this new adventure. The other part—which was grounded with love for her extended family—shrank back, dreading another parting. Her eyes clouded with tears. "I *must* get home. Try and understand."

"I do—I do," Roberta said slowly, understanding, although her mind was elsewhere. "I wish we could be together forever—I mean before we get to heaven."

Dear Roberta. "Remember, you are coming home," Courtney reminded.

Roberta looked out across the cape, watching a drift of clouds floating over the sea as they caught and held stripes of emerald, sapphire, and rose-gold from the sun-warmed water. "Courtney, I—I wish we could be bound together—one family, in a very special way. You know, the way there used to be in parental agreements—"

Courtney frowned in concentration. "I fail to understand."

"Oh, I know about your childhood. I know about the arrangements—the hateful exchanges of money for title or beauty. That is hardly what I mean—"

"What *do* you mean?"

"I mean," Roberta said, swallowing and seeming to measure every word, "that I have chosen in my heart a wife for our son," she gulped.

"Our Blessing!" Courtney exclaimed.

"You mean you—"

"No, no! I was calling her by name. Oh Ro, you are not thinking straight. This is the nineteenth century. People choose their own mates, live their own lives—and my past has nothing to do with it."

But even as she spoke, Courtney knew by the ring of ice around her heart that the words were a shade less than true.

"Promise you will think about it, just *promise*," Roberta implored.

The idea was ridiculous, unworthy of thought. "I can make you no such promise—you know that. Children are not pawns to be pushed forward for protection of the king and queen. They are not our property, in fact. We have dedicated our families to God who lent them to us for training." Her own heart was pounding wildly. Had she sounded too harsh? "But you are kind to want us closer," she said softly. "Oh Ro, please, I had no intentions of upsetting you so—"

There was a flurry of activity outside the old carriage house. Efraim was directing the men to port, paying them, and handing a generous fee to Old Alfie, whom they would never see again. She should thank him, say goodbye. But there had been enough farewells, and the final one remained. Actually, it had come. Efraim and little Yada entered the door.

"Ladies—" Efraim began but was interrupted by his son.

"Why is my mother crying?" Yada demanded fiercely. Then, bursting into tears himself, he ran to comfort Roberta. His eyes accused Courtney.

The emotion on the tiny face tore at Courtney's heart. She must not leave like this. And yet, what could she do?

"What is it, little sister?" Efraim whispered, putting his arms around Courtney. "You look as if you two had seen a ghost—"

"In a way, I guess we have," Courtney said, choking back tears. "It is just the emotional stress of saying goodbye. You know," she tried to say lightly, "how we women are."

Then, in the circle of her brother's arms, she, too, began to weep. "Hurry home to us—oh, Efraim, I must not leave Roberta and Yada in this state. I—I—"

"Roberta," she said with a trembling voice, "I will think—of—something." Her reward was Yada's shy smile.

# CHAPTER 6

# A Key to Many Colors

Efraim had arranged for her return ticket to the Pacific Northwest and taken her bag to the station. The carriage house was cleared of everything, so why look back on an empty room which—like the rest of the estate—had provided only shelter? Her adored father was long since gone. Efraim, whom she loved equally, would be joining her and Clint again—praise the Lord! And Lance—well, she and Lance had shared only a childhood. Otherwise, Courtney could lay claim to no degree of intimacy with another. Perhaps it was the ghost of what might have been which caused her to hesitate before pulling the protesting door closed behind her. That and the feeling that, although she was leaving her past forever behind, she was taking its memory with her (thanks to dear Grandmother Glamora) to weave into her present—a richer present, watering the roots Cousin Bella had planted.

The momentary heaviness was gone. With head high and spirits lifting at the thought of what lay ahead, Courtney marched out resolutely—a little relieved that she was a stranger here and there would be no curious eyes peeking from windows of the few remaining houses. She touched the pocket of her crisp white blouse, making sure that the little key Mr. Ashbury had given her was still pinned securely to her underbodice. She made no mention of the key to Efraim and Roberta.

They rode the short distance to the station in the strange silence that descends prior to farewells. Then came the departure, the last waving of handkerchiefs, and the warning whistle of the train as it strained forward. Courtney wiped the already-polished window for one last look at the setting which had never been *home* at all.

Courtney glanced around, appreciating how traveling had improved since she traveled to the West for the first time so long ago. Then she settled back to watch the passing scenery, interested only in that each picture framed by her window represented a turn of the wheels closer to home. Her mind did a joyous leap forward as she and Clint gave a new personality to their home—correction: *old* personality. Smiling a bit, she dozed, thinking as she drifted off that she had all but forgotten Roberta's emotional plea. The idea of a prearranged marriage was preposterous, totally out of keeping with her sister-in-law's common-sense approach to life with all her legal expertise. Unless, of course, it could be another way of holding onto the child she adored so much . . . too much to let go . . . too much to recognize his own needs and preferences. The idea bothered her, but she was too far over the threshold of slumber to give it further thought.

But the idea surfaced somewhere in the strange dream which came, causing her heart to pound and her palms to grow damp. Courtney awakened with that bothersome feeling that she needed to recall the dream's details, but it had drifted back into her subconscious.

When the dream came the second time, it left fragments which she tried to piece together like a puzzle. She could piece together the setting, but the characters and circumstances dissolved in the long, dark hall through which she seemed to be traveling from door to door in an effort to find the key which would fit into one of the locks.

Again and again, the dream recurred, growing more vivid each time. At first, it had left only a haunting presence. Now, it was frightening. Real. So real she knew that behind it lay a mystery which, when revealed, would make a crucial difference in her life.

The dream was always the same. Courtney was walking down that long, long hall. Somewhere in the distance a blue-green light flickered, perhaps signaling the hall's end. But in between lay scarves of ghostly fog which moved restlessly, changing shapes to obscure the light, clinging damply to the cold doorknobs, sometimes wrapping Courtney's face as if to suffocate what little breath she could manage in the dank atmosphere. Somebody or some*thing* was trying to extract a promise—then a multitude of doors....

"Open ... open ... open," the groans of a thousand doors pleaded in ghostly whispers that joined in hoarse song to further chill her bones. Open? But she had no key.

Key? What was she carrying? Why, an oversized bracelet of keys of all shapes. Even fully awake, Courtney found keys confusing, having little aptitude for abstractions. In the nightmare, the fumbling was intensified. She was trying, trying, trying, while the groans that she felt had been uttered for centuries grew louder, more demanding, even threatening—as if from empty tombs. The darkness thickened.

And then she dropped the bracelet. Looking back for an exit, she saw that the door behind her had closed. She was trapped! Dropping to her knees, she ran her hands over the slippery shards of the floor, feeling them penetrate her palm. She sensed no pain—just despair. Panic clutched at her throat, but her mouth was too dry to allow a scream. Then, blessedly, she remembered the little key the caretaker had placed in her hand.

Yes, it was there! Seeming to float down the dark tunnel, Courtney found that the key fit not one door, but many. "Choose—choose—choose the one which sets us free!" So the changing chant meant one choice?

Then, as is the way with dreams, the fog thinned and each door was revealed, vividly colored and transparent!

Inside the violet door lay riches akin to a king's storehouse; behind the green, heartbreak; the blue, the faces of loved ones—her family and friends as well as those who had gone on before; and, finally, a white light so bright that she knew that behind it was a heavenly being. If only she could reach it . . .

But the doors were elongating into scarves again, their colors blending into a blindingly beautiful rainbow arching above in the dark dome to touch the darkness below. If only she could find the rainbow's end and mount its stairs, surely she could climb out of the storms which preceded it, avoid its tears, basking only in the light of the heavenly being.

*Move, Courtney, move!* But before she could lift a leaden limb, Courtney awoke as the train came to a jolting halt. She was home!

# CHAPTER 7

# Homecoming

❦

Can anything match the joy of coming home? Courtney, surrounded by loved ones, thought not. Was this the manner in which the angels rejoiced when God's children crossed the heavenly realm to be reunited with Him? Surely there was a similarity.

The family was there—all of them—at the station! This she had never expected, and the joy and surprise—mingled with an overpowering fatigue due in part to the troublesome dream—were almost too much. Her knees buckled and she clung to Clint when, ignoring the stampede of children, he sprang ahead to clasp her in his arms, murmuring little words of endearment with an abandonment foreign to his nature. Usually in public they were Mr. and Mrs. Clint Desmond (or simply Clint and Courtney to close friends), and at home they were "Mommy and Daddy" (or Mother and Dad as the children grew older), reserving their far deeper relationship for the privacy of their bedroom. But then, they had never been apart like this before!

"I will never let you go again—never, *never*, NEVER!" Clint whispered almost fiercely.

"There will be no need, my darling. That part of my life is closed. I belong here with you—and oh, my goodness! Here they come!"

The children had made a tight circle around their parents and were chanting almost wildly:

Ring around a rosie,
Pocket full of posie,

Ashes, ashes,
*All fall down!*

With the last line, they pounced onto Courtney, tugging at her skirt, vying for her hands, and squealing with delight. Donolar, whose plane of thinking was often at the children's level, stood aside. Courtney saw from the corner of her eye that his face revealed a look of longing although his agate eyes were without expression.

Jordan, who looked enough like Donolar to be his childhood memory, followed her gaze. "Come on, Uncle Donny! You taught us the song—no sillier for you than it is for us."

Dear Donolar. It must be dreadful for him, sometimes being a child held captive in a man's body and wondering in which world he belonged. At the moment, he had no identity problem. He took the hand of his niece, as like Donolar as her twin brother, and—with a surprising gesture—reached out his free hand to Brother Jim.

"Praise be!" The booming voice of the big preacher echoed up and down the deserted platform. When his bride (still "Miss Lizzie" to him as well as to her students) joined the group, Courtney lost count. Mandy, Mrs. Rueben, Cara Laughten and her stair-stepped family (one child a year for the 12 years her John was alive) and—could it be? Surely the cinders of the backing-up train had damaged her eyesight. She squinted, tears clearing her vision. He was still in the welcoming circle—the rabbi himself. A little stiff, as if he had forgotten how to play, his eyes danced along with clumsy feet as he joined the merry group. Obviously he felt foolish, for he kept looking over his shoulder for an audience as the chant recommenced.

Courtney's pilgrimage was all but forgotten as, laughing and teasing, they all piled into whichever buggy was closest. Contentment settled over her as Clint held the reins in one hand and put his other arm around her shoulders; Blessing sat on her lap, temporarily reverting back to babyhood (although tomorrow she would be "going on six"); and Kenney squeezed in beside her. All they needed, she thought, giddy with happiness, was Mouser and her kittens.

The children talked nonstop, asking as many questions about their cousin as Yada had asked about them. There was no opportunity for conversation with Clint, but Courtney did observe the countryside as they journeyed toward home. Surely it must have grown lovelier during her short absence. The colorful rock walls looked even more powerful, shouldering the great waterfalls rushing over their walls like an army of giants and quarreling their way into the mighty Columbia or dividing into chatty little streams such as they followed now. How it sang through the ferny dells! Why had she failed to notice that the once-new cabins now looked like a part of the landscape, vine-clad as they were with fat rock chimneys and yards overgrown with flowers? Up, up, they seemed to be climbing, the little hill being steeper than she remembered. And on top, a castle, or so it looked to Courtney, with its freshly scrubbed windows catching and holding the pink of sunset's afterglow. Well, it *would* be a castle when the soft rugs were laid, the empty bookshelves filled with ancient volumes she had shipped, the handsome furniture polished and put into place. She tried to remember it all: the teakwood table . . . the ivory carvings which must have come from China . . . and the silver urn to be filled with yellow rosebuds from Donolar's garden.

"The earls and dukes with high ruffs and headdresses in the gold frames will look just right along the stairwell—" Courtney caught herself murmuring aloud. At the amused lift of Clint's right eyebrow, she felt herself coloring. "I am so sorry, but oh, there is so much to tell you. Oh Clint, I have brought home a real treasure!"

"A *buried* treasure, Mother?" Kenney's eyes enlarged comically, then he settled back with a teasing smile. "A lady pirate, huh?"

Blessing looked at her brother in dismay. "You shouldn't say th-things you do not mean or you may be th-ory—*sor*-ry."

Courtney smiled tenderly. Their youngest was learning to live with the loss of a baby tooth. Already a pearly tooth, looking too wide for the doll-like face, was visible beneath her rosy upper lip.

"Blessing does not *say* things—she *paints* them. That's what Miss Lizzie says. Do you look at her pictures, Mother?"

"I have not had the privilege," Courtney said as they turned in at the gate. "You will show me, sweetheart?"

Blessing gave the matter some thought. "They're just pwe-*pre*tend pictures. I just pw-pretend to be the people I dwaw—*draw*. I can be anybody I want to be —Wittle—*Little* Bo Peep or a Fwairy-F-*Fairy* Princess—it's just pretend pictures."

"Pretend pictures?" Clint said slowly. "Now, I am no artist, but I have a hunch that is what art is all about. How about a pretend kiss, sugar?"

"Oh Daddy," Blessing giggled. "I'll give you a weal one!"

———

Mandy served chicken and dumplings from the long oilcloth-covered table in the kitchen, fussing over every detail as if it were a full-course dinner served in the dining room (which one day it would be!). Brother Jim's prayer was mercifully brief, but those at the table—obviously by plan—rose like a vast, uneven wave, and sang fervently, "Praise God from Whom All Blessings Flow."

And then everyone began talking at once. Questions... questions... and Courtney basking in providing answers. Praise God, indeed! Memory of Roberta's request faded—forever, Courtney would have supposed. She was wrong.

# CHAPTER 8

# Reconstruction

❧

Homecoming was all Courtney could have wished it to be, a dream-come-true. Even the two towns, merged into one, looked clean and decent. There would always be a line of division, everybody said—translating into the truth which was that they chose it to be so. Oh well, they said philosophically, 'twas like that smart Miss Lizzie said, they could live "separate" together in something the schoolteacher called "mutual symbiosis." Might as well call the place "Twin Cities." Although they had signed that merger, what they had in common would fit on a pinhead with room to spare. So according to reports given on her arrival home, the saloons (*without* "bed and board") would stay on the port side; the church, in the valley. There was to be a town meeting the week following, Clint said with some concern, but tempers had cooled and there would be no shooting out the lights and that kind of foolishness.

Miss Lizzie confided proudly that the children had voted at school favoring a name which Brother Jim planned to propose: "Young America!"

"I like that!" Courtney said with genuine enthusiasm. Admittedly, of course, her mood was so light she liked almost everything.

Certainly, she liked the plans for expanding their new home. Hour after hour, she and Clint bent their heads together by lamplight after the children were in bed to work on the books and plan. The economy was changing—better in some ways but worse in others, Courtney

44

understood from Clint's explanations. Transportation had a lot to do with it. There was a time, Cousin Bella used to tell them, when the stagelines "made a killing." Revenues came largely from passengers who fattened the purses of investors. True entrepreneurs (out for "a quick buck," Doc George had always added) charged anywhere between 50 and 100 dollars for the shortest of trips. Railroads drove the stagelines out of business and continued to do reasonably well. The big thing now, however, by way of transportation was the growth of waterways since Washington fronts the sea. The Columbia River itself was a deep-sea harbor of the first order, allowing produce and products—whether gathered together over rails, roads, or rivers—to leave by sea. Courtney herself remembered when curious gawkers gathered to gape at the few seagoing vessels. Now at the river's mouth there was a steady procession of great freighters steaming in and out, exchanging goods with all parts of the world.

"Is the Columbia really a safe harbor in time of storm, Clint?" Courtney asked at one point, thinking of her lovely possessions.

"As long as the jetties are maintained, yes. It was dangerous back when ships carried sails and moved only with the wind. The channel was shallow and shifting then, due to deposits of sand. It is dredged deep and clean now. Say, you are worrying about that furniture needlessly, my sweet. Instead, it is best for us to decide just where we are to place it."

Clint meant in regard to building on to their new home, she knew. But her own mind kept drifting back to the visions she had at the old New England carriage house. The visions were just how she wanted it to look—like that original setting she knew existed somewhere in the past. It was an impractical dream—maybe a bit foolish since undoubtedly fragments of imagination harked back to castles with pepperpot chimneys and a houseful of servants—but somehow perhaps they could duplicate the visions.

"The way I am seeing it," she said dreamily, "we would need to hire two dozen carpenters—and you would need to purchase a marble quarry!"

"For you I would do that—only it would mean selling off the very ground on which the beginnings of this rambling house-to-be sits. We *will* need to add on."

"I had thought of doing it gradually," Courtney said slowly, still living out her visions—the future as bright as the summer sun.

She seemed to be floating from room to room, mentally running slender fingers over smooth marble—wherever it was to be used—of some magnificently imposing home she knew so well, although she had never seen it. The neoclassical facade captured the vibrant spirit of—what was it? Oh yes, the late Georgian period. Its furnishings, although palatial, seemed perfectly at ease. The frilly priscilla curtains in the kitchen would retain the atmosphere of the original cabin, Courtney dreamed on. That was fine, symbolic in a sense of the feeling the Desmonds wished to create—one of hospitality to all persons, a message that differences were not only accepted but welcomed. Arabella Kennedy Lovelace had done her job well in preparing her successors to carry on the traditions of love and hospitality.

Suddenly, Clint broke into her private world with a laugh. "I have never seen you more excited, Courtney. Your face has the look of a lady prospector wresting gold from a just-discovered vein. Am I a part of this dream?"

"Oh darling, you are the center of it! I want it for us all, just as your aunt wanted a gathering place, a sort of neutral ground for the valley and a home, a *real* home, for our children and the generations to come." She paused, biting her lower lip, "Providing you share that dream—that is essential—"

Clint laid down his pencil and looked straight into her eyes, so dark now with excitement, and let her drown in the deep blue lake of his own eyes. "I do, my darling. You know I do. Expansion, building on, has been my plan from the beginning. It came a bit sooner than I expected, but I think we can swing it. The newspaper and bank are flourishing, and I am giving serious thought to selling off some—*some*, not all—of the timber above the south wheat fields. We will discuss it. The mine is holding its own, and we can always hope for a bumper crop of grain. Efraim can advise me when they get back—" Clint then shifted the subject. "We want more than a glorified shack, and we want to make sure that it is decent in size—enduring and, well, I guess a little elegance will do no harm. Certainly, you have earned it!"

"I have done nothing to *earn* anything. It all comes by God's grace."

Courtney was unaware that Clint's smile came not from her words, but from the little-girl look of a child allowed to go on the Sunday school picnic although she has been playing hooky. The smile was fleeting. "You are right, my love—very, very right. But I think the Good Lord knows that our four are clamoring for rooms of their own and that Mandy and Mrs. Rueben have shared an uneasy peace long enough. I heard an argument between them yesterday that set bells ringing in my ears. Fussing, fuming, firing insults like bullets—calling one another *decrepit*. Sounds like a word borrowed from Miss Lizzie's vocabulary—oh yes, that reminds me. I suppose we will be having her and Brother Jim joining us in the family circle—for dinner, that is, so counting Donolar, that will be—"

"Oh yes, yes!" Courtney's voice rang out like Christmas bells and she went on with her vision. "Here by the fireplace, the secretary. And the enormous globe should go nearby so the children can mark the places they think some of the heirlooms came from. The Sheraton armchair will be for you in the library, opposite the Hepplewhite desk . . . and oh, wait until you see the ancestral paintings. I wish we had some pastoral scenes—oh darling, it will look so grand, and," she giggled, "elegant, but a little uncivilized!"

"A glorified shack, built with the lasting foundation of love!"

———————

"The two towns have changed very little," Clint reported of the town meeting, "except in size. Unified, Young America—they went for the children's suggestion!—boasts close to ten thousand, counting a wide circumference, of course. So wide it almost reaches Portland! Washington's largest settlement, in a sense, but too sprawling in design and philosophy to be considered the major city. More than a river divides us."

"How large is it?" Courtney asked in dismay.

Clint shrugged tiredly as he shucked off his jacket. "Somebody asked the surveyor. His answer was 80 miles in all directions as the crow flies—then added that it is twice that on horseback as the trails wind and double back 'like a barrel of hissing rattlers'—which I sometimes think Old Town across the river is filled with!"

Courtney sucked in a deep breath. "I had hoped all that was behind us. I wanted our children to grow up in peace and harmony."

Clint unbuttoned and removed his collar slowly, his mind elsewhere. "That would mean moving away and"—attempting to tease—"that would be dangerous. I overheard one fellow tell another that any quitter had better ride out at midnight, keep moving, and never look back."

"Silly talk!" Courtney said with spirit. "We are staying, of course. We belong here."

Stripped of his shirt and bare-chested, Clint reached out and drew her to him. "Madonna, my courageous little flower," he said with a rush of affection. "What would I do without you?"

"Never try to figure that one out," she cautioned with a light laugh. "Ouch, you brute! Let go of me and I will hang up your tie."

"Let it go until tomorrow—and kiss your mayor-husband."

"Mayor! Oh Clint—you mean—tell me," she gasped, trying to avert a kiss.

"That can wait until tomorrow, too."

———————————

That autumn Clint's grain crop exceeded his most optimistic predictions. Courtney assisted Mandy in preparation of meals for the hungry threshing crew in the summer kitchen. The big, good-natured cook, tired of "that woman a-fussin' " (referring to Mrs. Rueben), was out-of-sorts and grumbled about the men's being "bottomless pits uh body'd neber be able t'fill up." Courtney boosted both women's morale by telling them about the new kitchen already under construction. Mandy rolled her dark eyes upward in anticipation and said " 'twas lack unto dat promised Mansion-in-de-sky"—and doubled her efforts and recipes.

Spirits lifted among wheat farmers, too, as grain went off to the mill. Whistling and singing, they set about preparing for planting next year's crop. Clint, looking forward to Efraim's return in the spring, turned under an additional thousand-acre plot where trees had been removed. Combining his profits from the real timber sale, the newspaper, soaring wheat profits, and the now-paying mine, the Mayor and Mrs. Clint Desmond found themselves the "best-off" couple in the Columbia River Valley. Brother Jim called a special prayer meeting to praise their Maker for the bounty. "It means," the big, once-bare-fisted boxer explained, "that we can go on with Your plans here and gather more sheep into Your fold, soon as we dehorn Satan and drive some demons out of the unenlightened in Old Town. And we'll do it, Lord, with You in my corner!"

He was right—in some ways. But heartbreak lay between.

------------------------

Meanwhile, reconstruction was taking place elsewhere. Kennedy School, the first nonsectarian school in the region, began to outgrow the benefactor's enlarged (at the time of her demise) dream. The end of the Civil War had not ended hostilities. Second-generation families, in fact, renewed the differences with frequent bloody violence, propelling another flood of immigrants. Some headed West to escape the furor that once divided the nation, others to carry on their differences on a new battleground. As if it were inevitable, the "Feds" settled in Old Town and the Union sympathizers sought a hoped-for peace in the valley, now called the New Town of Young America. The neutrals huddled into small groups of frightened recluses. Among them were the Mormons, Mennonites, and a group calling themselves "Separatists." Valley folk looked on in dismay as Young America became history-repeating-itself, the North and South of the western frontier.

"War is declared," Clint said in perplexity. "So far it is only a ground swell of feeling, a war of words—but that is the atmosphere which preceded the four-hour bombardment of Fort Sumter, starting a war."

"We will deal with it as we have dealt with all else," Brother Jim declared stoutly. His wife took a more narrow view, seeing the situation from the perspective of Kennedy School's only teacher.

"I have set all your children to work," Miss Lizzie told Courtney one afternoon. "Were it not for the Desmonds—" she paused to throw up thin but strong hands. "Just know that their education is not suffering," the tired teacher begged. "For rest assured that the teacher learns more than the student!"

Courtney and Clint spoke reassuring words. Anything they could do to help?

Nothing more really. Well, there was one thing more.

Miss Lizzie hesitated, her tired expression changing suddenly to one of animation, making the plain woman rather lovely, Courtney was surprised to observe. "Yes?" Courtney, marveling, encouraged.

"I know how busy and involved you two are, but I do hope that you find time to help your children recognize and develop their talents. You do know they are gifted?"

Miss Lizzie's hands wadded her handkerchief, betraying a certain uneasiness. Had she offended by pointing out the obvious? The gestures all but spoke aloud.

"We know that they are alert and, as proud parents, I guess we think of them as bright—but *gifted*?" Courtney tasted the word. Good gifts came from God, and a strange little fear ringed her heart. Was she up to being custodian of such treasures? She was almost afraid to ask for an explanation. When it came, she was even more unsure of herself. Another totally new set of challenges.

"I will work from the bottom up," Miss Lizzie smiled uncertainly. "Although Blessing will not be entering school until fall, she has shared her drawings with me. While I am no real connoisseur of great art, I sense a certain something—"

Courtney nodded when the teacher paused. "Kenney says the same."

Miss Lizzie smiled broadly. "And *that* one—my, my!—what a young scientist, particularly in biology. He will make his mark."

"Thanks to Donolar who saw the aptitude before his parents."

"Donolar, yes, the boy—man—has been invaluable in helping the Laughtens with the *two R's*—and something more. I credit him with exposing Jordan to great literature, even though Donolar's ciphering is meaningless. Jordan's interest and instant recall amaze me. He is wanting to direct a Shakespearean play, *The Merchant of Venice*! Imagine an 11-year-old—"

"Twelve!" Jordan announced proudly from the doorway of the Desmond cabin's small living room where Miss Lizzie had been grading papers when Courtney went in search of Blessing who sometimes wandered too far with her crayons in search of Uncle Donny's butterflies. "I—we, Jonda and I—had birthdays."

"Jordan," Courtney chided gently, "were you eavesdropping?"

"Well," he said guiltily, making a circle with his left ankle-high brogan. Then, diplomatically, he paused, favored the ladies with his winsome smile, and said brightly, "So I wish to thank you, Miss Lizzie. I hope you will give the play some thought."

With that he was gone like a brief whirlwind, leaving his mother and teacher laughing, all reserve and concerns gone, as well.

Miss Lizzie wiped her eyes. "I adore him—as well as his sister. Jonda, as you probably know, is gifted musically. Except for the scale I have taught, the child—young lady—has had no training but is able to play the old organ by ear, as well as the priceless violin the Laughten children brought to show. Do you have a teacher in mind?"

It was Courtney's turn to be flustered. "I—I had no idea—"

"Of Jonda's talents? She is shy about revealing them. If you wish, I could tutor her. I am not gifted, but I know music and—"

"Oh bless you, yes!" Courtney sang out gratefully, her heart already leaping ahead to all she would have to tell Clint. And then she frowned slightly, feeling a tug at her heart. How could she and Clint have become so involved that they failed to see beyond the children's outward manifestations of behavior—failed to recognize their gifts?

"If you are feeling guilty," Miss Lizzie said kindly, "don't! Parents are so busy with nourishing and training their children—good parents like you—that they hardly have time to become acquainted with them as *people*. You have given them of your great gift—love!"

Tears rushed to fill Courtney's eyes. "That we have given."

"And more," Miss Lizzie said, awkwardly leaning forward with a rustle of stiffly starched petticoats to stroke Courtney's hand. "You have taught them the value of one world which must learn to get along or perish. I wish you could watch them mediate differences between the more quarrelsome children. The way they relate to one another as a family is a revelation."

Courtney gasped. "Are you sure you are talking about the right children? I mean—" she caught herself and blushed.

Miss Lizzie was repeating some anecdotes to support her statements, but Courtney's thoughts took her far from the scene. She was seeing again the wee, blond tyrants Vanessa had all but abandoned. The two angel-faced two-year-olds who spent their days thinking up devilment, creating chaos everywhere they went—partners in crime, while dreaming up dangerous games with Mandy's knives that gave every indication of being designed to destroy each other. When and how had they changed? True, she and Clint had agonized together, worked gently with the twins, and their own two who joined the family circle later, and prayed without ceasing that they would meet their needs, change their attitudes...but when had it happened? Miss Lizzie was right, however. There had been not a single report of misbehavior while she was away. *So there could be peace at home in a troubled world?*

Well, there *would* have to be reconstruction in her own mind as well as in the house and in the community—as well as praising the Lord!

"...and so I am hoping the school population is stable now. One more would be the straw that broke the camel's back," Miss Lizzie was saying. Well, why mention that

she would be getting one more—Yada? Courtney realized then that the Glamoras' return to their cabin would
leave Brother Jim and Miss Lizzie homeless.

# CHAPTER 9

# Setting the House in Order

❧

Clint and Courtney, inwardly bursting in pride, outwardly handled Miss Lizzie's assessment of their children casually. Clint delighted Donolar by asking that he spend some extra time with the boys.

"Miss Lizzie feels that you are a great help—a home teacher, really. When your sister's shipment comes, there will be a lot of new books for our library—maybe some to share with the school as well. Jordan likes literature, the Bible, Shakespeare—"

Donolar nodded, curls bobbing childishly over his unlined forehead. "He shall know the truth and the truth shall make him free—that's Bible, not Shakespeare. I will tell him all about the life cycle of my butterflies, too—"

"Thank you, Donolar. You are very understanding. But I had hoped you would help Kenney more in that area. He seems to be our biologist. And, of course, all of them need your work in literature, but Jordan especially. The girls—"

Again Donolar nodded. "They like my roses, but Jonda is afraid of bees and Blessing likes to draw pictures of butterflies instead of talking to them. The butterflies and bees like Jonda's music."

Courtney, listening from the bedroom window where she was preparing a column on furniture arrangement for the woman's page of *The Territorial Gazette*, smiled. It was unsettling but amusing that her brother whom so many (including his mother) found "strange," understood some corners of their children's minds better than their parents. "One thing is certain, though, Lord," she whispered in a quick prayer, "we have not spared the Word or Your love or ours—"

There was no time for an Amen as Clint, laughing, burst through the door. "You heard?" At her nod, he ran uncertain fingers through his hair and erased the smile. "I felt as foolish as when I tried to explain the birds and bees to the boys and found that the Laughtens had beat me to it. But, you know, that is proof that God had a wise plan in regard to families and friends. None of us do the job alone. We all need each other—which reminds me," Clint pretended to protect his face from any object she might throw, "I am almost afraid to tell you that I have a note here—and now, I have misplaced it—"

"The mind is the first to go!" Courtney quipped, then covered her own face. "Can you remember by whom the note was written?"

"Mind your manners! Of course, I remember. It's from Efraim."

"Efraim!" Courtney dropped her pencil. "*When— what*—tell me!"

Clint's shielding hands dropped to his side. "Two main things. He, Roberta, and Yada will be home at the next recess—unfortunately after Christmas but around New Year. And none too soon. It seems that the powers there object to Young America as a name for a town—"

Everything had looked so bright. Now it lost a bit of its promising glow and Courtney, whose heart had given a leap of joy at the prospect of her brother's return, slowed to normal. "What have they to say in such matters? Young America is the name *we* want—"

"It is a little hard to understand, harder yet for His Honor, the Mayor—that's *me*—to explain to the council. I will have to rely on history and their respect for Doc and Aunt Bella's account of statehood. Seems there was a tough time trying to push through a name for the state."

"I remember," Courtney said slowly, tapping her front teeth with her pencil. "Early settlers wanted 'Columbia,' but for some strange reason Washington, D.C. went for another Washington—sort of a namesake, old-timers claimed with some bitterness. Congress declared it was for the nation's first president that they proposed it. The Senate made out its own version of the territorial bill before Washington could become a state officially." She paused in puzzlement before adding, "But a town is different."

"Unfortunately not, if we hope to collect revenue. Efraim is preparing a lengthy editorial which explains everything better than I am doing—something about the name being in conflict with America itself."

"How silly! Do they quibble there as much as people do here?"

Clint laughed. "More, according to your brother."

---

It was six months to the day of selecting the architect—whose unblinking eyes, wide expanse of a mouth, and sparse straight-out moustache waxed to perfection, gave every appearance of a catfish—that he accomplished a miracle with only the help of field hands, a few miners for hire, and volunteers from the church. With Courtney's help too, of course. Closing her eyes, she was able to see again every minute detail of the great, rambling Mansion-in-the-Wild, including the wrought-iron fence laced tightly around the entire building like a too-tight corset. Almost comical, the Mansion had achieved a certain dignity and welcome which forgave its transgressions of poor taste in design. The finished house, a prototype of its predecessor, outdid it in beauty due to architect Alexander Pope Heston's expertise. Courtney, looking at the finished product, was overcome with emotion. The children, Mandy, and Mrs. Rueben were in their glory. And Clint, in wild abandon, tossed his hat in the air with a whoop. Pleased as punch, the beaming builder took them on a grand tour.

Bouncing about like a fish out of water, the man pointed out the fantail light above the massive front door, the fetching balcony above, with triple windows flanking it on both sides like compound eyes. The circular window nested under the peak of the roof was his own idea. Here there should be flowers; there, shrubs; and, of course, fruit trees lining the circular driveway which, fortunately, remained intact after the rubble of the fire was cleared away. Inside, the wood paneling and marble-top tables complemented one another. The library, Courtney's favorite room, was shelved from ceiling to floor with lighter wood on two papered, well-lighted walls, wherein would be encased her treasured books. The Persian rugs would add warmth and there would be pewter pitchers filled with Donolar's roses everywhere. The entire east wing would be bedrooms, and the walls along the stairway would be resplendent with portraits. Cara would help with drapes and—

Mandy took one look at the newly painted kitchen and burst into song. Not to be outdone, Mrs. Rueben began opening closets and banging them shut, drowning all song, and resorted to her native German. The few words Courtney was able to make out led her to know that here would be stored linens; there, china and silver; and "zee vun near'st der kitchen she's fo' der brooms—for vich I be needin' der padlock!"

"It is wonderful, *wonderful*," Courtney breathed as Clint placed the agreed-upon fee in the flouncing man's extended hand. "So, if there is something we can do for you—" she hesitated.

Alexander Pope Heston stood taller than he was, chest inflated. Mentally, she saw him fanning fingers forward—thumbs tucked beneath the red suspenders in victory. "Just tell all guests that Alexander did it!" He might as well have added, "the Great!"

The architect picked up his plans and rolled them into a scroll. "Perhaps I can use portions of this—in case Representative and Mrs. Glamora need a hand. His editorial alerted the readers that he will be returning; and I am supposing they will wish somewhat more lavish quarters than the cabin the preacher occupies. Not that he's a swell-head like some claim—begging your pardon, ma'am."

"Swell-head—whatever gave you such an idea?" Courtney said faintly.

"Never mind!" Clint growled. "You are out-of-order, Heston."

Confused, Mr. Heston looked for the nearest exit. "I apologize, Mr. Desmond. I only thought—well, with your being mayor, perhaps you, uh—should know that Mr. Glamora has taken some unpopular stands—"

"With which I agree." Clint's eyes were flashing.

"Yes, yes," the architect replied, backing toward the front door. "I only wanted you to know the talk in Old Town—hoping it would be helpful in preparing you—"

"Preparing us—for what?" Courtney urged, her heart pounding. "If there is trouble—"

"We will handle it. Good day, Mr. Heston," Clint said by way of dismissal. "I will show you out—thank you—and here is your hat."

"Should you have been so curt, darling?" Courtney asked as soon as the horse and rider were out of sight. "We need to know—"

"I know already—and you are not to worry your pretty head." Clint was making an effort to speak normally, but his eyes showed concern. "If I seemed to rush our talkative guest away, it was to tell you some far more exciting news. Your possessions have arrived!"

Courtney's squeal of delight brought the children back. Courtney wondered if any of them slept a wink that night. She heard the children talking but made no effort to stop their chatter. Her own eyes were focused on the beams of the bedroom ceiling. Christmas was near at hand. The furniture was to be arranged. Efraim, Roberta, and Yada were returning. How could she get it all done? "I can't, Lord," she whispered in the darkness.

"Of course, you can—*we* can—you, me, and the Lord," Clint murmured.

# CHAPTER 10

# Unnatural Curiosity

❦

As the dockhands transferred the bulky cargo of furniture and other possessions and carefully loaded it onto the waiting wagons, Clint was too preoccupied to take note of what Courtney observed uneasily. At first, there had been a knot of men, strangers to her, looking on as if they had nothing better to do. Natural, she supposed, although their eyes shifted somewhat *un*naturally. First to her, then to Clint. Then, as if to disguise their interest, the men talked in low voices—or were they plotting? If so, what did it concern? Why should they take an interest in this particular shipment? Ships unloaded at the docks daily. Given a moment alone, she would tell Clint.

She became more uneasy as the crowd of men enlarged. There were no women among them. The streets, usually so crowded, looked almost deserted. Her apprehension grew as one of the men, bearded and dirty, spat on the boardwalk and doffed his hat mockingly without speaking. Quickly, Courtney turned away without meeting his eyes.

On the way home, the children monopolized the conversation, planning with Donolar about books and their new interests, then wondering aloud what their cousin Yada would be like. Maybe he would wear a velvet suit and a peaked cap with a feather in it. Brother Jim then joined the conversation, explaining to them just what their responsibility was in "helping this laddie to adjust."

"Remember that Yada is not an Indian," he cautioned.

"Would that make a difference?" Did Courtney imagine it or was there a shade of resentment to the statement in Jonda's voice?

"Yada is Yada, my cousin, huh Mommy?" little Blessing asked softly.

"Yes, sweetheart, your cousin—that is, in a sense—" her voice wavered a bit as she wondered just how to explain the situation.

"Yada is adopted," Jordan took up the conversation. "But so are we!"

Again, Jonda spoke with a hint of resentment. "And does *that* make a difference, wise brother?"

"Yes, wise sister, in a way, it does. Our parents are related to us, while Yada—"

"—is Yada!" Blessing said again. "And I will love him."

"You will all love him," Courtney assured them. "There is no need for concern, Brother Jim."

"*Loving* concern only. The boy will need us all in helping him sort out just who he is—with his Hebraic heritage, mother's Indian upbringing, and our responsibility as Christians."

"Swift Arrow will help," Jonda said. Her cheeks turned pink, and Courtney wondered why.

"True, very true, my daughter—as will my good friend, Tobias. He will give us a hand, just as he has on the reservation," Brother Jim promised.

"Rabbi Epstern? He is Jewish," Kenney spoke for the first time, "and he is very smart—knows a lot about biology and calculus."

Brother Jim nodded. "And we're battling the same devil! We understand each other. By the way, did you know that Swift Arrow has accepted Jesus as his Savior and is helping teach some of the Indians we are unable to reach? He wants to unite with the church—but—"

"But what?" Jonda asked hotly. "He has every right. He loves God—"

"And *you* love him!" Jordan blurted out, reverting back momentarily to being a "brother."

Courtney was too startled to see the tears spring to her daughter's eyes at her brother's betrayal. What was the meaning of this? The wandering conversation had given her already-exhausted mind too much to digest. Would these children never cease to amaze her? She felt so close to them—and yet so far away. Did all mothers feel like this?

The chatter was still in progress. Swift Arrow had taken on a new name. Somebody giggled and was reprimanded by one of the other children. New name? Courtney remembered the ivory-skinned lad with blue-black hair.

What was it? First John, that's what it was—the talk continued.

Yeah, and his brother—well, not really his brother, but a *blood* brother like he had been to Rose Wind, Yada's mother—his brother was Second John. And then there was Third John—at least, if he decided to accept the Lord's invitation—

Courtney looked speechlessly at her husband, hoping for reassurance. Clint was paying attention to his driving, but from the corner of her eye she saw that his face shared her concern. There would have to be a long, long talk with these young ones and then a long, long prayer for guidance by their parents in private.

———————————

Christmas came and went. There was the gaudiest tree ever. With the children in charge, not a needle of the sweet-smelling fir was visible. But they were happy as they strung popcorn to drape over the already-groaning tree, singing carols as they worked together in harmony.

Courtney looked ahead happily to next Christmas when they would have everybody, absolutely *everybody*, in for a feast the way Cousin Bella used to do. Everybody? As she prepared the stuffing for Mandy's hens, her mind went back to the small boy who stole the wild goose for his starving people. Swift Arrow...First John...where did he fit in?

# CHAPTER 11

# Understandings

❧

"I am trying to make some sense of the conversation the children had as we were returning from the dock," Courtney told Clint that early-January night as they stood on the front balcony admiring the scene around them. A star arced across the sky on silver wings and vanished.

The winter had been unseasonably mild, nothing at all like the District of Columbia weather Roberta described in her frequent letters.

"Did you make a wish?" Clint asked, speaking of the star.

Courtney pressed her dark hair against his sleeve, looked up at him—knowing the dear planes of his face even in the darkness—and smiled.

"The only wish I have is a longing for our prayers to be heard and that we can meet the needs of each child. I wish they would not grow up so fast—there, I *did* make a wish, after all."

"God will hear our prayers—give Him time," Clint said reassuringly, then—pressing his lips to her hair— "Um-m-m, do I smell violets?"

"A little cologne in my rainwater shampoo," she admitted. "But we *will* smell violets soon. Donolar has planted big double ones along the walk. They will be in bloom by the time Efraim and Roberta are home. The children are broken-hearted over the delay, but trains are unable to battle the snow over the Divide. They shipped the furniture—"

Courtney's voice trailed off as she recalled the peculiar actions of the onlookers at the dock—another problem which somehow seemed like it would tie in with concerns about the children, the unrest in the cities, and something else she tried in vain to recall. But it eluded her.

"In a way," Clint said slowly, "the delay may be a good thing. Efraim has time now to give all the new laws a thorough study, and Roberta has renewed her interest in law—good that she is attending court sessions. I found the account of their living quarters most amusing," he laughed. "Apple boxes beneath a mattress is hardly the 'bed of ease' her father wanted for his only child."

"Ro would settle for anything to be near Efraim and Yada—or maybe I should have reversed those names. She idolizes that child—"

Again, she stopped. This, too, might create a problem, although she had made no mention of the conversation with her sister-in-law about an arrangement for Yada and Blessing's future. Removed from the scene, which had disturbed her then, Courtney dismissed the idea and hoped that Roberta had done the same. Probably the words meant nothing. Certainly less than Clint's arm around her as together they watched the changing scene in awe.

God seemed very close when a golden rim of moon poked inquiringly above a night-purple mountain to rose-tip the ruffles of light snow on the surrounding trees and fill the night with breathing shadows as a little wind rearranged the branches. As they watched in near-reverence, the moon rose slowly, sailing like a spirit freed from hampering restraints. In a way, she envied it. If only human beings were so free—

Something had captured her attention. For less than a moment a tower, an ethereal violet in the moonlight, loomed in the vicinity of where Rambling Gate once stood. Then, like the shooting star, it, too, was gone. Just a trick of the imagination, of course, but it served to bring back the niggling sense that something was un-finished. Violet . . . the door in her dream . . . what had purple represented? Riches? But what—?

Involuntarily, she shuddered.

"Cold, darling?" Clint said with concern.

"A little," Courtney admitted, "but I guess I am more scared than cold. I know we agreed to let matters take their own course, be patient, keep our hearts tuned to the situation—"

"—but you are still bothered," Clint finished for her. "It is mostly about Jonda, unless I miss my guess. Jonda and the Indian lad? Jonda has a good head on her shoulders—probably just now awakening to the injustices in the world, nothing more. Of course, she *is* maturing. Have you had a mother-daughter talk—not about Swift Arrow—John, I guess he goes by now—but—"

Men had a harder time with such things than women, Courtney thought with a secret smile. But when it came to big things—

"I am glad God created a woman for Adam instead of a male companion," she said suddenly. "It solves every-thing—almost."

"Agreed—no matter what prompted that observa-tion. Oh, I understand. Never mind our decision. Talk to Jonda if it will make you rest easier. I can see that you two are open about life. Good!"

---

Heavenly days had followed the arrival of the furni-ture. The excitement of unpacking, uncrating, arrang-ing, and rearranging. Surveying the near-completed job, except for the drapes Cara Laughten was working on, Courtney had not been happier since before the tragic fire. The furniture looked so inviting, so homey. It begged for company. And the slabs of marble made into table-tops, shelves, the stairway landing, and covering the foyer, lent a look of opulence to the entire decor. Even

Mandy and Mrs. Rueben ran out of breath praising the results—the cook taking great pride in the open-fire range and the entire set of granite cookware, while the housekeeper fluttered from closet to closet like a bird looking for a nesting place. Adequate storage space for the first time—room for everything except dust and "meddlers, dem wot tamper mit der contents."

So from time to time the two would bring down wrath upon the head of the other, but for now a shared enthusiasm brought peace.

All this Courtney reviewed as she waited a little apprehensively for Jonda to meet her in the library. Courtney had invited Jonda's approval of the ancestral-portrait arrangement. She thought herself prepared, but Jonda's entrance was disarming. So beautiful, so guileless, and so trusting. Half-woman, half-child that she was, Jonda strolled in (when had she become so graceful?), the amethyst gimp bringing new lights to the pale-gold hair, making her violet eyes appear even more dreamy than usual. Fleetingly, Courtney wished her niece (whom she thought of as a daughter) had chosen another color. The shade was a reminder of the dream—a diluted version of the "riches" door's purple.

"Lovely, Mother," Jonda said in admiration. "I wish I knew who they all are. It would make me know more about myself," she said, going from painting to painting. "Sometimes life confuses me."

Courtney felt confusion rising around her too. Somehow their roles had reversed. The child was the mother and had taken charge.

They talked at length about the ancestors. When the conversation lagged, Jonda smiled sweetly and said, "Now—truly why am I here? Is it about John? I thought you knew we were friends."

Courtney inhaled deeply. Then, following Jonda's lead, she used a direct approach. "How good of friends— is there something I should know, darling?"

"Only that my brother was right. I am in love with him."

Courtney gasped. "In love—oh Jonda, you are too young—"

The violet eyes widened. "How old must one be to know? In the Bible girls were married very young, and in *Romeo and Juliet*. Even you and Dad knew when you were very young. But just love me, understand—oh Mother!"

And then they were in each other's arms.

# CHAPTER 12

# And On to
# Other Matters...

❦

After their discussion, there was a closer tie between mother and daughter. Nothing was settled, and yet everything was. As long as there could be openness, there would be understanding—even though, secretly, a million misgivings churned in Courtney's mind. Although Jonda was only 12, something in the girl's manner was so sincere that Courtney knew there was deep love in her heart for the boy she called John, and wisdom far beyond her years. No silly giggling, no whispering among friends, a calm self-assurance that brought the bloom one usually observes in young ladies twice her age.

Courtney herself realized that always she had envisioned Jonda floating down the aisle of the new church clad in gleaming white satin, a frock Cara's caring fingers would fashion in a deftly simple style. The veil would be a drift of mist over her golden hair. There would be soft strains of Lohengrin's "Wedding March"... sacred vows... and tossing of the bouquet of white lilies and roses from Donolar's garden—just the way she and Cousin Bella would have wanted it. At the thought, there was an unbearable tightening about her heart, a missing of her wise cousin's counsel—and yes, misgivings about the groom.

Just who qualified for the groom was unclear. But was it—oh dear Lord, was she prejudiced?—an Indian? Clint would say she was premature with such thinking, but so was Jonda's maturity. She must sort out her feelings. Not just hers, but those of other people, for here there was family involved and the entire settlement was so closely knit. Everyone would be affected. *But later, Lord, please later....*

And then her mind flashed back—as if a screen were spread before her eyes—and projected memories of the talk between her and Roberta. "Children must live their own lives ... choose their own mates ... make up their own minds." How glibly Courtney had mouthed the words to Yada's mother.

Weary of trying to resolve the unexpected challenge in young Jonda's sudden maturity, Courtney turned her thinking to the satisfaction she felt regarding Jonda's absorption in her music. Most of her after-school time was spent at Miss Lizzie's ancient piano. Although the sharps and flats were off-key to the trained ear and one of the ivory keys stuck when touched, somehow she was able to coax music from the instrument, Miss Lizzie reported. All the old hymns Jonda could play by memory, bringing to them a vibrancy that even the authors would scarcely have believed. On and on she played, even as twilight shadows crept into the small living room and she could no longer see the notes on the more difficult pieces the teacher had provided. And then, dreamily, she would compose music wild and sweet, as if to reveal her very soul—sometimes joyful, often sad.

"My husband," Miss Lizzie said affectionately of Brother Jim, "has no knowledge of music and, if the truth be known, probably not the slightest interest. However, with Jonda's playing he sits up and listens—even says Amens to the lovely hymns and sometimes sings with her. Lovely voice that girl has! As for my husband, once he has sung his heart out, he arranges his big frame comfortably, with aid of pillows, in that high, straight-backed chair and dozes off—sometimes noisily!"

"I do hope our daughter is no nuisance—"

"Oh no!" Miss Lizzie smiled, almost mischievously. "It is a relief to have my protégé—may I call her that?—give both of us some rest: him from pulpit-pounding preaching and me from his snores!"

Courtney tried hard to put the friendship of Jonda and John out of her mind to give herself and Jonda some thinking time, but trying was not enough. Little things kept cropping up. There was the dining room, for instance. As yet, it was unfinished. The polished furniture looked lonely—like a store-window display—without the draperies, big bowls of Donolar's roses, a roaring fire, and *people*. Already Mandy was at work on the bill of fare for the first dinner, timed for when Mr. Efraim and Miz Roberta arrived. Praise be, the table was even larger and wider than Miz Arabella's, as there was bound to be more gathering 'round. Courtney had nodded at Mandy's observation, wondering what she would say if Jonda wanted to include John. That question set her mind traveling in even wider circles. What about the lad's wanting to attend (*unite with*, Brother Jim had said) the church? Would the congregation welcome him? *Stop crossing bridges before reaching them*, she warned herself.

It was a blessed departure from tormenting questions when, without warning, Roberta's beautiful piano arrived—none of the other furniture, just the piano, the most important! Jonda ran loving fingers over the mellow wood and rippled a thumb across the keyboard. Then she sat down and played for two hours before the instrument was moved from the foyer to the music room—the children's private hideaway where each pursued his or her talents, sometimes alone but more often together, concentrating without conversation. That Jonda was dedicated, there could be no doubt.

Clint was happy in a detached sort of way, his mind divided in so many directions. The steam-operated mill he had ordered freighted had arrived. It replaced the primitive arrastas that Jose Hernandez, the faithful Mexican worker, had improvised. The new mill would be safer and would crush the rock for extracting ore in a fraction of the previous time. Thanks to the rapidly expanding population, demands for *The Territorial Gazette* doubled, then tripled. Clint, dividing his time between his various enterprises, was on the run every hour of daylight. Evenings he divided between working and planning expansion of the church facilities, meeting with the fact-finding committees suggested by the school board of trustees, and his mayoral responsibilities. Meetings ... meetings ...

That left little time for his family—and certainly no time for Courtney to trouble him with her apprehensions about the children (for he was right, everything did seem to be going smoothly). Although the colored-door dream had returned, she would feel foolish to ask him or anybody else to interpret it. As far as ogling men were concerned, she should be accustomed to that. So she carried on busily, devoting her time to the house, the children, and taking on more and more responsibility in writing the newspaper columns. In fact, Clint's assistant editor was so pleased with her writing that he no longer asked Clint to edit her work. She wrote about the seasons—their beauty and what the busy homemakers could do to shorten their hours in the kitchen and garden by planning ahead and how to make use of canned and dried meats and vegetables. She wrote about activities in the two communities, seeking help from women she knew in both Old Town and New Town. She wrote about women's role in politics, speculating that one day they would be given a voice just as they now were allowed to vote on local measures. And she wrote about equal rights for all peoples regardless of code, creed, or color. On this, she boldly invited other women to write in their opinions. The inpouring of scribbled notes was her reward, although Jonda laughingly agreed that it would take the Rosetta stone to unsnarl the hieroglyphics. It was a scathing letter from Widder Brown, representing those who shunned association with the Indians, that lighted the fuse to a bomb ready to explode. Clint broke the news with concern.

"Old Town is looking for trouble, according to talk around the mine," he said. "They blame Efraim, women's 'interference'—and well, our association with 'half-breeds.' Yada—or Jonda's friend?"

# CHAPTER 13

# A Changing Atmosphere

February bowed out after coating the countryside with a sheet of ice. All night the snow fell heavily, and the first morning of March came in with an icy wind puffing out its cheeks. Trees bent beneath its force, sending needles of snow to sting noses of those who dared venture out. Clint was among them. Clad in a heavy mackinaw and wearing a furry hat with earflaps, he rubbed his hands in anticipation of the biting cold.

"I wish you would stay home with us. The school is closed so we could pop corn, make chocolate, do family things—" Courtney said, wistfully looking at the roaring fire he had built in the living room.

"I do too, sweetheart, but Jose needs help erecting the new mill. It is urgent to make the changeover. You know how important it is to do away with the arrastas. You know how unsafe they were."

Yes, she knew. It was an accident caused by the makeshift means of mining that caused his temporary blindness and almost ended their marriage—or had his long convalescence strengthened it? After all, her mother had tried in vain to destroy the relationship. Now Courtney knew, with a sudden surge of certainty born of love, that nothing could.

"It is wonderful what we have built together," she said, standing on tiptoe to turn up her husband's collar.

Clint nodded as though he barely heard her, his mind already at the mine. She watched him fumble in his pocket for his gloves which lay on the highboy. Reaching for them with a fond smile, she glanced about the room. How she loved it! In the long oval mirror she saw reflected an image of the self-consciously quaint and charming room love had put together and held in its arms: dancing flames from the fireplace turning to pure gold the age-old settles beside it and the crane extended from above...old-fashioned rockers...the piecrust table (centered by Donolar's arrangement of spruce branches and bright-cheeked rose hips)...rag rugs flanking the polished wide-board spaces beyond the Oriental carpet with the fluffy white bearskin rugs between...and the handmade spinning wheel in the corner. Just a jumble of styles, colors, and periods—the effect was delightful: as warm as the comforting fire, as welcoming as their love—and as ageless.

As Clint, grinning with a little-boy look of embarrassment, pulled on his gloves, there was an icy draft around their feet—a signal that someone had entered the room noiselessly.

"Sorry," an astonished Jonda murmured. "I—I was unaware that you were here—or I would have knocked—"

"You are always welcome, darling," Courtney assured her. "It is nice to have you home."

Jonda inhaled deeply, delicate nostrils flaring ever so slightly. "Sometimes I wish," she said in a small voice, "that I could be here always—away from the world—"

Clint looked at her in surprise. "I thought you enjoyed school and your friends. Is there a problem, Jonda—something you need to talk about with your mother and me?"

Pushing back her cloud of golden ringlets, Jonda looked from one to the other as if fearful of upsetting them. Then exhaling her sucked-in breath, she said haltingly, "School is fine and I love my music—"

"But your friends?" Clint looked at her with concern.

"There is something wrong," she burst out. "Please no more questions—I—I don't know—"

And she ran from the room.

"What do you make of it? I am worried about her, Clint."

"I will look into it—talk to her again—but we will not push her—"

"You are hesitating. What is it, Clint?"

Clint looked deeply into Courtney's eyes. His own were tender, but knowing. She would worry more if he left something unsaid than if he said it. "I am wondering if there is any connection between Jonda's comments and the changes I have noticed at the council meetings. There is a sort of—well, hostility. It could be only a small matter or—"

"Or?"

"Or it could be a sort of conspiracy. I have been reviewing some of Efraim's editorials and interviews under "The Washington Scene" column. You know yourself that the valley's populace has changed since he and Roberta went to Washington. We have always been the melting pot here, but somehow we have managed to accept differences—at least, until both sides of the river filled up with malcontents, the embittered, and the failures. Even the neutrals seem unwilling to join beneath a single flag. Underneath it all, I sense a push for political power—people who think themselves to be leaders and in reality are puppets of some driving force—you understand?"

Courtney nodded. "I guess it has always been like this, people trying for power, trying to dominate others. Every so often civilization is set back by it. But darling, what makes you suspicious?"

"I wasn't going to discuss this, but I need a colleague. I found a directive mailed out from Washington, D.C. Of course, it could have been mailed elsewhere and rerouted. If it came from Washington, somebody here is serving as a misguided satellite. But you need to know that there are those who feel your brother is responsible for the trouble."

*Efraim!* "That is impossible," she said through frozen lips.

"I know, but there is such hostility among the new factions here, refusals to accept each other at face value, that it has created suspicion among those who used to trust one another—the minority groups—Mexicans, Chinese, Jews, and Indians."

Courtney's heart stopped. "Jonda," she whispered, "—John."

Clint took off his gloves to smooth her hair. "I have upset you—"

Courtney reached up to pull his head to her shoulder. "Oh my darling, I *want* to be a part of your life—never, ever hold anything back. Let me worry with you if that is what it takes—"

Clint chuckled, his breath warm against the part in her hair. "Our Jordan would call you a valuable stage prop—oh Courtney—"

"It makes no difference what title you hang on it. I want to be a part of your private genius!"

"Hey!" Clint laughed, pushing her away gently and putting on his gloves again, "that is a big word. Let's not abuse it. This family has its share already."

Again she was seized by the longing to delay his departure, an emotion Clint read in her eyes. "Don't tempt me, woman! Tell you what—I will finish at the mine and get home early."

Courtney nodded, a lump in her throat. Then she watched him as, head braced against the wind, he turned into the woods. The road was too slippery to risk riding a horse. It occurred to her suddenly that there could lurk threats more dangerous than the storm in the woods.

--------

The storm lasted for two weeks, growing worse before it became better. Wheat farmers welcomed the drop of the mercury as exactly what they needed to lock the seed into its winter bed. And, of course, it gave them time to gather around the potbellied stove of Tony Bronson's Company Store, the only place in the growing New Town to retain its original name, proprietor, and clientele. There they whittled, complained about the government, and solved the world's problems. Anything, they said good-naturedly, to get away from their "brawling women." Davey Hightower said, over a game of checkers, that he outright quoted to his wife Proverbs 21:9 about it being better to dwell on a housetop than with one of them brawlers in a wide house. The game stopped while the men laughed until Davey soberly relayed Symanthia's answer. "She taken Brother Jim's text, she did, and throwed Proverbs 15:18 about a wrathful man stirring up strife then hammered it home comparing a slothful man to a hedge o'thorns—making me downright skeered she was a-gonna toss me right in a briar patch!"

The "slothful" of Old Town spent their time with what Brother Jim called "unregenerate drunks." The preacher himself visited some of the saloons trying to seek out the "backsliders" and separate them from the confirmed alcoholics. "Seemed useless," he reported, "depriving them of liquor would be putting a bullet in their heads, the devil's got such a hold on their souls." But he said frowning, what bothered him was the talk and then the lack of it. "Acted like they were planning the Boston Tea Party," he said, puzzled, "until I put in an appearance. Then there was silence, dead silence. They just sat there like sacks of meal. Something's going on, I tell you...."

Unsuspecting housewives went about their business, complaining about being unable to put out a white washing. Everybody knew lye soap alone couldn't do the job. Took the sun to bleach the yellow out. And it was so cold that even the flatirons wouldn't heat on live coals!

Mandy and Mrs. Rueben weathered the storm surprisingly well, although the newfangled pump (installed on the wide back porch) froze and "Matilda," the cook's prize hen—usually a sensible fowl—lacked the judgment of "Bertha," the housekeeper's goose. Imagine hatching out chicks so early! Mandy brought hen and chicks into her spotless kitchen and used an abandoned crate covered with burlap as an incubator.

The big house, "magnificently furnished," brought the two women closer than Courtney remembered ever seeing them—proving once more that peace could be achieved in a world of unrest. There was no complaining about the increased work although it was five times greater than the other house had been. This they denied, of course.

Mandy complained of one thing only. "This place ain't a-gonna be happy 'til it's got company wid lotsa foks gathered 'round dat big ole table. Hit's a-gwine t'be a great day in de mawnin' w'en Mr. Efraim and Miz Roberta gits heah—'cep fo'—"

"For what, Mandy?" Courtney asked through a mouthful of pins as she tried to adjust the kitchen curtains Cara had completed.

Mandy hesitated and apologized for mentioning the matter at all. Then, with her avaricious appetite for delivering news, she blurted out, "Well y'all knows dat fetchin' cleanin' woman wat comed heah-bouts as wat some foks wuz a-callin' de 'Black Widder,' her man bein' kilt mysterious-like? Works parta de time fo' foks in Ole Town and gits de lowdown—not a whit lack mah frien' Hannah—"

"Der vun mit der face plain as der fryin' pan," Mrs. Rueben interjected.

Mandy nodded her frizzled head. "Yessum, dull lack w'en it ain't polished—but now Hannah she's honest, works harder'n most 'n keeps uh civil tongue in 'er cheek—"

Courtney climbed down from the stepladder on which she had been standing and removed the pins from her mouth. "What is this leading up to, Mandy? Cleaning ladies do not come in matched pairs—"

"Sho' nuf," Mandy broke in, "ain't no twins, 'cordin'

t'de good Lawd's plan. Well, now, de widder woman's doin' wat servants should'n oughta—tellin' wat's a-happenin' in de householes—so's dat whur de tales 'bout our Yada begun."

"Yada?" Courtney felt a choking in her windpipe as if she had swallowed one of the pins, cutting off her ability to make a sound. But somehow she found the voice to ask, "What about him, Mandy?"

"Dat he ain't a-gonna be 'lowed in school—bein' de wors' kinda mix breed—'nuf t'break mah heart, him bein' so sweet 'n all—"

Mandy paused and drew such a long breath her ample bosom inflated dangerously. Courtney pinched her chin in concentration. So Yada—dear, sweet little Yada—was part of the problem. And there was more to come, she knew, by the sudden explosion of Mandy's breath.

" 'n hit's breakin' dis ole heart o'mine de thangs dey's a-sayin' 'bout—uh—'bout mah li'l Jonda, po' baby—all 'cuz dat widder—"

The pin in Courtney's throat traveled downward, stabbing her heart. "Gossip, Mandy—ugly and against God's will," she choked without waiting to hear more. That it had to do with Jonda's friendship with the Indian lad there could be no question. She must try and dismiss it from her mind, only she was unable. The damage was done, arousing suspicion in her own mind. *Was Jonda meeting John secretly?*

The roads were passable by the last Sunday in March, and a pale-yellow sun made a half-promise that the worst was over. Settlers knew without being told that Brother Jim would be preaching. Eagerly, they clustered before the service to catch up on the latest news. Courtney's spirits lifted—until Mandy nudged her to whisper, "See? Dar she is!"

Beautiful, yes, except for the boldness of eye and looseness of tongue, a young woman ducked and ran. All eyes turned Courtney's direction—and then turned away. So the lines were drawn. . . .

# CHAPTER 14

# The Truth

Spring arrived without an overture. One day it was winter, the next it was spring. The rains continued, but they were soft and warm, bringing a million trilliums, white violets, and new fern fronds to the woods; daisies, Indian paintbrush, and wide-eyed daisies to the meadows. Cows brought home new calves. Mandy's lima beans poked up inquisitive heads, and Donolar's roses filled the air with sweetness.

Warm April sun unlocked the earth, and wheat "as thick as the hair on a dog's back" gave cause to the farmers to be jubilant. All nature seemed in tune, and history began to repeat itself.

Jonda—just as Roberta before her had done—began to take walks between her long hours of practice at the piano. Longing for an opportunity for them to be alone and talk, Courtney offered to accompany her. Jonda always shook her head, sometimes a little sadly as if she almost regretted growing up. Her words were always the same, "I need to be alone with my thoughts." Courtney, equally sad, watched her daughter disappear out of sight. It came as no surprise that she traced Roberta's footsteps—the footsteps which led to (what was it called?) the Path of Springtime Moons? Where they found Rose Wind and where John, then called Swift Arrow, had taken Courtney to find Grandmother Old, the aged squaw who cared for little Blessing when she was stolen away mistakenly because she looked like Yada.

She wondered if Jonda would consider it spying if she retraced the journey, found Grandmother—who truly had proven to be very wise—and consulted her. No, that would be meddling—or was it meddling to check on a child so young? These questions she took to the Lord, trying to be patient as she waited for a solution. It was slow in coming.

One bright spring day in mid-April Clint came home unexpectedly, announcing that he had word of a man in Old Town looking for a newspaper job, and would Courtney come along? At last—a chance to be alone with Clint, a chance to talk. Quickly she changed from a housedress to a lightweight skirt and yellow taffeta-silk blouse with a ruffle of petals at the neck. Her reward was Clint's soft whistle.

"You look exactly like a daffodil," he said at the door.

His compliment made her feel frivolous, young again. And then she saw that Brother Jim was in the buggy awaiting them outside. Much as she enjoyed his company, her spirits plummeted. No talking today. . . .

The men found William Jennings in a bar, drowning his troubles—which were numerous, all of them were to learn later. His wife had died of consumption, his topsoil had blown away in a Kansas windstorm, and his cattle had been stolen by poachers. So here he was—penniless.

"And drunk!" Clint said sternly. "Now, you listen to me. If you want a job—a newspaper job—you are to dry out and stay that way. Do I make myself clear? Hang onto that lamppost for support until I can get the buggy—and watch your language. My wife is with me."

"I can work," the white-haired man in need of a haircut and a bath said thickly. "I am a newspaper man—an editor, a g-good one."

When he hiccupped, Brother Jim boomed, "Man, would you rather have your veins run with printer's ink or alcohol? You'll have to choose!"

Courtney felt the urge to giggle. It was as if she had a sudden vision of this man's brain fermenting like

Mandy's dill pickles and now shedding its juice, letting him come alive. His eyes narrowed then widened as if he were seeing light for the first time.

"You must be the parson," William Jennings said as if just awakening, "And you, sir, must be Efraim Glamora, owner of *The Gazette*. But I thought you were in Washington—I worked on *The Post* there once—"

"No," Clint corrected. "I am his brother-in-law, and I expect this newspaper to be doubling its circulation by the time he returns. I am part owner, but my other interests make it impossible for me to carry on alone. And I need some time with my family."

"So do I—some time, money, and education for my lad—as well as some exposure to religion, parson," he said to Brother Jim.

"The best exposure you can give him is to *bring* him to church."

William Jennings hung his head, then lifted it with determination. "I will and that's a promise. And, Mr.—I didn't catch your name—"

"Clint—Clint Desmond." Clint extended his hand. "Courtney, this is our new editor—I think. My wife, *Mrs.* Desmond."

The animated editor-to-be bowed to Courtney. "I am Willie," he said with simple dignity. "Let me assure all of you that I have what it takes—the grit, the spit—to put all other newspapers to sleep. I'll clean up this town. Justice! That's my theme song. I would die for the blindfolded lady! I'll remain sober as a judge."

"You'll need to do better than that, Willie," Brother Jim growled. "Judges around here are the watering holes' best patrons."

Willie nodded. "When do I start, Mr. Desmond?"

"Clint, please. We need a friendly relationship and you may find us a bit more informal. Get yourself cleaned up and your boy in school," Clint said, placing a bill in his hand. "Monday all right?"

Monday was fine! He and Tadwell, who was nine, were certainly obliged. And from Monday on, time was to tell, Willie made good his promises.

The trio was almost home when, as they shared a laugh over Brother Jim's comment about hoping to see Willie next time "looking like a bar of soap after a hard day's washing," two figures, hands laced together, shoulders touching, walked slowly between the trees. So lovely they looked that the arrow-straight dark youth and his golden goddess could have been a painted-in part of the green vale. So young, so innocent, and so in love—

*In love?* Why, it was Jonda!

Brother Jim put a restraining finger over Courtney's lips. "Pass in silence," he pleaded. "It is as pure as washed wool. Tobias and I have talked—"

Clint all but stopped the buggy, but Courtney motioned him on. The wheels moved noiselessly over the thick carpet of dead pine needles. Courtney sat frozen until the Path of Springtime Moons took the pair out of hearing distance.

"Has Rabbi Epstern dared to try converting Jonda to the Jewish faith?" she asked between stiff lips. "We were led to believe that the boy had accepted Jesus—wanted to unite—" her voice broke.

Brother Jim placed his rough, ham-like hand over her knotted-together, icy ones. "Say his name, Courtney—it is John," he said kindly. "We must accept him before asking the congregation to do so. And you need have no fears—about *anything*, my child. Tobias would never try imposing his ideas on anyone—and couldn't if he wanted to. The law of their faith prohibits women from becoming Jewesses unless their husbands are Jews. Not that Jonda could be blown about like a straw in the wind even if John had elected to—"

"John?" Clint's voice expressed shock. "How could an Indian—"

Brother Jim appeared to be wrestling with a decision. What was he holding back? Clint's unasked question was answered after a very short hesitation. "It's all very complicated, and I was hoping the truth could remain with John himself—where it belongs. But folks have made so much of this—mostly, because they're riled up about everything in general—that maybe you ought to know."

"*Ought* to?" Clint's hands tightened on the reins and his voice shook with restraint. "We're Jonda's parents. We have a *right* to know."

Big Jim's round head bobbed up and down in agreement. "That's just what Tobias said. But well, you see, John has a Jewish heritage—being only half Indian. His father, a soldier at the fort, was killed in battle with another tribe, more war-like. His Indian wife and their child returned to the reservation for protection."

"The father was Jewish, I gather?" Clint said in resignation. "You are right—it is complicated."

"But John chose to accept Christ not as a prophet, but as his personal Savior. I talked with him, read the Bible to him—showing him how the Old and the New Testaments tie together. But it was your Jonda who prayed with him—"

Tears welled up in Courtney's eyes and spilled onto Brother Jim's hands. From someplace in her heart where dreams are stored the vision returned. A green door swung open to reveal a cathedral with soft moss for a carpet on which there knelt two children—too young to be in love, but were. Overhead the pines made music wild and sweet—like Jonda's playing. *Oh dear God*, her heart whispered, *what is the answer?*

She would always believe the Lord felt that He had kept her waiting long enough. As if by divine instinct, Courtney knew that Jonda had been aware of being detected and, having nothing to hide, she would come to her mother.

She was right.

The timing was perfect. Jonda came into the bedroom shortly after Clint left for work. There, in the privacy of the half-dark, she cuddled close as she had done as a Goldilocks-toddler, frightened that the bears were going to gobble her up as punishment for trespassing.

"I am in love with John."

"I know, darling," Courtney answered, drawing the budding young body to her. "You have no need to work at convincing me."

"I think," Jonda continued, breath warm and sweet on Courtney's face, "that I loved him back when he came into our lives—took the goose—because he was forced to choose between theft and love of his starving people. Or is that really stealing?"

"I am not sure, Jonda. Mothers are less wise than their children sometimes. But what surprises me is that you remember. I thought I was the only witness. Neither of us said a word—how did he know?"

"Where the goose was—or that we would not betray him? I—I showed him the fowl, and he trusted us on the other—just as we trusted him to guide us to Grandmother Old's hiding place where our Blessing was."

A streak of dawn laid a pink finger on Jonda's golden hair and outlined the dimpled, vulnerable face—so open to hurt. "You thought I was too young to remember? Oh Mother, I remember it all. Sometimes I think my memory was developed before I was born—along with all the heartaches of coming here, feeling so abandoned that I took it out on all of you—and yet, all I ever wanted was to be loved—"

"I know, my precious Jonda, I know," Courtney whispered, tenderly pushing the rose-gold ringlets from the Dresden forehead. "I guess those of us who are robbed of our childhood grow up faster. I did—"

Jonda's response was an impulsive reaching out to throw both arms about Courtney's neck. "Oh Mother, you are so wonderful, so understanding. You believe my heart can know—even though I am going on 13—"

Courtney smiled against her daughter's hair. Going on 13 sounded so much more mature to the youthful ears. And yet—

"If you are looking for approval to be friends with John, you have it, darling. But are you able to leave it at that for now?"

Drawing Jonda even closer, Courtney told her about Lance. How, so eager to be loved, that she had attributed qualities to him that were sadly lacking because he, too, was searching for love. How, although he would remain forever in the tender memories she had folded away, she knew now what true love was—the give-and-take of it, the sacred, God-given gift.

Courtney wavered when Jonda interrupted to say, "But Mother, you were barely 16 when you met my father and fell in love the beautiful way you describe. What would you have done if—if somebody—or some circumstance had forbidden your love? Would you have loved again?"

How could she answer? And how could she tell Jonda that there was a difference—when perhaps none existed?

"I guess," she said weakly, "the difference is that our love had the approval of those around us." Courtney paused just short of adding that the very difference was what almost tore her from Clint's arms—how she had felt pushed, even while being hopelessly in love—how overapproval could be as threatening as love of the forbidden fruit.

"You're thinking of all the problems our love will bring—is already bringing," Jonda said softly. "We know them all, feel them already, realize that our families and friends will be affected—"

"The problems have begun already, and I wish I could take all the hurts you face away. I want only your happiness, but I must make a request, my baby—forgive me, you have outgrown that word—it's only that I love you so dearly that I will always see you as one of my babies."

"I want to be." Jonda's voice was filled with tears. "The request?"

Everything hinged on the next words. Leaning on God for strength, Courtney said haltingly, "That you and John will stay as you are, give yourselves time—and lean on God. He alone is wise."

# CHAPTER 15

# Uncertainty of the Future

❦

The season moved into May. Along the brink of the little brook separating Donolar's Isle-of-Innisfree from the rambling Desmond house the mayflies hatched out, swarming dully as if waiting to be swallowed up by the silver-streaked trout that leaped eagerly to oblige. The children, taught by Uncle Donny to cast out lines, furnished many a treat for the family dinner table. There really should be a fish fry, Mandy suggested. Maybe that would serve as an open house, she hinted.

Courtney's heart picked up speed. The subject was one she had tried to avoid. Such a short while ago, everything had hinged on a housewarming as a means of letting the settlement know that this house, like Mansion-in-the-Wild, was to be home to all. But a certain reserve shook the very foundations of her soul now. Her feeling that they were objects of suspicion to all became more and more evident. In fact, she wondered what would happen if invitations were extended and nobody came. Perhaps it was better this way, a sort of postponing, rather than having the alienation be made complete. Or was such thinking foreign to Jesus' teaching? His parable, for instance, about the king who invited guests to his son's wedding then proceeded to prepare the feast to which nobody came. The host then sent servants out to invite the uninvited, the good and the bad. Somehow the message seemed significant, but how or why?

Toward the month's end, Roberta, Efraim, and Yada arrived, unannounced like the spring. The children, out fishing, heard the clatter of the loose board on the bridge spanning the creek which fed Donolar's moat. The turn of buggy wheels announced company, and the company was just who they had waited so long to see.

"Yada, Yada!" all screamed at once, surrounding their cousin like a small army. Questions. Embraces. Laughter. And the family was all together again.

And together they remained for the next several days, denying Courtney and Roberta an opportunity to be alone, although both longed for a private talk. Well, it could wait. For now, Courtney enjoyed the joy of togetherness as the four of them tried in vain to catch each other up on the high points of the news above the children's noisy play.

Efraim was pleased with Clint's hiring of William Jennings, and even more pleased when he learned that, yes, the editor had stayed as dry as a bone. And what work he was turning out—somewhat controversial, but then these were times of controversy—

"I understand that I am the center of it—my reports from Washington," Efraim said tiredly.

"Only *one* of the centers. The atmosphere here seems charged with several. But yes, I would say that the reports of bills you introduced regarding better provisions for the Indians are a disturbing factor. Of course, I have held my ground, because I agree with you. This is not a popularity contest. It's an issue to which we will have to apply Christian principles."

"We may be fed to the lions before it ends."

"Could very well be," Clint said soberly. "We, Courtney and I, seem to have become involved in a *personal* way—but that can wait for an explanation—"

Roberta's eyes questioned Courtney's over their husbands' heads, but Courtney made no effort to communicate. This took some thinking. Best now to let the men discuss the bank, the mine, and the wheat. Eventually, the talk led to housing. Why, Roberta and Efraim were to stay here, of course, Courtney and Clint chimed in together.

"We expect to plunge in on building immediately," Roberta said with stars in her eyes. "There should be another house where Rambling Gate stood—and I want the children to be together (her amber eyes sought Courtney's significantly). Also, Old Town is no place for living, although I want to resume a law practice—Old Town's no place for Yada either."

At that very moment Yada's laugh rang out, followed by Blessing's.

"Love at first sight," Roberta said with satisfaction.

---

Efraim and Roberta, after touring and admiring expansion and redecorating of what once was only the Desmond cabin, asked for the architect's name. Clint gave it with some reluctance.

"Alexander Pope Heston knows his business but not his place. He steps out of it sometimes. There is something about the man I dislike."

"No matter how unsavory, or whether he sympathizes with our cause," Roberta said, dreamily caressing the smooth woods and marbles around her and obviously seeing visions of her own home, "we want him. Right, Efraim?"

Touched by her enthusiasm, Efraim squeezed her hand affectionately. The gesture translated into consent, Courtney supposed. But she was genuinely concerned for the first time when Clint, who almost never tampered with the decisions of others, warned, "Just be careful what you say around Heston. The future is so uncertain—"

Courtney was unable to hear the rest since Roberta had interrupted to ask in a little aside if Courtney had found what the mysterious key unlocked. "Doors," she blurted out, regretting it. How foolish she would have looked if she had added the rest of her dream: "doors to many colors." "Actually," she said instead, "I had forgotten about the key. It is in the rolltop desk. You and I can experiment sometime."

"*Time* reminds me," Roberta broke in, "we shipped the seven-foot fruit-wood grandfather clock to mark time for us, and my eastern-made love seats which I want Cara to re-cover with mauve velveteen. Just wait until you see it all! It will all be so romantic—and we will color our garden with petunias...flower beds... hanging baskets...borders along the walk. Donolar can be our landscaper."

When Roberta paused for breath, Courtney said, "He will love that—as well as salvaging the healthier fruit trees. He has checked on the survivors of the fire already and by thinning the apples—a new way of increasing the size of the fruit, he says—Donolar coaxed more and better apples than our own sparse crop."

"He has changed so much, as I am sure you have noticed."

Actually, no, Courtney had not noticed. Now that she thought about it, however, it came to her that there had been no babbling or strange, otherworldly talk for as long as she could remember. "Maybe," she said slowly, "the change comes from having responsibility."

Roberta listened with interest as Courtney told her with ill-concealed pride how well the children were doing and the part Donolar had played in helping them to make the most of their talents. Courtney paused in embarrassment when she realized that the men were listening.

"Never mind, little sister. You have every right to be proud parents. With a little humility, you might say you do a perfect job!" Efraim teased.

*Perfect? Oh no, there is Jonda*, her heart whispered hauntingly.

"Everything will turn up roses!" Roberta declared with a knowing smile, "in spite of what you men fear.

How dare you quarrel with 'The Star-Spangled Banner?' I brought some sheet music of the anthem for Jonda, by the way. Sooo—let's be 'dawn's-early-lighters' instead of 'twilight's-last-gleamers'," she smiled gaily.

"Maybe you should transpose your mood to a lower key," Efraim said slowly. "Eloquent—but 'bombs bursting in air'? The future *is* uncertain."

# CHAPTER 16

# Naming of a City

In the whirlwind days that led into summer, both Roberta and Jonda gave every appearance of being either blissfully happy or determinedly cheerful. Courtney, a cloud of doubt hovering over her usually sunny heart, wondered if they were dodging reality or if she herself was a borrower of trouble.

Roberta had seemed so eager to be alone with Courtney at first, whereas she now avoided it, devoting herself completely to planning the house with Alex Heston. "Oakwood Knoll" it would be called, because the great house was to sit atop an oak-dotted hillock overlooking the millstream, site of Rambling Gate and its painful memories. The mood would be light, she planned aloud when the Glamoras and Desmonds were a foursome (always, it seemed). It would be totally different from the heaviness of formal fringed drapes and massive furniture. On and on she planned the cozy comfort of the 12-foot old-rose couch and matching pillows—with blue tassels, of course, picking up the color of braided rugs. There would be bric-a-brac shelves for innocuous collections, Roberta added, rambling on about every detail down to the cookie cutters. And a dog, oh yes, an *enormous* Belgian sheep dog . . . black and probably named for his breed, *Bouvier de Flanders*. While Courtney and Clint would welcome the masses, as had Cousin Bella before them, she and Efraim would maintain a sort of cloistered privacy, a retreat from the world.

Courtney longed to tell her sister-in-law that there could be no retreat from the world, and neither should there be. Furthermore, there should never be here where neighborliness was the goal upon which the future depended. Coutney tried to remind her that not all stories had happy endings. . . .

How, she wondered, could there be a happy ending for her daughter? Jonda, too, wrapped herself in a world of love's young fantasy. How the child's face had lighted when she asked permission to bring John, whom Aunt Ro would remember as Swift Arrow, to dinner, to let her see the changes and share her secret. Courtney had agreed haltingly, asking only for time to prepare Roberta—that opportunity had not come.

"Does Roberta know about Jonda's infatuation?" Clint asked once.

"Oh darling, it is more than that," Courtney responded, taking the opportunity to explain about her long talk with Jonda, then went on to say that Roberta was so busy buzzing around that it was doubtful if she would really hear the story even if Courtney told it. Roberta's behavior at the Sunday worship service bore out Courtney's conviction.

Brother Jim, fully aware of the lack of congregational warmth toward Jonda, took for his text: "But whoso shall offend one of these little ones which believe in me, it were better for him that a millstone were hanged about his neck, and that he were drowned in the depth of the sea. Woe unto the world because of offences!"

There he paused, mopped his sweating brow and made mention of "everlasting fire" before bursting out, *"Is it well with thee?"*

Did anyone other than Ahab, the smithy, and Tony Bronson—and, of course, Cara's brood—shout, "Yes, yes!"? If so, Courtney failed to hear.

"It is not," he said sorrowfully. "What will it take for you to come back to the narrow way that leads home? How long will you be bigots? Do you not know that the

Creator made men, *all* men, in His image? What are ye—
'little lower than the angels' or—or carpet tacks that
have to be hammered on the head to be of any account?"

Over and over, he pounded the pulpit as if to drive
home his point. It fell on deaf ears—including Roberta's.

Oakwood Knoll took shape quickly. The character of
the man calling himself Alexander Pope Heston had
little to do with his genius, Courtney mused. Not that
she liked the looks of the unsavory hands he hired—im-
poverished miners who, according to Brother Jim, did
more prospecting at the new Waterfront Saloon than in
the hills. One man in particular disturbed her. Dirty,
foul-smelling, with eyes which spoke of overindulgence—
looking for the world like raw oysters still in their
shells—that rambled from one valuable to another as he
inquired in a whiskey-slurred voice "whar's Oakwood
Know whar them rich gov'ment foks" was located.

Without opening the screen door, Courtney showed
the man the trail and hoped to hurry him along. He
refused to be hurried, tarrying to ask for reassurance
that the trail was safe. "They's talk 'bout them owners
holin' up with scalp-huntin' Injuns," he leered, leaning
so heavily on a pillar supporting the front-porch landing
that she feared the roof would collapse. "You be one
o'them, too—I understan' y'er kin foks—'course, me
now, bein' a peaceful man, tote no grudge er weapon."

"The trail is that way," Courtney said curtly, pointing
in the direction of the new building and closing the door.

Repulsive as the man was, what bothered her was
that, intoxicated as the man appeared, his eyes had
inventoried every item visible from the front door. It
occurred to her then that Mr. Heston and all his workers
had access to every secret of the two houses and their
contents. Even so, his ideas concerned her more. Renewed hatred for their red brothers could lead only to
tragedy unless it was stemmed. But how?

The summer rocked on. Roberta and Efraim divided
their time between setting up offices in New Town,

attending to the newspaper and bank in Old Town, and supervising the finishing of Oakwood Knoll. All these topics dominated the conversation, and added to it was their shared concern about the unexplained delay of their furniture's arrival.

"Somebody had better set out to rediscover America," Efraim said. "Maybe the Great Circle route is leading the ship round and round—"

"Or the earth is square, after all," Yada, overhearing, teased.

"Be patient—as I am trying to be with the renaming of the city," Clint said several times. "Government aid is suspended until we reach a decision. Are you girls coming along to the town meeting?"

Roberta pretended shock. "You mean to say, your Honor, that you skip my column on women's rights? I am advocating it tooth and toenail."

Courtney bit her lip. "I hope you get better results than my invitation for letters from the ladies for the "Women Involved" column. There was total apathy."

There was total apathy at the meeting as well. Courtney and Roberta were the only women in attendance. The only sign of faint interest was the few who sent their proxies by their husbands—some verbal and others scribbled on the back of used envelopes.

Attendance by the men was gratifyingly large. However, most of them were armed and dangerous—with words. The discussion was long, loud, and often insulting. To the surprise of everybody, it was Roberta's suggestion and unexpected (even to her husband) pitch she gave in its favor that held appeal. No longer was she "Glamora's wife," "Aunty Ro," or more explosive titles such as "that Injun lover's woman." She was all lawyer, eloquent and persuasive. Momentarily, the men were silenced.

"Think it over before casting your vote, gentlemen. We want something we can mouth with pride. What about New Hope?"

There was discussion then which threatened to incite a riot, since at least half of the men in the smoke-filled room were looking for a reason to fight. Finally the suggestion won, but by less than a landslide. Some objected to the proposal's coming from New Town; others, that it came from a woman. Clint suggested a compromise why not East New Hope and West? Courtney was thankful it was not North and South!

# CHAPTER 17

# Tragic Ending of a Beautiful Love

❦

The august body known in the nation's Capitol as "fact finders" accepted the name of New Hope. Victory, if not conviction of its worthiness, united the people east and west of the river to some small degree. They actually took a certain pride in the star-spangled banner which whipped in the early autumn breeze above the town square where a courthouse was under construction. In that, Courtney took some comfort.

She was comforted, too, by the little domestic bustlings about her own home. Mandy's capable black hands squeezed together green tomatoes, shredded cabbage, and red-hot peppers for pickledilly as she hummed hymns while pepper-induced tears streamed from her dark eyes. Mrs. Rueben's sneezes were amplified for the cook's sake as she saved and measured the dwindling supply of lye soap and scrubbed away on the washboard at the summer linens to be packed away in flowerlets of lavender from Donolar's herb plot. Donolar prepared dropping rose petals for potpourri, and the children excitedly chattered about the opening of school in October. That was providing families could spare their offspring—dependent upon whether apples were in the cellar, hay in the mow, corn husked (some shelled and placed behind the kitchen stoves for testing seed corn—that which sprouted earliest being the best for seeding. After all, could a body put much trust in buyin' in the bulk, even if need be, since Tony Bronson had them newfangled produce scales that was a-bound to weigh heavy?).

Most of all, Courtney was comforted by the growing relationships within the family, although it chafed her to realize that the wider family—the settlement—had been heretofore growing farther and farther apart. She had prayed so often about the matter, finally coming to realize that it—like Jonda's love for John—God alone could work out in His way. So, trying to put such matters from her mind, she watched as Blessing and Yada lost some of their babyhood ways and started the long journey into adulthood. Roberta was wrong, she felt, in trying to outline their future together, but it warmed Courtney's heart to see the closeness between the two children. She and Clint had shared many a laugh between them at Yada's devotion, following Blessing's every footstep. He was like a song in search of music—waiting to be sung, and Blessing had not heard. In fact, she had taken to quoting Tad Jennings, son of the editor of *The Gazette*. Tad wanted to be a feature writer like his dad (not a bad idea Clint said, in tribute to Willie's work), while Blessing proclaimed that she would " 'lustrate." Yada adopted an air of superiority, saying that he probably would be a missionary and visit all the exciting places Paul had visited, living dangerously. At that point, Blessing always wavered. That might be "funner" than newspapers.

But inside herself Courtney still felt the dark cloud of work unfinished. Clint sensed it. "Patience, darling—maybe you will feel more cheerful when we christen our home. We were going to—remember?"

Courtney nodded sadly. "I—I had thought of something with a welcome, but I am uncertain now."

Clint ruffled her hair. "It will work out—just you wait and see. I had thought of . . . would it sound silly to call it 'Longacres' or 'Green Acres'? I have it! Let's propose to the children a combination of the two. Would you settle for 'Welcome Acres'?"

Courtney loved it. So did the children. But that was only a first step. She must talk to Roberta, help Jonda, then concentrate on renewing relationships in the valley of New Hope.

Evenings grew chill with the pledge of autumn and the evening's damp lingered until mid-morning. The cidery smell of windfalls lingered in like manner when apple harvest was through. Migratory birds were on the wing and Courtney felt a vagabond yearning she was unable to identify tug at her heart one particular morning. Cloudless, the October-day sky was painted a rich, solid blue except for the gray chiffon scarves of fog knotted loosely at the necks of the tallest mountains. Gazing skyward, she remembered Cousin Bella's almost unfailing prediction: "Mist on the mountain—rain in the making."

Yes, the rains were soon to come. Did that account for the feel of restlessness, the urge to get away—or did the need go deeper? It was as if, above the sudden sound of wild geese honking their way south, she heard a voice calling. What she needed was a good walk!

As if Roberta had heard the message from Courtney's heart, she poked her head into the library at that exact moment. "Isn't it time we had that long-postponed talk?" Roberta asked, her voice as bright as the autumn skies.

"And *walk*!" Courtney replied eagerly. "Oh Ro, I am glad you came."

Shawls about their shoulders, the two of them hurried away, giggling at their escape from household cares, walking on tiptoe, pointed toes of their high-top shoes slicing the dew noiselessly.

"Pick up your skirt, Courtney," Roberta whispered. "Let's leave no telltale trail of where we're off to!"

The lighthearted departure was to linger forever in Courtney's heart as a mocking prelude to tragedy. A good play does not fool its audience, she remembered the drama teacher telling her in finishing school. The audience must have some hint, some clue. Life should be the same. Give little warning signals. But there were none as she and Roberta gaily looked over their shoulders at the narrow slices their high heels cut through the grass, laughed again, and high-stepped to the needled path leading into the forest. As if by instinct, they turned toward the green glade where they first had seen Rose Wind.

Then they sobered. "I guess you are remembering," Roberta said quietly. "When I think of the miracle of Yada—I want to talk further—"

"Roberta," Courtney interrupted, "there is time for that—and happy as I am for you through God's blessing, I need to tell you a related story—about our Jonda—"

Courtney plunged in, words tumbling over themselves, often tripping her tongue. But Roberta understood. "You are telling me that Jonda and Swift Arrow— John—are in love? It is hard to believe. How have I failed to see this—to suspect? Tell me more."

Courtney was never able to oblige.

The thickness of the canopy of leaves, still tardily abundant and verdant with summer although those exposed to more sun were tinted with gold and crimson, created an eerie near-night darkness. Courtney found herself shivering even before she heard the lumbering crash followed by the heavy *stomp-stomp* that could belong only to a four-footed animal.

Grabbing the rough bark of the nearest tree for support, Courtney reached out and grasped Roberta's arm. Both of them stopped to stare ahead in horror. A short distance away stood two figures silhouetted but recognizable in the semidarkness. *Jonda and John!* And around them circled an enormous brown creature, its bloated body coated with matted fur, its saw-toothed mouth opened hungrily to emit a menacing growl, and its eyes sending darts of red fire to light the dimness.

Jonda and John, his protective arms around her, stood like statues. Even in her fear, Courtney recalled that Jonda had told her that she had persuaded the boy to give up all weapons since he had accepted Jesus, the Peacemaker. Unarmed, they were helpless victims of the grizzly bear.

Fear such as she had never known crept along Courtney's neck like the thousand legs of a slithering centipede forcing entrance past her chin-high collar, wriggling down her backbone, then dividing into two segments—each segment traveling beneath her cotton hose to bind circulation at her ankles . . . draining her blood . . . rendering her unable to move.

Then Roberta grasped her shoulder firmly and motioned by pointing a thumb backward. No, no! She must scream—not run. Help her precious Jonda. But no sound would come when she opened her mouth. And then, having lost the power to think, she moved backward slowly, slowly, Roberta's hand still clasping her shoulder. Once her feet became entangled in wild raspberry whips, but she was unaware of the pain—only of the red stains on her skirt. Was it juice from the fruit or her own blood?

The bleary-eyed animal turned fiercely their direction at the crack of a twig. Then, sniffing, it turned its attention back to its original prey.

"Don't move." Roberta hardly moved her lips, her whisper was so faint. "Don't move—or it'll attack us—or them."

Hypnotized, Courtney saw the yellow eyes focus on the very spot where Jonda and John still stood. Then with a forest-splitting roar, the brown monster rose on all fours, jaws snapping, and sprang toward Jonda and John, knocking both to the ground. John, agile and lithe, leaped to his feet and with bare fists attempted to stall off the deadly attack by grasping the upper jaw of their attacker. Blood spurted from the wounded animal as Jonda tried to rise to John's aid.

"Run, my darling, *run!*" John's words carried a command as the brown bear raised a heavy claw to paw at its attacker, jerked him down, and with another roar of fury, clamped down with deadly fangs.

The nightmare was too horrible for Courtney to watch. She must rescue Jonda.

But there was no time. A shot rang from an unseen source—a shot so straight and sure that the bear's jaw grew slack and the animal fell—dead.

There was no time to rush forward. Another shot rang out in a blue-white flash that left a fiery trail. John fell backward to the ground, eyes seeking Jonda's for a fleeting second, then closing, a small circle of crimson on his chest.

With an agonized scream, Jonda threw herself across her fallen warrior shielding him with her own body. "Don't die—don't die—oh, my darling, *stay!*"

Half-rising, she ripped off her white blouse and leaned forward to press it against the wound. But a button became entangled with her skirt, and it was the split second of jerking upright to try to free it that saved her life. A volley of shots lit the forest, all striking their target: the dying Indian boy.

Why, *why*, WHY? The bear was dead. A human being lay dead . . .

Even as Courtney rushed to the scene in spite of Roberta's determined grip, she asked herself the question. Maybe even then she knew that the animal had not been the intended victim—that it was a trap. One day she was to learn that the bear had been injured purposely just enough to craze it with pain. Feverish, the animal would strike back in primitive instinct. But for now all she could see was the desperate need before her—her daughter's grief, her pain.

What happened next was a blur. Instinctively, Courtney laid her shawl over the lad's beautiful face, watching in horrible fascination as the bullet-riddled body issued a torrent of blood. She pulled Jonda's head to her bosom and rocked her to and fro . . . tried to soothe her delirium by humming a bar of the lullaby which used to induce sleep. . . .

Courtney's mind registered nothing. Even so, through the white haze of shock, she heard—in that strange sense of detachment—a faint stirring in the raspberry vines, then Roberta's angry scream.

"Stop—stop right where you are, you—you weaselly little coward! You will pay for this! No punishment would be too great—"

Whimpering penetrated the white haze and Courtney was vaguely aware that the voice of the man cowering in the face of Roberta's fury was familiar. "I never dun nothin'—nothing' a-tall, missus—"

"Nothing? I guess in your whiskey-shrunk brain, murder *would* be nothing! Look at you! Just look—" she hissed.

Courtney, still sharing the maze of shock with her daughter, continued to hum and to rock while casting a look over her shoulder at the scene which had to be taking place in another world. A woman, grasping the bosom of a small man's grease-creased shirt, was shaking him as a dog would shake a rat. It was funny. She and Jonda should laugh.

"You gopher, you *murderer*! You sneaking drunk! Look at that face—bloated like a barrel of new wine without a vent—"

"Have mercy—I dun nothin'—jest a pore miner workin' fer ye—"

Ah, now the voice gave Courtney her clue. This viper was the man who stopped by Welcome Acres on his way to work for Alex Heston. Only something was not right— something important, but unimportant . . .

Courtney was to stay with Jonda. Roberta was going for help, and God help this man.

Roberta must be speaking, but the white haze had descended again. The white haze which shut out the rest of the world. In it there were only mother and daughter. Alone. So she nodded, time taking her back, making her hope that all voices would cease so her baby could sleep. . . .

Blue jays, which had ceased their raucous cries and flown away frantically when the guns shook the green silence, returned to resume their quarreling. How like man they were—didn't they know a child must rest?

The next thing Courtney remembered clearly was Clint's loving arms around her. Jonda, their brave little Jonda, had gone to tell Grandma Old about the tragedy, to ask permission for a Christian burial.

"Brother Jim and Tobias are with her, darling. They have lost a valuable ally."

*The valley had lost a friend* . . . Jonda, her love. But Courtney could say only, "Hold me."

# CHAPTER 18

# "Sown in Dishonor...
# Raised in Glory"

The ceremony was simple. John was laid to rest, sadly but swiftly (in keeping with his Indian name) returned to his Maker. Although nobody put it into words, there was obviously tacit accord in the Desmond household that the service should be private. Jonda, with calm dignity beyond her years, asked both Brother Jim and Rabbi Epstern to officiate. Clint and Jordan would please stand beside her. And would Donolar please select for her his most perfect red rose?

The little group clustered together for consolation in the small cemetery beside The-Church-in-the-Wildwood instead of the grounds by the new building. Almost symbolically, a dark cloud obscured the sun as Tobias read from Job chapter 24:

> Men groan from out of the city, and the soul of the wounded crieth out.... They are of those that rebel against the light.... The murderer rising with the light killeth the poor and needy, and in the night is as a thief.... For the morning is to them even as the shadow of death.... They are exalted for a little while, but are gone and brought low ... and cut off as the tops of corn.

In contrast, the sun broke through as Brother Jim read from 1 Corinthians 15:

> Behold, I shew you a mystery. We shall not all sleep, but we shall all be changed . . . in the twinkling of an eye . . . for the trumpet shall sound, and the dead shall be raised incorruptible . . . and this mortal must put on immortality. . . . Death is swallowed up in victory. O death, where is thy sting . . . thy victory?

White-faced, Jonda walked to the graveside in a way that broke Courtney's heart, while swelling it with pride. There, Jonda paused, lifting tragic eyes to the hill beyond, before dropping the scarlet rose.

All eyes followed Jonda's gaze. There was silence and in it a feeling of both fear and expectancy. Courtney herself felt it—a strangeness as if the old world were destroyed and a new one born. Was it irreverent to wonder if the people, believers, and skeptics, at the foot of the crucifixion cross had experienced this emotion?

Another cloud crossed the late-afternoon sun, brightening the thin cradle of a honeysuckle moon in the western sky. A little wind sighed through the pines. Then it, too, was silent. Was the scene of mortal making? The small group waited, and watched with Jonda.

And then from a far distance there came a soft and mournful chant—rising faintly and then drifting away, leaving spectators to wonder if they had heard the song at all. And then, like a rising sun, they crept, a long line of men, women, and children, clad in native mourning, ascending the brow of the scrub-thorn hill which set the reservation apart—weaving, winding, chanting their ancient funeral dirge.

At the top they stopped. With indrawn breath, those in the cemetery waited as a once-powerful, now-withered man, as old as time, stepped forward—feet faltering but shoulders straight. The chief priest as Courtney recalled from her encounters, and she knew by the faces of Brother Jim and Rabbi Epstern that her guess was correct. They stepped out to meet him, dignity matching dignity. The old man extended a gnarled hand in which he held a beautifully plaited garland of autumn flowers, grasses, and thorns for the "waiting place" of their fallen brave. Then the three returned to their appointed places.

Again, the waiting. As if by signal, the tribe parted, standing in two lines as their sad chant recommenced. Their mission appeared complete.

And then the unbelievable! Between the two lines came two young warriors taking a long stride forward, pausing, then stepping again. Behind them they trailed an enormous cross.

Jonda squeezed her father's hand and Clint stepped out to accept their tribute. There should be some way of thanking them, acknowledging their symbol of Christianity. But already, in the gathering twilight, the Indian brothers and sisters had turned home, a single line of shadows against the moon-brushed shoulder of the hill. The old man waited, a lone figure bowing in salute to their acceptance. Then he, too, was gone. But behind them remained a trail of song...different now... louder...triumphant...almost frenzied in a certain secret glory. The cross told Swift Arrow's story, as they understood it.

Jonda's face, though white with grief, reflected the glory-shine as she plucked the petals from the second crimson rose Donolar provided and dropped them one by one into the gaping hole.

"Good night, my love," she whispered, her voice audible in the silence. "Jesus has borne you safely across the Great River."

Then turning to Courtney, she said in a near-normal tone, "Let's go home. I have known love—enough for life." She was so young—but so right.

----

It pained Courtney deeply that nobody from the valley

came to the service while the Indians, whom they suspected, feared, and sometimes hated, had shown com-
passion in the only way they knew. They, too, suffered a
great loss. And then she realized that no matter the *why*
of the rebuffs she had felt of late, there was no way in
which the former friends could have known. Perhaps
she had been wrong in being so hasty to agree to keeping
John's death so secret.

And Jonda (*Oh, praise the Lord for Jonda!*) behaved
like an angel of mercy—comforting the family instead
of begging comfort for herself. There were no awkward
moments, no tiptoeing or whispers, and Jonda refused a
black wreath at the door. Wasn't John with God?

"There is only one matter, Mother," she said calmly to
Courtney. "I wish to go away—not far, only to Portland to
a School of Music...."

Courtney nodded wordlessly, pondering at the fragment of a Scripture: "...sown in dishonor...raised in
glory...." Who knew...save God?

# CHAPTER 19

# Unfinished Story

❦

It took two weeks to piece the story together. Even then, it was unfinished. Jonda was more help than Courtney whose mind remained unable to accept the terrible circumstances of John's death. At the time, she had thought only of her daughter. Now she knew that she must concentrate as Clint and Roberta urged her to do. The culprit must be identified in court in order that justice be served. That failing, the Indians would take matters in their own hands.

Courtney shuddered at the possibility.

"Oh Clint, I am so sorry. It was all so grisly," she grimaced time and time again, "that my mind goes blank with the horror."

And always his answer was the same: "No apologies, sweetheart. You behaved marvelously, and recollections will come back. I only thank God that you and Jonda are all right."

"But there are steps we must take—I *have* to remember—"

"You will," Clint assured her. "And steps *are* being taken. Roberta never slowed down. She brought the little quisling to the sheriff—"

Courtney, who had been lying down in an effort to rid herself of a nagging headache at the time of that particular conversation, sat up with a start. "*Quisling*—why that? A traitor? Who is he anyway—I mean, what is his name?"

Clint laid her gently back on the bed and, pouring water from the pink-flowered pitcher into the matching basin, wrung out a washcloth and laid the cold compress across her eyes. From behind the dark screen, Courtney tried to relive the memory, grimacing again and again as the scene became clearer. A man ... Heston's helper ... carrying a gun. . . . *No, there was no gun.* And there she stopped, trying vainly to put something in place. Something which bothered her even then—

But Clint was talking, giving her answers. "Grub Brewster—the only name anybody has for the man, and it sounds fitting by any definition—may *be* a traitor, a tool, or both."

Again, the flash of something unrecalled, buried in the subconscious. Unable to unearth it, Courtney said slowly, "I can be sure of only one thing, Clint. It was no accident—but there was no gun."

"Right. And nobody has been able to find one—or a motive."

"You suspect something—something big?" Courtney was remembering Clint and Efraim's talk of a conspiracy beginning at government level.

Clint nodded, saying it was too early to speculate.

The flashback continued to recur as Courtney went about trying to restore a semblance of order at Welcome Acres. Mandy and Mrs. Rueben were jumpy and overprotective of the smaller children. "Sumpin' awful—turble-awful's a-gonna happen. Ah dun feels it in mah bones. De Good Lawd tol'rates jest so much fer transgressors afore steppin' in. Alas, Babylon! Ah's bound on keepin' His li'l lambs safe."

Courtney thanked the motherly black woman and suggested that she give some thought to Thanksgiving baking. Jonda wanted to leave just after Christmas. The gleam that the mention of Thanksgiving brought was erased by mention of Jonda's departure. Mandy began to weep, dabbing her eyes with the long apron wrapped around her ample middle and tied in front.

"Mah baby—mah po' white chile, bloomin' out afore uh time t'bud."

Mandy's words were true. Courtney was keeping a close eye on Jonda, watching for signs of a break. There were none. Were it anyone else except Jonda, the behavior would have been pretentious—melodramatic. But Jonda was prematurely a woman, whether by design or circumstances. She wore no false faces. Dear Jonda—a thoroughbred through and through.

Nevertheless, Courtney consulted Clint. Was Jonda all right in his eyes? Clint had answered without hesitation. Very much all right. Then he had frowned. "It is Blessing who concerns me."

"Blessing?" Courtney's heart lurched painfully. "What is wrong?"

"She is so young—so open to hurt. And I overheard her confiding to Donolar that the same thing could happen to Yada—"

"Oh Clint," Courtney whispered. "The thought had not occurred to me. If this awful thing is prejudice—or a conspiracy—"

"Now, now, no worrying, darling. Just be careful and keep an eye on both of them. Efraim and Roberta are so engrossed in the track-down that the thought has not crossed their minds—probably for the best."

Courtney swallowed, trying to still her heart. "I will watch—and Clint, is there any progress?"

"Little, except that others have joined the cause. Brother Jim has recruited a trusted few—as has Tobias. Both are filled with righteous anger, Tobias saying 'an eye for an eye.' I'm afraid he would show little mercy. Then Willie's editorials have opened the whole matter, which forced the sheriff to order in the militia—"

Then there was going to be more tragedy. How did she know? By the multitude of doors swinging open before her. The green door, which had closed when John entered, had swung open again. The green door—leading to *heartbreak*!

"Courtney, Courtney, what is it?" Clint's voice came from far away.

How could she tell him—make him understand about the dream? She must locate the key, find what it opened, see where it led. Only then could the story be finished.

# CHAPTER 20

# New Findings

Kenney was sharing his mosses with Courtney, some of his explanations lost on her half-listening ear as her eyes searched the garden for Blessing and Yada. Locating the two, she had turned back with a smile when there was the distant rumbling of hooves. Two riders, silhouetted against the darkening sky of evening, were racing toward Welcome Acres. At a distance, she was unable to make out their faces. But Brother Jim's old black hat identified him and there was no mistaking his companion. The wind snatching the long beard and tossing it over the rider's shoulder said plainly, "Rabbi Epstern." She rushed to open the gate, knowing that there was news—perhaps bad news.

The men began talking before dismounting from their sweating horses.

"There's trouble, Courtney." Brother Jim panted excitedly. "The bruiser calling himself 'Grub' has escaped the jail—strong-armed the half-wit guard and has headed from West New Hope to East—"

When he paused to draw a breath, Tobias took up the conversation as he pulled his wind-snarled beard in place. "We fear that he may seek revenge—or destroy the evidence."

"What evidence?" Courtney interrupted. "You mean—"

Both men nodded. They meant those who might testify against him, witnesses. *Witnesses.* Courtney's blood curdled. Witnesses meant Jonda, Roberta, and herself. "Then he is guilty?" Her words were almost inaudible.

"No trial...claims innocence...but Heston volunteered damaging information..." the voices trailed away as they pulled her inside the house.

Courtney walked as calmly as her thudding heart would allow into the kitchen while the two men positioned themselves at the front window. It was obvious that they knew more than they had told her.

Mandy looked up with a broad smile, wiping her hands on her apron when Courtney entered her domain. "Mincemeat pies," she said with pride, "but I dun thank dey's a-gonna be no stuffed gooses fo' dinnah cum Thanksgivin' cuz uv—"

Courtney nodded, trying to be calm and avoid worrying Mandy. Too many memories for Jonda. Pheasant or grouse instead. "Where are the children?"

"Got dem'seves wid dat Uncle Donny 'foah light o'day." Mandy raised her flour-dusted hand and pushed impatiently at a skein of hair escaping the bright-red bandanna, leaving a white trail across her forehead, before pointing to Innisfree. "Dey's plannin' on lookin' fo' cones—startin' early-like on sumpin', sum kinda reaf fo' Chris'mas—y'all knows 'bout dem reafs wid candles—"

"Advent," Courtney supplied and ran the short distance to Donolar's cabin. There, in quiet tones, she asked that they postpone the searching party as—well, she had something else in mind. Her eyes took roll quickly. Jordan, bent over some kind of list. Kenney with his spread-out mosses. Yada and Blessing, heads together, drawing a picture of what the finished wreath should look like. But *Jonda*?

"I need to find Jonda." Courtney pressed one hand against her breast under the heavy shawl, an attempt to steady her voice.

Engrossed in their tasks, the children did not look up. Hadn't seen her all morning. Nothing unusual. Jonda took lots of walks—

Courtney raced back toward the big house, reaching it just in time. A lone figure, clutching an oversized Confederate jacket against his chest, emerged from a clump of bushes at the edge of the woods. Underneath the coat, the man wore nothing except long johns, dirty and ragged from long wear in hiding. Courtney knew him instinctively, and then recognition of the hunched-over man's face came. *Grub Brewster!*

There was no time to think further. Things happened too rapidly. First, there was a shout from the front window.

"Move a hair and you're dead!"

Did Brother Jim actually think a desperate man would mistake the walking cane he aimed for a gun?

Tobias Epstern apparently thought the bluff would work. "Now, now, good brother," the rabbi said in falsetto, the artificial highness contrived to reach Brewster's ears.

Brother Jim raised the stick higher. " 'An eye for an eye'! You said so yourself. *Higher!*"

The cringing man lifted his already-upraised hands another three inches, parting the coat to reveal a naked belly. "Don't shoot, I'm beggin'—I ain't guilty, I swear—"

"And don't you go swearin', you big mouth—" Brother Jim growled.

"Show mercy, good brother—'Return good for evil,' " Tobias' voice extended to perfect tenor, "*Your* words, I believe."

"Not *my* words, friend! The Good Book's—from the Sermon on the Mount."

"Th' Hebrew man's right—show mercy. I wouldn't harm no man, not even uh redskin er Jew like some other folks plan doin'! Have mercy 'n I stand ready t'tell ye—"

"Shut up!" Brother Jim shouted in fake rage. "Start moving this way. Arms up. This thing just could go off with a little encouragement! The likes of you are entitled to no mercy. Forward. *March!*"

"Aye, aye! 'Blessed are the peacemakers.' "

Tobias said *that*? Incredible! Some part of Courtney stored her surprise away to be examined later—along with the rest of the unfolding scene. It would be comical under less critical circumstances.

Slowly, Grub Brewster moved forward. And once more something jogged Courtney's brain.

# CHAPTER 21

# Tragedy—and Truth

❧

Inside, wrapped in a blanket supplied by a reluctant Mrs. Rueben who determinedly squeezed her eyes shut either to avoid seeing the man's nakedness or the sight of his dirty body's contact with her spotless cover, Grub Brewster talked rapidly. And indeed, he did have news—news that curdled the blood of those who listened.

"You gotta lissen," he said through chattering teeth. "Yore lives are at stake—you *gotta* lissen! They dun gonna blow up th' harbor—'n in port wuz all them fine fixin's uv th' Glamoras'. Flyers is bein' handed out all through Wes' New Hope—them what hates others who're below 'em—you know, that's what Heston sez— that them what's dif'ernt has t'be wiped out—"

"Heston?" Brother Jim's face went white. "The harbor—"

"Let the man talk," Tobias said quietly. "Something tells me that he just may be telling the truth—probably a new experience."

Encouraged, Grub Brewster moistened his thin lips and for the first time lifted his eyes. Pitiful, Courtney found herself thinking that something in the eyes which looked for the world like freshly broken eggs, the yolks floating in their watery substance, could plead for life. But the harbor...Roberta and Efraim...*Jonda*? Sympathy was premature.

"That man Heston ain't what he 'pears on bein'. Jest hired me on so's he'd have uh fall-guy—takes me fer a simpleton, but I'm willin' t'cop'ate with th' lawmen iffen

120

you can git me off—'cuz I ain't guilty o'nothin', I swear—
beggin' pardon, parson—*please* hep me."

"You've told us nothing so far, Brewster," Brother Jim
rumbled. "And your time is running out. What was the
mumbo jumbo about the harbor? Make it short!"

The little man seemed to shrink before Courtney's
very eyes—an Alice-in-Wonderland creature ready for
the rabbit hole. "I—I dunno much—jest that Heston's
hired a gang aimed on dynamitin' th' shipment—gittin'
back at Glamora's standin' up fer sumpin' I don't understand—sumpin' in that Washington place. You gotta
promise me," he was pleading again, " 'cuz they'll be a
lynchin' iffen they ketch me agin. I had t'come to Miz
Desmon' here, hopin' Heston did'n find her first. The
gang'll blow th' harbor t'tarnation, 'cuz they're after
Glamora's woman, too—her bein' a witness on that
killin'—"

"You claim innocence—get your story organized!"
Brother Jim's voice now held a real threat, the kind that
went with a red face.

The account was disjointed, hard to put together, with
many a blank space on matters the man obviously knew
nothing about. Heston had framed him on that fateful
day which snuffed out John's life . . . that man took him
along on what Heston claimed was a squirrel hunt and
sent him on ahead to shake the bushes to bring the
animals into firing range. Then, boom! Oh, it was awful—
him left standing there and being discovered. Only it
was Heston who did it, and it was Heston organizing the
blasting. Clever man, Heston—clever and cruel. Figured
on himself "spillin' th' beans" so he best get rid of witnesses "what knows he's a-lyin'." "Me, I ain't no killer—
don' own me no fire-piece—cain't even shoot straight
'cuz I gotta eye put out in th' war—you gotta *hurry*!"

"He is right!" Courtney blurted, the fragment which
had bothered her suddenly surfacing. Grub Brewster
had carried no weapon that day—just as he had been
unarmed the day he stopped for directions to Oakwood

Knoll. Afraid of the Indians, he had said, and himself without a gun....

Courtney's words changed the situation completely. At first her two dear friends looked dubious. But her word was good and they knew it. So, with a flurry of activity, they had Grub Brewster cuffed and astride a horse, with the blanket still wrapped around him.

"I look like uh Injun," the man whimpered. "And Heston'll kill me on sight—hates 'em—'n knows I'll be bound on tellin' th' truth—"

"You'd better be!" Brother Jim barked as he straddled his own horse. Courtney handed him the reins.

"One moment, good brothers," Tobias said solemnly and, with eyes closed, began a prayer in Hebrew. His prayers were generally long. This one was brief. "I asked our Jehovah for mercy—only if you are speaking the truth and keep your sacred promise to speak it to authorities. The Almighty does not look with favor upon those who swear falsely."

Without waiting for further explanation, Brother Jim and Rabbi Epstern (admittedly with a bit of pomp) rode away, leading the third horse. Brother Jim looked over his shoulder with a warning.

"Get inside and lock the door!"

Still dazed, Courtney turned toward the house. Too late it occurred to her that the men were unarmed and facing possible danger. Cupping her hands to her mouth, she shouted in an effort to stop them, but they were swallowed in the darkened woods. *Jonda—where was Jonda?*

The question was answered too soon. There was a moment of great joy when Clint came riding from the direction of East New Hope, missing sight of the two other riders who had galloped back to West New Hope to turn Grub Brewster over to the law enforcement officers. Behind Clint rode their Jonda! Courtney was so overcome with relief that she failed to see the dark shape of a man leaping from a horse which had been tethered in hiding—for how long? Her heart stopped.

With the agility of a panther, the man had grabbed Jonda, pulled her from the horse and, face twisted in rage, yelled, "She's my ticket out!" *Heston!*

# CHAPTER 22

# The Purple Door of Peace

❦

Courtney would never forget Jonda's calm as, like a golden Christmas angel, she sat in the glow of the lamp that Alexander Pope Heston had commanded a white-eyed Mandy to light, as if nothing were out of order as he held them captive in the kitchen, barking orders.

"You nigger woman, don't just stand there. Pack me some grub—"

Mandy stopped dead in her tracks. "*Colored*," she said boldly. "Did'n nobody learn y'all no manners? 'Ask and ye shall receive' 'pends a heap on de way it's ast fer!"

The man cursed and fired at the ceiling. "Next time I won't miss—and I'm talking to all of you! While this washerwoman follows orders, you two," his head inclined first to Clint and then to Courtney, "back up to the wall—not that close, ten paces apart—and freeze!" Heston grabbed Mrs. Rueben's arm in a vise-like grip. "Prove to me that a foreigner like you can understand. Your life depends on that. Gather the money and jewelry you find on your master and mistress."

*Nigger...foreigner...master and mistress.* So Brewster was right. Alex Heston was a part of a gang—small or far-reaching—of bigots organized to wipe out those they felt were inferior, including the Indians.

The puzzle was coming together. To escape apprehension and probable conviction, he would stoop to anything in order to make a getaway. He had killed once. He would kill again. Courtney felt the blood drain from her heart and knew her face had blanched when the man's bloodshot eyes turned toward her. "Seen a ghost, have you, Madam Desmond? You'll see a lot more if you put me in jeopardy. Tongue-tied?"

Courtney did not answer. Her only concern was for Jonda. Dear, sweet Jonda whose silver-blond hair shone like a halo in the pale light of a sliver of moon slanting through the window. Then her worst fears were realized.

"You're right, great lady," Heston spat out, following her gaze. "That Indian-loving daughter's coming with me when I ride out. One of you show your face at the door and she's a goner. Savvy?"

He had positioned himself behind Jonda, one hand on his holstered gun. "Anybody else here?"

"No," Clint said truthfully. "The children are at a neighbor's—"

"And the holy men?"

"In town—West New Hope—on business."

"Expect any of them home? Value your lives, you'll tell me. If I have to flush them out, they'll get it, too. Are they expected?"

Courtney shook her head vigorously, praying that the children would remember her instructions. Brother Jim and Tobias knew nothing of the crisis here. Cara would have no way of suspecting trouble.

And then, as Mandy bustled about gathering apples, cookies, and sourdough biscuits inside which she was stuffing cold sausages, she raised her head to look Courtney straight in the eye—slowly, ever so carefully, inclining her head slightly toward the east window just above Jonda's head. Courtney, pretending a sneeze, was able to follow her gaze. What she saw turned her blood to ice, rendered her unable to move a muscle. For there at the window were three look-alike faces: Donolar's expressionless eyes alongside Jordan and Kenney's which sparkled with something between fear and excitement.

If only she could wave a warning hand. Had Clint seen them? Risking no movement, Courtney saw from the corner of her eye that the signal came from Donolar and the children—a finger-to-lips signal, and then they were gone. Whatever they were up to could lead only to further trouble—trouble too horrible for the mind to spell out. So Courtney concentrated on the slice of moon, dusted now with a thin, white cloud. In the deadly silence, her ears picked up the sound of a night bird, a quail—Donolar's signal. Then there was something more. Was it the sound of her own heart or the distant sound of hooves?

There was no time to answer her own question. Clint moved ever so slightly as if shifting his weight and in so doing caught her eye for a flickering moment. Words had never been necessary. Courtney knew instinctively that something or somebody was at the back door. Again, the fake sneeze and the turn of gaze. Miss Lizzie!

Surely, she must be wrong. Why would the teacher be out at this hour? She knew her husband's orders. A second shift of her eyes confirmed the first. Miss Lizzie—and, *oh no, it must not be!* In Miss Lizzie's guardian-angel arms were the dark, dimpled faces of Blessing and Yada!

The drama unfolded quickly, and anybody watching the actors on stage would have agreed that it was a perfect performance. The door burst open and, with Blessing and Yada in lead, they trooped in without visible signs of fear. Just a warm welcome for the "guest."

Both descended upon Alexander Pope Heston in a natural manner, clearly rehearsed so as to arouse no suspicion. Each reached for one of the startled man's hands. "We love our house," Blessing said sweetly, all but crawling on his lap. "So do we!" Yada chimed in. "You must see it when the furniture comes—"

That was when Jordan, the born actor, looked at his father to ask, "What is the sheriff doing outside, Dad? Is something wrong?"

"What?" Heston's throat rasped with fear as he tried to shove the children from him.

But Clint was too quick for him. One leap forward and he had pinned the man to the kitchen floor. The gun spun from his holster. Mandy kicked it beneath the stove, sending an enraged Mouser and her ever-increasing family of kittens hissing all directions. Mandy threw the rope she was preparing to tie around the knapsack to Clint, and Mrs. Rueben silenced Heston's oaths with a wet mop.

Courtney was too desensitized to feel. She could only react, grabbing the children one by one into a huddle and whispering little words of endearment—too soon! Alex Heston, experienced at scuffles to save his scrawny neck, had managed to loosen the knotted rope.

"*Clint!*" Courtney let go of the children and sprang toward her husband, only to feel a powerful hand twisting her wrist. She screamed in pain as Heston kicked the kerosene lamp from the cook table.

There was an immediate explosion and flames shot to the ceiling, beautiful in their treachery—twists of rainbow colors which lighted the room, illuminated horrified faces, and sent purple shadows dancing.

A purple door—the door of peace. Was there peace in death?

"Hold it!" The voice was very much *alive*, and the purple door was filled with familiar and unfamiliar faces. Surely not one keeper of the peace remained in either West New Hope or East.

Moments later, having extinguished the fire, those who had been held prisoners and the characters in the dramatic rescue stood watching the law enforcement officers ride away with the man "Most Wanted."

"Oh, you foolish, foolish children!" Courtney sobbed. "You naughty kittens—"

"You shall have no pie!" Donolar, Blessing, and Yada giggled.

# CHAPTER 23

# Suspense

Every story must have a beginning, a middle, and a close. The beginning was over. And now, although a thousand questions were asked and answered, the end was yet to come—on this, all agreed who had taken part in the melodramatic "play," of which Jordan claimed to be producer. Courtney wished with all her heart that it could have been the finishing chapter.

"How did you know there was trouble—and how did you find your way in the darkness?" Clint asked of Miss Lizzie, after a we'll-settle-some-of-this-later look at the child-actors.

Obviously proud of her role, Miss Lizzie stepped completely out of character. Usually a reserved and controlled woman who was admittedly dedicated to behaving the role thrust upon her—"submissive wife, austere schoolmistress, and God-fearing model"—she squared angular shoulders and talked breathlessly, a sparkle in her spectacled eyes.

"Worried about my Jim, I suspected trouble and tuned my ears for it. Night riders are a rarity, so when I heard hoofbeats, I counted and the sum added up to about four leading me to know that there are more out there—that this beast-in-architect's-clothing had more than the cowardly Brewster as devil's helpers! Maybe extending beyond this valley, exactly the way the city editor paints the picture—"

She looked to Clint for approval. He nodded. "Go ahead, Miss Lizzie."

Miss Lizzie rummaged through her enormous bag as if searching for words to put her into the spotlight she had earned.

"It's gone—I was sure I had a propaganda sheet too professional to be turned out on local presses. Oh well, the point is that Donolar, brave lad that he is, followed orders to a T, not allowing the children to return to Welcome Acres, you know. Instead, he came for me when he knew there was trouble—in the dark, all by himself!"

Courtney felt like applauding her brother who stood against the kitchen cupboard like a soldier called to arms. But there were questions. Compliments, reprimands, or whatever was called for must wait.

"Then," she said slowly, "the two of you came here in the dark? Even in the face of danger—those men on horseback—?"

"Not just the two of us. As if the Lord sent that gig, we had ourselves a ride. The driver, in fact, helped the posse once we were here—not that we could not have managed, with all the rehearsing the children were doing and a wee bit more coaching from me."

*"Gig? Driver? At night?"* Clint looked skeptical, his eyes narrowing in concentration. *Were this anybody except Miss Lizzie—*

Basking in the spotlight she was sure she had now, Miss Lizzie became even more animated, her face looking almost feverish as she swished her skirts with the right foot which crossed the left to where her ankles showed. Courtney suppressed a smile. Did Miss Lizzie know that, in her excitement, the unthinkable had happened? That her ankles were in full view—something she would have declared indiscreet in another woman? It was a first for the teacher, but so was her talkativeness.

"The man had taken a wrong turn and asked for directions. That is when I became very bold, along with Donolar. I just asked him outright—a stranger—for a ride. On the way I whispered the story and he drove like—well, he drove fast. Once here, we crawled—

*crawled*, mind you, on our bellies—uh, stomachs, right through the grass to Innisfree. The stranger stood guard while I helped plan our strategy, even though I felt a little uncomfortable with pretending that the sheriff was here. Still, as Jordan pointed out, it was only a play, you know? The boy is a born director—and I guess you know the rest about how bravely we handled the production. Oh, and one thing more, we were protected, which is to say we were armed. I grabbed a pitchfork from the gig—"

"Pitchfo'k? Lan' sakes alive!" Mandy almost dropped the poker she was using to stoke the fire in the always-hungry cookstove. "Coffee's dun a'ready. *Pitchfo'k*," she said as if viewing a corpse.

All talk stopped as suddenly as it began. The rumble of hoofbeats could spell danger. "Get down—stay in the shadows—*now!*"

The children, aware that as yet their parents had withheld approval of their behavior, made no further effort to come up with something inspired. They dropped to the floor, followed by the adults. One sound or motion could put them all in jeopardy.

The horses stopped, as did all breathing in the warm coziness of the coffee-scented kitchen. The only sounds were the cheerful singing of the tea kettle and an occasional grace-note of the crackling fire.

And then voices. *Familiar* voices! Brother Jim singing lustily . . . Tobias chanting a nonstop prayer . . . and—*Oh, praise the Lord*—Efraim and Roberta. Courtney sprang to her feet and ran to Clint, "Oh, darling, darling, *darling*, surely everything is all right—"

Their own children ran to be gathered into the waiting arms. Yada burst out the back door with an uncharacteristic whoop to be gathered into his mother's arms. "It's all right, sweetheart," Roberta was whispering.

Then all was bedlam—all bodies melding into one. How fitting, some faraway part of Courtney's jumbled mind was thinking, ". . . parts of one body. . . ."

But the other part was straining to hear Efraim's account of how by secret ways that he was unable to discuss they discovered the plot to blow up the harbor. Yes, all was well—for now. But—and there he stopped.

# CHAPTER 24

# Life Goes On—Differently

❦

Nobody participating in the episode which led to conviction on a multitude of charges of Alexander Pope Heston and some lesser ones—such as his dirty utensil, Grub Brewster—was ever quite the same. It left them shaken yet grateful to be alive and together again, determined to make the most of each day while waiting for they knew not what.

On the surface, all was well. The matter was never mentioned between Courtney and Clint, but on occasion she saw worry flood his face and cause the usually placid blue-lake eyes to cloud over like troubled waters. Perhaps it stemmed from his reporting to the East New Hope city council that the government was arranging to hand back to the Indians some of the lands taken over by the whites, or his suggestion that lumberjacks spare more trees so as not to leave the forest floors scarred and unusable for future generations. The opposition—the majority—had replied, So what? Who gave a fig that the sawed-off stumps gave every appearance of a graveyard? All this concerned Clint, she knew, but she had a feeling that the real worry stemmed from something deeper. Courtney was concerned because the children seemed to have matured too rapidly, changing from childhood to near-adulthood without the carefree in-between stage they deserved.

Roberta agreed about the children, and she and Courtney lightened the atmosphere at every opportunity, making little of their appearance in court to identify and testify against Heston and a bit begrudgingly help clear Brewster, who had turned state's evidence.

Miss Lizzie, having tasted a moment's glory, found it as sweet as Mandy's honeycomb and, to her husband's bafflement, became involved in Roberta's push for women's rights. Roberta herself declared that she would set up a law practice in East New Hope, one of her causes being to lead a growing national movement toward achieving for the "weaker sex" a stronger image and eventually a place in the Constitution itself. Yes, she meant a voting franchise!

"What this place needs is a real revival," Brother Jim declared.

"Right you are, dear husband," Miss Lizzie's words were ingratiatingly sweet, as if saccharin-sprinkled. "With women leading the band!"

Brother Jim scratched the full moon on top of his head where the hair used to grow. Going ten rounds in the ring with another pugilist was one thing, taking on a ring full of sassy women was quite another. The new converts were always the most zealous. Quoting Paul's view of a woman's place could lead to a knockout blow. Even Tobias surprised Brother Jim by making mention that there were women judges before Paul showed up.

Roberta selected a two-room office in a new building near Tony's Company Store. The location, she confided to Courtney, was the closest one to the school. She could keep an eye on the playground from her upstairs window and have Yada come there when the school day ended. Courtney wanted to pursue the talk, but decided against it. Maybe Roberta was right in her vigilance, rather than being overprotective. Times were uncertain.

Two days after taking the office, Roberta asked Courtney to accompany her and Efraim into West New Hope for selecting some pieces of furniture from her old office. While Efraim took care of business at the bank, Roberta and Courtney stopped at *The Gazette* office.

Willie Jennings' round head (white hair now in a disciplined puff-cut, parted in the middle, and slicked down on both sides) bent over the press, oiling gears before starting the weekly run. He looked ready to jump for joy at the sight of them. "Oh, mankind! What an editorial I'm running—sure, *sure* to ruffle some feathers, my supporting your cause! But," he hesitated, "you ladies better sit for this one."

They sat down slowly and waited for Willie to go on. "I'm running some pretty dynamic stuff—excerpts taken from leaflets put on my desk by mistake, or could've been on purpose. No idea who dropped them, this place being to West New Hope what Tony Bronson's Store is to East. You know, a place to gather, exchange gossip, or just plain waste time—folksy but dangerous—"

Willie handed the materials to the two women. The leaflets appealed to the city council (combining both towns), churches, and (both Courtney and Roberta paled to read this) *students*! The thrust was an overthrow of the government to clean out the clutter on Capitol Hill, and to start with fresh new blood—*pure* blood from *white Americans*!

"Yes," Roberta said thoughtfully, "I guess that would serve to raise the ire of mothers, make them see the necessity of having a voice in local, state, and government affairs. But—"

"The truth is, Willie, Mrs. Glamora and I are uncertain that we are welcome anymore. The center of unrest seems to be our husbands—"

"And our own children," Roberta added. "Tell us, Willie—have you any suspicions who heads this rebellion? Are you holding something back?"

Willie frowned. "I have a couple of suspicions, but the best weapon one in my position can hold is his tongue."

"That applies to us all, but my mind keeps going back—"

Courtney finished Roberta's sentence, "To Heston's gang."

The editor wiped his ink-stained fingers and tossed an oily cloth to a nearby table. "That would be the obvious, but there are those—"

"—who blame our husbands," Courtney said, light dawning suddenly.

Roberta gasped. "Efraim and Clint! Blaming *us* would make more sense." She stopped, eyes narrowing, "Maybe they do. Willie—"

Willie did not meet her eye as he picked up a bundle of clean paper in preparation for starting the machinery. "Like I said, I hold my tongue. It goes deeper than that puffer of an architect—that I know. To mastermind something this big would take influence—money—brains—"

"We qualify," Roberta said without arrogance or rancor.

"What do *you* think of us, Willie?" Courtney asked bluntly.

The man's head jerked erect, disturbing the carefully controlled sides of his hair—a matter he corrected quickly. "That the men I work for put God, country, and family above all else—and that their wives are without blemish. That sums it up!"

"Thank you, Willie. But what should we do? Tell Efraim and Clint...keep still...call in the militia to guard our children?" Roberta's voice rose and Courtney put a restraining hand on her arm.

"I don't know—I just don't know," the editor said helplessly. "I only know that I'll continue to probe, to fight, to support all of you. We will win—it's just that we're all jumpy."

"And with just cause!" Roberta said, rising.

"Aye! With just cause," Willie said quietly.

When Efraim entered the door, it was to announce that two wagon-loads of furniture would arrive at Oakwood Knoll tomorrow. Courtney found solace in his news. It would give them all something different to think about.

And it did. Aside from what Willie had told them, Courtney felt a domestic satisfaction in concentrating on such small decisions as to whether the loveseat would look more inviting alongside the library fire or beside the window where those seated could view the potted petunias and the nasturtium border along the walk.

Only one thing disturbed the newfound calm for Courtney: Her dream of colored doors was back.

# CHAPTER 25

# Call to Arms!

"A body'd a-thunk capturin' them outlaws woulda made headlines!" Valley folk shook their collective heads. "But no, instead comes this puzzlin' call to arms 'gin uh enemy we dunno."

Men clustered together with voices lowered and labored over *The Gazette's* article and the editor's stinging editorial. Sure, they'd known something wasn't right— make that a heap o'things—but it was like a secret, everybody suspecting this one or that. Maybe 'twas just as well to flush the traitors out of the brush. Still and all, best not panic. No need in the womenfolks knowin'....

The women knew—Roberta saw to that. In a surprise move, she announced at dinner two weeks after the talk with Willie Jennings that she intended inviting the women to come to her office. They would cooperate where their children were involved. Courtney cast an inquiring look at her husband. He and Efraim were nodding. Brother Jim turned palms up in resignation as if the referee had declared him the loser. After all, he liked old Willie's manner of speech. "We are a peaceful valley, and there is decency, respect, and love of God and country behind the masks we wear. What we see on the surface only masks the truth. So let us strip away the masks...be vigilant...let some of the belly-laughers who think we are ignoramuses choke on their own bile, the gag stick in their throats."

Editor Jennings had boldly quoted the flyers left on his desk and told of pleas for youngsters to become "involved" and dangers that involved "messing with the minds of children." Dangerous, he said. Dangerous like communistic tactics, meaning that people only voted the way they were told—if allowed to vote at all. Well, this valley was not destined to follow leaden-eyed like a flock of woollies! No siree, 'twas the Good Lord's will that they be out in front.

Courtney and Clint heard the children's prayers and retired to the privacy of their bedroom. There he took her in his arms.

"You look worried, my little madonna."

It had been some time since Clint had called her that, and just hearing the endearing term made her feel better. Moments before she had felt as if she were facing a firing squad. Now she felt safe, protected, loved. Whatever must be faced, they would face together.

Lifting her dark eyes to meet his, Courtney stopped her gaze at sight of them in the narrow Venetian mirror which framed them like a portrait. Courtney saw the glow of excitement that had returned to her eyes and decided that she looked less like the famous painting than Clint had recognized in earlier years. She looked like—who was it anyway, that resemblance she saw? Oh, one of the portraits she had brought from Waverly Manor. Her jumbled thoughts went back to her encounter with Old Alfie Ashbury for no accountable reason. What had become of him—and, for that matter, the key he had given her? Why had she thought of this now?

The vision was so brief it failed to interrupt their conversation. It faded, leaving the memory of the dark quarters of *The Gazette*, its floor nail-scarred around the potbellied stove where a cross section of the population gathered. Around Willie's desk, papers were knee-deep; but the desk itself was uncluttered. How could anyone have left papers there unknowingly? It was no blunder.

"I *am* worried—or *was*. This conspiracy—if there is one—scares me. It has divided the two towns, alienated us from our friends, and created suspicion to the point that—well, I almost hold things back, wondering why you have failed to question *me*."

Clint laughed deeply the way she loved, the kind of laugh that sent her blood flowing with renewed warmth. His laugh was the only one ever she had heard with an I-love-you in it. Some laughs could be insulting. Clint's laughter was a high compliment, as were the words which followed.

"*You?* Why, you are incapable of dishonor. I would trust you more than myself! And," he paused then and in the mirror she saw the familiar cloud cross his face, "try to put such ideas out of your pretty head. Division is the game they play. When there is no trust, they move in. Stop fretting, my sweet. Agreed?"

Courtney nodded. "I must. I found a gray hair today."

Again the laugh. "Good! How wonderful that we grow old together!"

---

Cara Laughten, hollows in her cheeks filled out and a look of determined peace in her once grief-glazed eyes, arrived first. Talk flowed easily between her, Courtney, and Roberta. Some of the women would show up, she assured them, while others—well, "they're jest downright shamefaced, but give 'em time. Fact is," and she pointed out the window to announce the arrival of Miranda Bronson. Tony's wife, always warm and friendly, wore new gold-filled spectacles perched too far down on her nose to help her vision. Above them, her merry eyes twinkled with anticipation. Here was her chance to be her own woman, to prove to her storekeepin' husband that she was more than his definition—a-stay-at-home and more than simply his conscience nagging him. Ahab the smithy's Maizzie tripped up the creaking plank steps hesitantly. Just how a thimbleful of womenfolk could keep bad blood from boilin' over beat the likes of her. But Ahab had wanted her here, and she *could* tell how her father helped get some building codes into force back in Denver. All because a few stuck to their cause, they were able to enforce these codes, too. No more canvas roofs, dirt floors, and whiskey-barrel smokestacks. This she could tell—if her tongue would allow.

The councilmen's wives appeared in a group, all eyeing Roberta suspiciously, faces turning purple with fury when she explained the danger of getting their children dragged into such a conspiracy. Why, it could lead to open rebellion, turn them against their parents.

There were seven late arrivals who, seeing the honorable councilmen's wives' fury, began to titter among themselves. Maybe tweren't jest that representative er his Honor, the Mayor's foolhardy notion...could be more'n idle chitchat. So their 14 eyes fixed on "that Glamora woman" as if attached by a single string. Oh, she was bright all right.

Roberta spoke eloquently—and won her case! The women left eating out of her hand, Courtney reported to Clint.

"Did she convince them?" he asked with interest.

"She had them taking notes. And Clint, they *asked* to meet again—"

Clint grinned. "Then maybe she should address the men."

"Oh, she would if invited—and Clint, listen to this. When Roberta asked the ladies to spread the word, they volunteered to canvass the valley and alert the neighbors—and—" Courtney paused dramatically, hoping to arouse her husband's curiosity (which she did!), "Widder Brown herself suggested there would have to be a larger gathering place—"

"And?"

"Here!" Courtney said with a near-shout of glee.

They went into each other's arms, Courtney's tears spilling over.

# CHAPTER 26

# Strange Thanksgiving

❦

Thanksgiving dawned, in Brother Jim's words later, "as clear as Hobson's bell." Snow fell heavily the night before, transforming the world into a white fairyland. Mandy and Mrs. Rueben were quarreling over the wood stove, each blaming the other for the smoke which it belched back into the kitchen, as Courtney and Clint stole out for a hike to whet their appetites for buckwheat cakes with the family.

Side by side they walked, laughing like children as they trudged through the frozen snow, falling, getting up, and winding into the forest. On and on they walked through the green tunnels of fir, pine, cedar, and hemlock. Some of the branches drooped with packages of snow like overburdened Christmas trees; others dripped with spikes of icicles, glistening in the bold sun which momentarily behaved liked Mandy's oven when the damper was wide open. Teasingly they dripped, only to refreeze.

As the couple entered a little clump of vine maples still strung with a few bright leaves, Clint paused. "Ever see anything so beautiful?" he asked. "Just listen to the silence." Courtney, spellbound, held her breath. Not a sound—as if the woods were deserted. Then low branches of the maples shivered to send a shower of snow into their upturned faces. And there, above them, were two beady eyes. A squirrel satisfying his curiosity, Clint whispered. Then, with a flit of his fluffy tail, the little creature was gone. The movement startled a lone deer from hiding. For a single moment, the animal stood like a graven image. Then it, too, was gone. So they were alone in a pristine world, Courtney thought happily, as she filled her lungs with clean, pure air.

*Alone?* Not quite perhaps. Clint was pointing wordlessly at fresh tracks which led directly from Welcome Acres' private trail to the turnoff for the reservation.

"What do you make of it?" Courtney whispered.

There was no time for an answer. Mandy's giant bell—which, suspended near the kitchen window, announced to the world that a meal was waiting when she set its iron tongue to clanging with a pull of the bell rope—rang deafeningly.

"Race you!" Clint laughed, breaking the tension.

"No fair—you have a head start," Courtney answered his challenge as she took a shortcut toward the smell of homemade maple syrup.

Jordan greeted his panting parents as they stamped snow from their boots at the door. "Was Jonda with you? She's gone."

The glow was instantly extinguished from Courtney's heart. Even Clint's reassuring words that Jonda had taken a walk failed to lessen her apprehension. A walk? Alone? Those footprints were too large to be hers. The sound of footsteps broke into her confused thoughts.

"Do I smell pancakes?" Tobias was shaking snow from his wide-brimmed black hat, wiping his dark beard, and removing his frock-tail cloth coat at the door which Courtney had failed to close behind her. "Praise be unto the Shepherd who preparest a table before me!"

Mandy grunted. "Ah dun preparest dis meal, Tobias, but ah'm a-warnin' we dun got sugah-cuah'd ham—swine, as y'all calls hit—"

"The rabbi can bless it," Kenney said solemnly. "Or is it still evil?"

Clint silenced them all with a glance. "Come in, come in!" he invited cheerily. "Brother Jim's overdue—so perhaps you will honor us with a blessing?"

The conversation turned to Jonda—and where were Brother Jim and Miss Lizzie? "A searching party is called for," Kenney offered dramatically. But it was Mandy's moan from the kitchen that said it so plainly that her words were superfluous. "Dey's outsmarted us'n a'gin—dun gone'n stole dis houshole! Dey's took mah fattest hen wat wuz stuffed fo' roastin'."

So history repeated itself again, Courtney thought wretchedly. While she concerned herself with political matters, she had neglected to think of those less fortunate. Maybe the men were right, after all. A woman's place was in the home, serving others—and that included her family! They must find Jonda—*now!* "Jonda—" was all she could manage.

"Let's approach this sensibly," Efraim said quietly. "This is no time to moralize. The Indians need to be fed—"

"And ministered unto," Rabbi Epstern added. *"Jehovah-jireh!"*

"The Lord will provide," Yada said with a nod, to which Donolar added, "Genesis 22:14."

Courtney and Roberta stared at one another in disbelief. Was this how Mary felt when she discovered her tender-aged Son teaching in the temple? Was this God's way of saying that their children, too, must be about His business?

Courtney had no clear memory of eating breakfast. There was quick conversation. Yes, it was wise to go to the reservation—clearly their duty. There was no mention of the possible dangers. Donolar would accompany the men—and yes, Roberta said, Yada had permission, a part of his "learning" (and her promise to Rose Wind, Courtney thought numbly). But the numbness was gone when Yada refused unless Blessing might go along. Blessing—*her baby*? How could Clint be nodding . . . didn't he recall? And why was she agreeing as if matters were in the hands of a Power greater than herself? But Mandy was packing an enormous basket. "Man don' go livin'

by bread—er fat hens—alone. Sendin' dem food'll save
'em fum de sin uv thievin'—'n please de Lawd, ah'm
a-guessin'. So git back heah fo' dinnah—strange Thanksgivin', dis!"

# CHAPTER 27

# Mission Accomplished— Almost

❦

The house felt empty robbed of those whom Courtney loved. For, in the end, Jordan and Kenney went along with the men. Reluctantly, Courtney stayed at home in case Jonda should show up or Brother Jim should bring some report. Even Roberta agreed that it was best. Mandy and Mrs. Rueben had everything under control. There was nothing to do but wait—the hardest part of all.

She hardly heard Roberta's talk of continuing the search for the culprit or culprits bent on stirring up trouble, endangering them all. Perhaps an emergency meeting of the women...and did Courtney know that Willie had a printer's devil?

Courtney rallied, momentarily pausing in her restless pacing. "A *what?*"

How did Roberta manage a laugh? "An apprentice. Jeptha something or other—good boy and making it possible for faster circulation of the newspaper. Tad is learning the trade and—"

*Tad*—Tad Jennings, the editor's son. Courtney welcomed a change of thought. The lanky, tow-haired boy, whose bone structure gave promise of later handsomeness, was Blessing's declared "beau." *Beau.* At her age! Clint had laughed at her concern. Nevertheless, Courtney had felt compelled to ask gently what happened to the friendship between her and Yada (and immediately regretted it...why, she was falling right into Roberta's trap!). Blessing had turned her great, dark, dark eyes, wide with innocence, toward her mother. Nothing had happened. Yada loved her and she loved him. But she wished he would stop opening doors for her, making her feel like a *lady*—scurrying around to pull out chairs, things like that which made the other girls titter. She was too young for *that*. She would rather draw Donolar's butterflies for Tad's stories.

Blessing summarized again by saying, as she had said before, that Yada was *Yada*—just that. He was her cousin—and did Mother understand?

Yes and no. Courtney wondered again how to explain the relationship. She was about to mention the matter to Roberta when the sound of voices wiped away all else. In her rush to the door, she stumbled into a chair, caught her petticoat, and all but fell. Yanking at it impatiently, she left a trail of lace all the way down the hall.

And that is how the mistress of Welcome Acres greeted the missing persons—all of them! *Oh, praise the Lord, all of them were there.*

———————————

For the next month the strange Thanksgiving dominated all conversation. Jonda, failing to find her parents, went to the cemetery to take the last of Donolar's bronze chrysanthemums to John's grave. There she met Grandmother Old who was in no condition to have made the journey. Yes, Courtney remembered the old, old Indian woman (nobody knew how many moons she was) whose skin was stretched across her bones so tightly there seemed to be no flesh. Now the old bones, too, had shrunk, bending her forward grotesquely like a misshapen *U*, but her mind was sharp. She remembered—and she still "knew things." Jonda, Swift Arrow's "Star Flower," would never love again. Best that Jonda go, Grandmother Old had agreed, to world outside. Nothing left for her here. Too late (no matter what the great men said) for Grandma Old herself to leave. Old women had no reason for leaving the only way of life they knew . . . and what would she be wanting for, except food? No, she and her half-wild cat would wait here until Great White Father came to take her to join Swift Arrow in Happy Hunting Ground. The withered woman had dozed even as she spoke, only to arouse and say, "Aiee, how is it that sleep is my master when there are words? I was wrong, dear little Star Flower, to think you were too young to know things, to experience man-and-woman love magic. And now (sadly) you will never love again." Again the dozing, the smell of old flesh, as the once-proud head drooped. "No—more—Love—I know things."

Grandmother Old had a convincing manner. How well Courtney knew. "But darling, her beliefs are different," Courtney began, but a glance at Jonda's sad face silenced her. "And then?"

Suddenly the private talk was over. Everyone seemed to speak at once. Brother Jim and Miss Lizzie, too, had gone for a walk—taking the back road to Welcome Acres. Catching sight of Jonda, they followed because of strange footprints running parallel to hers in the snow. Who knew what some drunken "blubber-belly" with too much hooch soaked in might do? Carrying 12 pound cakes, they changed plans at the sight of Jonda leading the half-frozen woman back to the reservation and—

The children began outshouting one another at that point, each with a different version of a beautiful prayer dance for ewe milk for a new mother who would die without it. The Great Spirit had turned a deaf ear, so the prayer dance became the prayer of death—a skin of milk failing to come. All would die. What mattered who went first? None had food . . . *Aiee. Ochone.* OCHONE!

"But food came," Tobias said triumphantly, "and Yada, whom I have taught the language, explained that it was the Good Shepherd who hears."

There was a bonfire and rejoicing. "*But* the tracks remain a mystery," Efraim said. Clint nodded, the cloud obscuring his face again.

# CHAPTER 28

# "Good Will Toward Men..."

Roberta and Efraim planned to move into Oakwood Knoll after Christmas. Courtney regretted the timing. Jonda would be leaving for Portland, something she was unable to face as yet. Welcome Acres, instead of being filled with family and friends, would be so lonely, losing the personality it never really had. It needed to be peopled. She wondered if, beneath its bold exterior, the great house's wooden heart might be aching like her own.

However, the change would be good for Jonda. Her welfare must come before her mother's. She wondered then how it would affect the other children—especially her twin brother. But it was not for himself that Jordan was concerned—it was for Blessing.

"She wants Yada to stay here," Jordan confided with a smile. "Fat chance. Right, Mother? I guess you know she tries to protect him."

Courtney had been helping Mandy crush sage leaves for spicing the holiday dressing. Immediately, she let go of the mortar and pestle. "Protect him? From what or whom, Jordan?"

The boy, who seemed to have grown two inches since yesterday, shifted his unaccustomed height for better balance before meeting her gaze. "I would have thought Blessing told you. There are all kinds of slurs made at school behind books and, of course, when Miss Lizzie's face is toward the blackboard. It's about his race, or what they think it is. Sometimes it's hard to turn the other cheek, you know?"

Courtney nodded wordlessly. Jordan went on talking, as—seating himself across the oilcloth-covered cook-table from her—he began cracking walnuts he had promised yesterday to do for Mandy's matchless walnut-carmel pies.

He asked if Miss Lizzie had told her that they were going to produce *The Merchant of Venice*. Had Courtney been listening, she would have gasped and said it was the worst of all possible choices. Jordan was going to direct it—even choose the characters. Jonda had refused to play the part of Portia but had promised to furnish original music—chamber music of the Shakespearean times . . . speaking of which reminded him: Did Mother know that there was going to be a new teacher?

New teacher? Courtney, still only half-listening, thought she heard right. New teacher—and she had heard nothing of it. Again the ache, the feeling of isolation. Yes, it *was* hard to turn the other cheek.

"He visited school, even demonstrated his skills for the Board. Maybe he's smart, but," Jordan giggled with a bit of the mischief remaining from his babyhood, "but this Mr. Haysack—Haystack—or whatever his name is, is no looker—except with his eyes! He just about wrote on the wall instead of the board because his gaze kept following Jonda—"

"What age is he?" Courtney asked for the sake of conversation.

Jordan, mistaking her meaning, laughed. "Young—but too old for my sister! Hard telling. I think the cane's for effect. Maybe he's older than I thought, what with the poker face and the funny hair. Sort of whitish—no, straw-like. Yeah, the name *has* to be Haystack!"

Later, Courtney tried in vain to recall all of Jordan's chatter. It was a treat for them to be alone, and she had allowed herself to be buried in her own thoughts. His words may have held some key—*key*? She resolved to check on the mysterious key this very day.

———————————

Later in the day, Roberta returned from her office. Her eyes held a spark of worry, but Courtney decided against questions. It was too easy to make a slip of the tongue, to make mention of Yada's predicament. Some day, when the time was right, maybe—and then she would marvel with his mother how a child so young had tried bravely to handle the hurts alone. For now, none of them needed more concerns. They all knew that the cup of scorn was overflowing in the valley already. One more drop and—

"Ro, let's try that mysterious key!" Courtney burst out instead.

Roberta met the suggestion with enthusiasm. Moments later they had slid back the slatted cover of the rolltop writing desk. Almost childlike in their enthusiasm, they began opening small drawers in search of the envelope holding the key. Courtney wondered why she was surprised when Roberta held it up excitedly. Somehow she had expected it to have disappeared. She could not have said why.

"Well, that is that!" Roberta announced after they had tried every keyhole. "But it was fun—took my mind off some problems."

With the announcement, she tossed the key aside. Courtney picked it up and examined it carefully as vague, fleeting fragments of the dreams came and went. Wait! She did remember something—something about a secret door, or was it a drawer? Slowly, then almost in a frenzy while the dream remained, she ran her fingers along the sides of the desk while Roberta watched in curious silence. Then, dropping to her knees, she began to explore the underside of the desk.

What was this? Just a scar in the ancient wood no

doubt. But as she pressed, there was a small squeak of protest from a countersunk screw—and out dropped a yellowed envelope.

Voices interrupted them. Clint and Efraim were calling. Neither of the searchers had taken note of the lengthening shadows. Best stuff the envelope back for another time. But Roberta had grabbed it and hurried down the winding stairs. "Eureka!" she cried.

Together the four of them puzzled over the contents. Just a single sheet of paper, and in an unrecognizable language.

Efraim bit his lip in concentration. "I believe it is Gaelic."

"Could be," Roberta agreed, looking over his shoulder. "Celtic—"

"Did any of your ancestors live on the Isle of Man—Scottish Highlands—Ireland?" Roberta asked Efraim.

He nodded. "Ireland. What did the key open, Courtney?"

Courtney realized then that the key had opened nothing. The little trap door had flown open with the pressure of her finger. Roberta answered for her. "Nothing," she said.

Well, what good was a letter in a language none of them knew, and a key that opened nothing? The search was over.

"Not on your life!" Efraim said with feeling. "It has only begun." His eyes suddenly lighted up strangely. "Courtney, think hard. What language did Old Alfie speak?"

The caretaker? "No language—he was mute. Well, he *was*—"

"Perhaps, but I was never sure. Once I heard—never mind. May I take the letter and the key? There is something I want to check out. Something—*everything*—could depend on it. No questions!"

"Except from me," Clint said, attempting a smile

when he caught sight of Courtney's white face. "Question: Who is as hungry as I?"

---

There was a lot to think about. But there was no time. There was decorating to do . . . baking . . . a tree to select. And the Christmas program! This year Miss Lizzie had suggested having the children tell the Christmas story by making use of the Advent wreath. The democratic Donolar, Jordan and Jonda, Kenney, Blessing, and Yada had volunteered. Rehearsals preceded devotionals at the evening meal.

The program was scheduled for Christmas Eve, and Mother Nature cooperated by changing the week-long rain into snow. The children already riding on the crest of a giant breaker, were unable to restrain their whoops of sheer joy at the first feathery flake.

Smiling, Courtney went up to the bedroom to dress. Lamplight spilled onto the tufted blanket of snow, turning the world to silver. Downstairs, she could hear Jonda's laugh (lighter now), the other children's shrill chatter, and Mandy's throaty crooning, joined by the bass notes of the men's voices. Family. Oh, blessed word! *Happy* family. Her heart was bright with Christmas, all troubled thoughts wiped out. Dropping to her knees, Courtney prayed that the whole world one day would know the meaning of the holy birth, open their hearts, and let love in. Then, quickly, she pulled a winter-white wool dress over her head, smoothed the crinoline petticoats beneath, and was struggling to match back buttons with buttonholes, wondering aloud why dresses were designed with buttons in the back, when Clint entered noiselessly. "My job," he said, stepping behind her. "We poor husbands are the ones who should be protesting."

"You love it!" Courtney said lightly, "but you scared me—"

She stopped as their reflection came into focus in the

full-length mirror. His eyes devoured her, causing the usual rush of color to rise in her cheeks. Yes, all the world's people should let love in.

"Stand still, you!" And Clint, without a hint of warning, wound a two-strand necklace of pearls around her neck. The effect was magical. The pearls matched the heirloom setting on her wedding-ring finger, and her dress! She was transformed, as Clint said adoringly, into a snow princess—his very own. If only the moment could last forever. But she must inspect the children's clothes . . . make sure they had washed their ears . . . and, oh yes, Roberta had asked that she pin a sprig of holly on top of her halo of braided hair once she had on her pine-green suit.

The church was crowded, and Courtney felt a thrill of pride as Jonda—looking like a Christmas angel in her draped-sheet robe—walked to the piano. The pride gave way to sheer joy as there was a spatter of applause. The applause gained momentum as, with her usual poise and grace, she played the time-tested carols while Brother Jim's voice—with more volume than talent—led the audience in song.

They had accepted Jonda. They were singing together. How quickly the Lord had answered her prayers, Courtney thought, as she reached for her husband's hand.

Then sudden silence and momentary darkness as light wicks were turned low and then extinguished. The next light appeared from onstage.

All week Mandy and Mrs. Rueben had worked on coloring tallow candles—with Mandy, for once, forced to allow the housekeeper to take charge. *Ach!* Twenty grains of cochineal and 15 of cream of tartar, plus a piece of alum the size of a cherry pit (from the "drugstore man") would make deep red—but careful! A gill of rainwater was needed for the rosy tint. Add indigo the size of a pea, and what have you? Purple!

Their efforts were not in vain. Nestled in Donolar's wide circle of evergreens, pine cones, and rose hips clustered three violet candles, one rose-pink, and a single colorless one, as white as the new snow.

Donolar's trembling hands lighted the first violet candle. And surely the spectators were robbed of speech when, in a loud clear voice, he said with scarcely a quiver: "The hope of the prophets of old."

As rehearsed, he stepped into the shadows as Jordan emerged and, with a flourish, lifted the purple candle from its bed of evergreens to set a second purple candle ablaze. "The candle of Bethlehem, a light in the dark." When he finished, it was Kenney's turn. "The candle of faith, a reminder of hope. . . ." Yada lighted the angel-of-love candle to mingle a rosy glow to the purple tongues of flame.

And then the final candle! With a rustle of ruffles, rainbow lights reflecting from her raven curls, Blessing completed her mission of lighting the white candle. In a sweet, childish voice, she said: "The white candle, God's gift of light—now and forevermore," and promptly burst into tears!

The audience, having sat in awed silence at the solemn ceremony, was caught unprepared. There was a sniffle here, a snort there, and then, like the little girl who would rather paint life with colors than with words, they gave way to tears—some sobbing without shame.

Well now, this was unplanned. And who said a change of heart should require rehearsals? The time was right, that's what, and Brother Jim was not about to miss his opportunity to announce that "out of the mouths of babes" had come the call for repentance. Christmas! What better time to kneel at the altar and offer up the only sacrifice acceptable to the Lord: the human heart in need of forgiveness?

The great bulky minister opened his arms so wide that it appeared surely all buttons would pop off his ill-fitting black suit coat. What appeared to be thousands surged forward as Jonda played triumphantly.

---

The Christmas Eve miracle was not enough, it seemed. The sun had scarcely begun its fiery Christmas Day journey across the bright vault of sky when the sound of singing wafted over the snow-wrapped hills. Louder it grew until, to the astonished eyes of the Welcome Acres inhabitants, it stopped at the frontyard gate. And there they were: the whole of East New Hope, a handful of West New Hope and, wonder of wonders, a bouquet of those from Tobias' Jewish believers, a black-and-white cluster of the "Separatists" . . . and could it be? Yes, it could! Bringing up the rear was Grandmother Old, supported by two braves. All were singing: "Peace on earth, good will toward men. . . . Glory to God in the Highest. . . ."

This time it was the Desmond-Glamora family who wept.

# CHAPTER 29

# End of the Beginning— Beginning of the End

❦

The beautiful Christmas marked the end of isolation. The hands and hearts extended by Courtney and Clint Desmond and Roberta and Efraim Glamora had turned the tide of hostilities back into the sea of hatred where such evils lie in waiting. Courtney felt God's pleasure in their continued faithfulness, their "other cheek" attitudes, their refusals to fall prey to unjust accusations and hurts when the darts of unwarranted slurs had pierced their hearts. Now Welcome Acres could be what they had asked God that it become: the heart of the vast valley—love's destiny fulfilled.

It also marked the beginning of the end of the presently fruitless search for those lighting the bonfire of division and adding fuel with carefully designed frequency. Clint and Efraim, with studied discretion, remained casual while keeping watchful eyes on members of the city council, business associates, and those in the high places of New Hope's city officials. Willie was less cautious. Using his seat in the editorial chair as a license to freedom of the press, his words bounced from sensational to scathing, fully expecting to attract a following while arousing the ire of weak links in the chain of those underground. That there were "bigwigs"— some powerful masterminds—at the bottom of a dangerous conspiracy, he was convinced.

And, now that the ice was broken among the women, Roberta was able to put the skills of her profession to good use. Their children's safety came first, even if it meant postponement of "putting up" wild-grape jelly. Who was to know the difference between it and that made from the garden varieties of grapes? Now, meals for their men jolly well better be on time but there were shortcuts ("least said, easiest mended" about the matter). The whole idea brought about renewed neighborliness as the good ladies shared their secrets and doubled their ingredients when baking, planning ahead to share bread and desserts as well.

There was another result of their organizing. Although it would be downright scandalizing to give such an idea voice, a new sense of dignity and worth lifted their heads a little higher. After all, nobody could say that their hands were idle. They mended while they reported and planned their simple strategy of watchfulness. There was nothing unseemly or unrighteous about their mission, was there?

And that smart Miz Glamora was so reassuring. Women could serve their families without being drudges, and it would be beneficial to their children for them to be well-informed. Interesting news, they said, as they patched overalls and mended black bloomers, that a few brave women before them had protested by pen and petition that women needed to have the right to participate in their husbands' world; that, wonder of wonders, somebody named Abigail Adams, the *president's* wife, dared ask for women's right to vote! Still and all, no more than a fourth of the *men* could vote " 'countin' them what could'n read," so with women being burdened with household cares, they were not as free as now. There was that fifty-niner, Susan B. Anthony, "a-kickin' up dust" about women's rights hampered by men who regarded women as slaves (How dare them!) . . . others who saw them as angels, goddesses, queens to be kept on a cloud, a pedestal, or throne (Now that was interesting!) . . . *but*, Roberta cautioned, change came slowly and (hesitantly), "We women are in narrow grooves, the vast majority of men accepting the Bible literally and placing us in an inferior position. Some churches say it is thrust upon us by divine decree. But even as I speak, a National Woman Suffrage Association which would allow us a right to vote in government elections is underway. Our time will come. But, for then as well as now, our concern which is at the heart of every mother is the welfare of our children—so be vigilant. It will require dedication, a few hardships—which we are accustomed to—and a lot of disappointments. But together we *will* win—together, I say, meaning everybody—men, women, children."

Yes, a beginning and an end. The end, if defined as the secret move to an international conspiracy, unfolded slowly—much, much too slowly to please those involved in solving it. But when the climax came, it was sudden. It was surprising. It made New Hope (under a new name) more than a dot on the map of Washington State. And, in a larger sense, it rocked the world.

But in the interim, life went on in the busy, prayerful valley, each day opening like a bright blossom. So bright it made one forget how long it took for a bud to produce such beauty, and the patience required to wait.

-------

Courtney's loneliness was eased somewhat by the whirl of activity. It served as a balm for her aching heart when Jonda, the youngest to enter the Portland School of Music and Fine Arts, waved goodbye to Welcome Acres. She was so young, so vulnerable.

"Our first to leave the nest," she whispered against Clint's chest.

"Chin up, my darling," he said tenderly. "Our Jonda is mature for her age—life saw to that. God has plans for her."

Clint was right, she thought through a mist of tears. And she would be home for holidays and special events— one of them being Jordan's production of *The Merchant of Venice* for which she was to arrange chamber music, typical of the Shakespearean times.

Clint was right, too, in saying that they owed it to the rest of the children to carry on, preparing them for entering the world as they had prepared Jonda. And now (more lightly) they were needed also in helping Roberta and Efraim settle in their new home.

Courtney realized with a start that he was right. This meant that they would be losing Yada, too. What a void in Blessing's heart—a void with which Courtney must help her reckon. *Well, Lord, keep my chin up. I know You want it high. Make this house Your house—and my heart will be less lonely*... was her constant prayer.

Oakwood Knoll, which once had seemed a far-flung fantasy, became a reality. Roberta's bubbling enthusiasm was contagious. She laughed at Efraim's teasing that the estate lacked the folksy American appeal, had no "down-home" flavor—looked more like some provincial style of King Gustavus in eighteenth-century Sweden or (daringly) like a Gothic fourteenth-century monastery.

"So?" Roberta quipped, *"Le roi le veut!"*

"The king wills it," Yada—who stood cross-legged with arms folded as neighbors wrestled with the upright piano—translated.

Courtney never ceased to be amazed that a child so young could manage so many languages. She wondered if he was managing his mixed heritages as well. Her brother showed no concern. "His mother means it literally—and I agree. We spell King with a capital *K*."

In the months following, Roberta's conversation was sprinkled with medieval colors: cinnamon, copper, bronze, gold... claret... persimmon. But she was not obsessed. Even as she sought Courtney's advice in arranging the *demi-lune* cherry table with its impressive *faux marbre* top, the hand-painted flowers and swags, and an endless parade of chintz-covered slipper chairs and poufed leather divans, her plans went beyond the three members of the Glamoras' immediate family.

Pausing to wipe dusty hands on a flannel cloth after

all was in order, Roberta said thoughtfully, "Courtney, I—we—want to erect a cross. After all," she smiled in reference to Efraim's teasing, "it dates a lot farther back than this hodgepodge of period furniture. Unless, of course, you and Clint plan one? You have prior claim."

"A cross?" Courtney was surprised at the thought. "It had never occurred to us—"

"Wonderful idea—wonderful, wonderful," Brother Jim puffed as he and Tobias dropped a massive sofa in the foyer. "Make it high—"

"*Very* high!" Roberta, ecstatic, promised. "And well-lighted with strings of lanterns for the night—guiding all the lost, in both senses of the word, to our humble abode!"

Tobias frowned in concentration and gave his beard a tug. "Do you think people will follow it?"

"We Christians do, good brother!" Big Jim said with pride.

Tobias nodded soberly. " 'Tis true—but I mean, can anyone find the road that leads to your cross?"

Again it was Yada who spoke. "Jesus did," he said.

Another four months passed before the full impact of Yada's words came home to Courtney. The Glamoras, the Desmonds, Brother Jim (after a rousing sermon) and Miss Lizzie—and Tobias by means of his own invitation—were enjoying a Sunday dinner of chicken and dumplings when the rabbi wiped his fork clean with a napkin in preparation for a second helping, laid it down, and spoke over Donolar's tall centerpiece of wild larkspur.

"I trust that you good people have been satisfied with my instruction of young Yada—not that much was new, just a reinforcement?"

Courtney held her breath, knowing somehow that the question was the shallow preface to deeper water. Efraim shared her premonition, if one could judge by his look of concentration even before his "yes."

Tobias cleared his throat. "According to Hebrew law, we should be preparing him for his bar mitzvah—"

He had no opportunity to finish. "His thirteenth birthday is years away!" Roberta protested, color high in her cheeks. "We wanted our son to be informed—as well as to know about his natural mother's Indian upbringing—but she chose to be a Christian—and—"

Roberta could go no farther. Efraim, placing his hand over hers, finished for her. "And Yada will choose his faith," he said flatly.

Tobias was unperturbed. "The *bar mitzvah* is only a ceremony, but it takes concentration to prepare a student for assumption of responsibility and religious duty. His thirteenth birthday *will* come."

Brother Jim could restrain himself no longer. "My friend, who is to say that 13 is the age of accountability? We are under the new law!"

Another debate was in the making—the first between the two men to be held in the presence of the children. Courtney sought Clint's eyes, but they were focused on Blessing. She followed his gaze and was seized by a sudden desire to desert her post. The child, whose dark, thoughtful eyes were filled with unexplained pain, needed comfort more than the group needed a hostess. But something held her back—some inner instinct that warned of her daughter's need to find an answer to whatever was troubling her. Courtney must wait for the *why* of the pain.

"Surely," Tobias said kindly but firmly, "we are agreed upon the Ten Commandments which go back to Leviticus—"

"Aye! But, good brother, let me correct your arithmetic. There are 11! Yada himself can quote John's proof—"

"Love needs no proof other than what the Good Book says. That we love one another as we love ourselves—" Tobias insisted.

"Ah," Brother Jim said with a hint of sadness in his usually booming voice, "self-love has destroyed nations. Look around you and see what brimstone it has rained down in this valley. Lives destroyed . . . land stolen from rightful owners...robbery...thievery...fornication... destruction of homes, timber, the earth's minerals. Love of self boils down to lust of the flesh. No, no! Do not interrupt me! You can be mighty pigheaded when it comes to listening. But, you see, I love you anyway, because of the new commandment which says—"

"A new commandment I give unto you, that ye love one another as *I* have loved you," Yada said with such simple dignity that both men fell silent. "The Jesus-commandment," he added.

"And *then* you can love each other," Blessing said, her tone matching his. And, with a bounce of dark curls that sent her blue hair-bow askew, she rose. "Please, may we be excused? Yada and I would like to play."

---

Miss Lizzie announced at the Easter service that the end-of-school exercises, in addition to the community picnic, would include production of *The Merchant of Venice*. "And this time, we invite adult participation." So if the ladies would circulate the news that Jordan Desmond would be producer? With herself and Mr. Haysacker directing, of course. She hesitated, then added, "Please inform Rabbi Epstern that *everyone* is welcome."

The school's chapel auditorium overflowed with a curious audience. Who would perform? Strange, its being kept secret. They strained forward as lesser characters came onstage. And one could guess after Miss Lizzie's simple explanation of the plot that the "intelleck, Miz Glamora" was bound on being Portia, the lady-lawyer. And Brother Jim was right for that Gobbo clown. But—could you beat that? The Rabbi himself playing Shylock, the Jew who demanded a pound of human flesh? Still, that young Glamora stole the show—made it all seem right with his explanation of something called "instinctive protest 'gainst race hatred." Religious-like.

Courtney and Clint watched through tears. One day Jordan, too, would be leaving.

# CHAPTER 30

# Had There Been
# a Black Door?

❦

Jonda came home for the performance which was to be talked about for years to come as a stitching together of the rips in the fabric of family neighborliness. Having given no advance notice, she simply appeared onstage with three friends from her school, and together they played the memorable strains of hauntingly beautiful but unfamiliar arrangements in chamber-music fashion. Her proud parents were to learn that Jonda herself composed the music—music, her instructors declared, which one day would make her famous. At this the golden-goddess replica of Vanessa, her mother, and her grandmother before her smiled sweetly, almost sadly, and replied that she would write even greater works. But they would not be for fame—the music would be for the Lord's work. She had felt His call.

Her cheeks glowed. Her eyes were bright. The heartbreak had left her face. For a fleeting moment, Courtney caught a glimpse of the blinding light of the white door from her dreams. . . .

Wistfully, Jonda tiptoed through the great house, her fingers caressing each piece of furniture as they caressed the ivory keys of the piano. She longed to stay a while, but she and the other girls must give a recital in two days, she explained. So there was time only to see Auntie Ro's house, tease Mandy into making her favorite chocolate cake (promising to stay out of the kitchen so it would not fall), and chat with the siblings she loved with so great a passion. Courtney, staying carefully out of their way, watched from a window overlooking the garden as Jonda slipped up behind Kenney where he was busily pouring a white liquid from one container into another with an absorbed look in his fair-skinned face. It was another of his endless experiments. "Boo!" his big sister said.

Kenney looked up happily and went back to pouring. "Someday," he said with that faraway look in his blue eyes, "I will come up with the formula that will kill pain—something other than this laughing gas dentists use when yanking out aching teeth."

"You probably will. What about a syrup for aching hearts?"

Kenney cast her a sideways glance. "Mr. Haysacker has one, especially prepared for you."

"Kenney!" Jonda chided, looking relieved when Jordan joined them to take his bows for directing the play—and received them.

"Miss Lizzie deserves the applause," Jordan said modestly, "but (standing taller) she *did* say that *The Merchant of Venice* demands a lot of skill in stage management. Of course," he smiled, "Shakespeare never constructed a better plot. Do you think the audience understood, Jonda?"

"Shakespeare's language is somewhat like the biblical writers'. Nobody understands completely, I guess—but the more we read or hear, the more we understand. Our wonderful friends and neighbors here deserve an introduction to both. I congratulate you. You made us proud!"

"I wish they hadn't laughed at my friend," Yada said as he and Blessing joined the little group. "Me, too," Blessing added.

Jordan bit his lip in concentration. "Try to understand, Yada, that they were not laughing at the rabbi—just at the part he played. You know, flying into fits of rage. Shakespeare wrote the play for Elizabethan audiences and things were—well, different then."

Apparently nobody had heard Donolar's footsteps as he crossed the bridge leading over his moat. Shaking his childishly curling hair in perplexity, he said sadly, "Nobody should laugh at anybody. Butterflies know better." Kenney nodded, as if surprised.

Jonda sighed. "Sometimes, my young scientist, animals are wiser than people."

Courtney's heart swelled with pride. "And sometimes, my darlings, children are wiser than their parents," she said from her hiding place.

---

"Any progress, girls?" Clint, who had been discussing with Efraim their lack of it, turned first to Courtney and then to Roberta. "We men have been unable to pick up a clue. Sometimes I think I dreamed the nightmare—even though I know better. In fact, the lack of evidence of a conspiracy against the government bothers me more than something concrete."

"The women have worked hard, but sometimes I wonder if there could have been a slip of the tongue, something which gave us away," Roberta responded. "That would send those involved underground—cause them to burrow like rodents."

Courtney found herself fidgeting, wondering if she should inquire about the key. Efraim seemed to sense her hesitation. "I have been unable to find hair or hide of Mr. Ashbury, Courtney. He seems to have disappeared into thin air—taking his knowledge of the key, if any, with him. It has been a year now, and even with the help of some dependable connections in the capital, nothing!" He spread his hands in despair, paused, and then added almost as if talking to himself, "Somehow I think there is a connection, but Old Alfie is an isolationist from the human race. It is all very strange—his silence, everything."

Strange indeed, and it was to become more so.

Some two months later, when the four of them saw Jordan off to Portland where he would study theater at the same school his sister attended, the watchful eyes of Postmaster Archie Sylvester caught sight of them.

The war had left Archie crippled bodily and emotionally. A spinal injury confined him to a wheelchair, and explosion of a cannon near his battalion had disfigured his face grotesquely. Embarrassment had reduced him to a querulous invalid. However, there was a glitter of interest in his eyes when he waved two letters, unmistakably intended for someone in the foursome. Were the letters too important to wait for mail delivery?

"That reminds me," Courtney said when the two men went inside the enlarged building which served both West and East New Hope for distribution of mail, "I have intended to ask Efraim if he found anybody who could read Gaelic."

"*I* did," Roberta said, her eyes on the post office. "A woman—"

The sight of Efraim's white face stopped further explanation. Clint's face, too, was chalky. Wordlessly each handed their wives a letter. Black edging told the story in advance of the opening. *Death!*

Startled by the postmark, it took Courtney some time to control the premonition that gripped her heart. Lance. Why, after all these years, would Lance Sterling emerge from her past to write her from London where he was painting so successfully? *Why?* She knew, of course.

"Let me help, darling," Clint said gently. Taking the letter from her trembling fingers, he quickly tore open the flap and returned the envelope. Even then she hesitated, although Roberta had scanned her own letter and was rereading the contents.

"My father," she said without emotion, "drowned—as I guess you know."

Courtney shook her head numbly. Dear Roberta. There had been no demonstration of real affection between father and daughter. He represented no great virtue or godliness. But he had been all she had by way of family.

Now he was no longer there. Death was sobering...
*anybody's* death.

"My mother—" Courtney whispered, "how will she
manage alone?"

From somewhere far away she heard Roberta's words.
"She will not have to, dear Courtney. Read your letter. Oh,
I'm so sorry—"

Sorry? Lance was sorry, too. It was his heartbreaking
duty to tell Courtney that her mother, unable to bear her
sorrow, had taken her life.

Was there a black door in the dream? Courtney was
unable to remember.

# CHAPTER 31

# Questions Without Answers

❦

Time was passing. The letter from Robert VanKoten's lawyer had raised questions to which Courtney was unable to find answers. Certainly her mother's demise following so quickly threw matters into a state of chaos, Courtney realized, wishing she were uninvolved.

"If we were there," Roberta said in an offhand manner, as if to avoid the complications of her father's will, "you and I would wear black for six months, cover our faces with veiling, and go through the hypocrisy of mourning. Servants would stand at attention—" and there her voice broke.

Roberta was deeply hurt—that Courtney knew from her own feelings of regret that she and Mother had never been closer. How well she remembered the Lady Ana's meaningless ritual of properly graduating to grays and dark blues, always aware that the colors were becoming to her fragile beauty and drew admiring glances from later suitors. As a small child, Courtney had asked the governess why someone could not mourn as properly in red—a question for which she had been sent to bed without supper.

Oh, the sham of it all! Well, something worthwhile had come as a result. She and Roberta had learned the meaning of *real* love, the value of openness, the refusal to be sucked into silly tradition, and—most important of all—how to draw their children close and pass that God-given legacy on to them.

"He had been ill, you know—my father," Roberta said on one particular morning as they had tea on Roberta's terrace. "And nobody told me. A near-fatal stroke—that's when he made out the will, giving all to your mother—"

Courtney gasped. "And nobody told us," Courtney said faintly, "the daughters."

Roberta did not seem to hear. "Nobody expected him to recover, but he rallied—rallied enough to change it. I was to have a portion, *providing* I was in Europe to claim it! His speech was impaired—perhaps his mind, as well. Father walked with a cane, but there is no cane for the tongue or the brain. He—he—there was a more massive stroke the second time—"

"Oh, Ro, I am sorry," Courtney laid down her silver spoon and leaned across the sun-warmed tea cart to place a comforting hand over her sister-in-law's.

Roberta tried to smile, then said a little bitterly, " 'Wipe that smile off your face, Roberta! Have you no respect for the dead?' Forgive me, dear Courtney—dear, dear friend—you do understand? We must face this together."

Their grief, Courtney supposed—but there was more. "Our parents' deaths raise so many questions. Even the lawyer is confused. You see, there is mention of grandchildren—and that affects both of us. Your children—Vanessa's—but I am not sure about Yada. Then the lawyer wonders who is heir when there is—uh, suicide—and is my son *really* a grandchild under the strange circumstances. Then, Courtney," Roberta's amber eyes reflected real pain, "*I* was to be there—" .

Courtney shook her head to clear it. "Have you talked this over with Efraim?" was all she could manage, shaken as she was by news of her own involvement in the legal tangle.

Roberta nodded. "I am supposed to understand. I am the lawyer. Oh Courtney, I am not at all sure anymore that I *want* to be liberated! Efraim and I want what is best for our son. Maybe it would be a chocolate cake baked by his mother with Yada licking the spoon—"

"You are a wonderful mother, Roberta. Stop accusing yourself. You are under emotional stress. Try to relax. Please—let's pray together."

Roberta's eyes filled with tears as together they knelt beside the vine-wrapped railing, clasping one another's hand.

---

Courtney's only concern was for Roberta. For herself, she wanted nothing. Clint, holding her close, said that he was proud of her, that she was totally unselfish—*and* that she was totally his!

It was good to see that Roberta relaxed. She invited the ladies' group for a grand tour of Oakwood Knoll, a treat they were to talk about for years to come. She then did a total flip-flop (as if to salve her smarting conscience) and asked permission of Mandy and Mrs. Rueben to teach her the art of making lye soap. Armed with a gallon bucket of meat drippings, she struggled with combining the fat and lye with a wooden paddle and boiling the smelly mixture in a black kettle over an outdoor fire. Spread in bread pans, it hardened properly and looked good enough to eat when, under Mandy's watchful eye, Roberta proudly cut the soap into squares and stored part of it in the smokehouse and took the remainder home. Good for Saturday-night baths, Mandy said, happy with her role as teacher. Good for healing poison oak, seven-year itch, and vulgar mouths—just rinse Satan's language right off the tongue.

The experience furnished many a laugh as Efraim teased her unmercifully. "It would wash away anything short of sin," he confided to Brother Jim and told Courtney and Clint (in his wife's presence) that he had washed his face with her potent mix, making the skin as taut as the strings on a banjo. "Just stick with your law," he suggested. Roberta obliged.

Several weeks later she told Courtney that she had written the lawyer, instructing him to hold the estate open. She had some thinking to do.

"Prayer did it," she said humbly. "It is as if God told me that there was no rush. 'Be still and know that I am God.' "

―――――――――――

Although Roberta was able to keep her father's will in probate, all else moved on. There were back-and-forth letters between Courtney and the twins, report cards for her and Clint to study as they looked ahead to Kenney and Blessing's future and—in addition to her church work and the ladies' meetings, which had developed into a "Patch-and-Chat Club" as well as Bible study—a letter to Lance. The latter she postponed until it could be postponed no longer.

Lance had done a portrait of her mother, he wrote. If Courtney wished to have it, he would be happy to ship it together with another that Robert VanKoten, Esquire had contracted him to do: a replica of their castle. Unfortunately, neither was completed before Mr. VanKoten's unfortunate death. If not, he would either put them in the gallery which used so many of his paintings or would sell them at an auction. He wished her well, hoped that she and Clint were parents of the 12 children she planned (surely she jested?), and assumed that one was named for him as promised. "Uncle Lance" had a nice ring to it—especially if assigned by one of her children. Lance signed his letter "With love," then added a postscript: "I am still a confirmed bachelor—or should I say I am married to my work?"

Courtney responded with a brief but warm note, explaining how the naming of the children came to be, congratulated him on his success, and told of her trip back to their childhood home, including her encounter with Old Alfie. That part was easy, but she found herself struggling with his question concerning the paintings. They seemed such a faraway part of her. Would it seem rude—even heartless—if she refused? After all, the portrait of her mother was also a portrait of the children's grandmother, as much a part of their undeniable past as Rose Wind was of Yada's.

It came to her then that perhaps Roberta and Efraim would appreciate the painting of the castle her mother had demanded of Roberta's father. Perhaps the castle would one day belong to Yada. Who knew? And for her own children's sake, yes, she must accept Lance's gift.

Roberta was delighted, as were the children. "I shall paint it, too," Blessing promised Yada, hopping up and down in glee while he watched, eyes shining with admiration. "Imagine, Yada—*imagine!* a real live castle of our own!"

Yada imagined. It was in his face. And, Courtney realized with a jolt, his mother imagined, too.

———————————

In due time Lance replied. His second letter was as shocking as the first. The paintings were on their way with his love, he said and—ever the gentleman—thanked Courtney for accepting his offering.

"Old Alfie?" his gracious note concluded. "It pleases me that you had a last opportunity to see him, Courtney—a last remnant of our childhood. You see, he too is dead. Rex Alverson, the only classmate with whom I have kept in touch, wrote that Mr. Ashbury's remains were found in the Devil's Cove. Foul play is suspected."

Foul play? Who would want to harm the helpless mute? Courtney was saddened. But Efraim's reaction was more than one of sadness. A cold draft seemed to have entered the library of Welcome Acres as, uncharacteristically, he began jangling the loose change in his trouser pockets. Deep in thought, he seemed to have forgotten Courtney's presence. Something warned her not to force a confidence.

Then suddenly her brother spoke. "Say nothing about this, Courtney. The carriage house could be where it all begins. We need that letter translated—*now!*"

# CHAPTER 32

# The Frightening Truth

The translation was slow in coming. Roberta's friend had gone to Colorado to visit her daughter. The daughter had a neighbor who knew the strange mixture of Scotch-Irish that Roberta's friend was unable to make out. Colloquialisms—wasn't that the word for "peculiar-like sayings"?

During the months of waiting, two important things had happened. Efraim seemed strangely changed, withdrawn. At times, he seemed about to speak to Courtney, ask her something—only to clamp his lips shut tightly. He was often away from Oakwood Knoll—a matter which disturbed her more than it did Roberta, who was struggling with her own indecisions.

"What is it, Clint? Something is wrong. Efraim seems to weigh everybody in balance—even us. What is going on in his mind?" Courtney asked.

"You know I am unable to tell you that, sweetheart." Can't or won't? Which did her husband mean? Was he, too, being secretive?

Efraim had asked that she say nothing. That must mean *ask* nothing as well. Courtney had resolved to wait until the men took her into their confidence. But, for all her resolution, an urgent voice inside demanded: *What is going on that you cannot share with your wives?*

Feeling that she had clenched her fists too long in order to hold her tongue, Courtney walked toward Oakwood Knoll one morning. The air was bracing, the sun unusually bright for February. Roberta had felt the same and met Courtney halfway. "Which house?" they both laughed. But Roberta's news would not wait for walls. "I have decided to go—it has been a year now—"

To Europe, Courtney was sure Roberta meant. The year had slipped by on invisible wings, marked only by the notches on the gallery post where Clint measured the children's growth.

"I will keep Yada—and I suppose Efraim will accompany you."

Roberta's answer was instantaneous. "Wrong on both counts! I will take Yada with me, and it is Efraim you can board. He is far too deeply involved in the investigation to take time out."

"I wanted to talk about that—" Courtney began.

Roberta gave no sign of hearing. "Efraim and I agree that the trip will be good for Yada. He can see for himself the 'homeland' of the Israelites—as well as Bethlehem-Judah. We would like to take Blessing—"

"Oh no!" Courtney cried out sharply. "Please, *please* do not put that in her mind, Ro. Once you pressed me into a half-promise—"

"Oh Courtney," Roberta protested, "you know me too well to think that one has anything to do with the other. It is still my dream, but this matter has to do with Blessing's future."

"A future she is far too young to decide. And no—a very *flat* no—I would never, never consent to allowing her to go that far from me. I can understand your reason for taking Yada, but the situation is very, very different."

Roberta looked at Courtney strangely. Slowly she nodded. "And I understand your refusal. But I wonder if you know what those two mean to one another. I doubt if Yada will want to come along without her. But rest assured," and she touched Courtney's hand lightly, "that I will make no mention—if you will look after his father!"

Their laugh was a little strange as each returned

home. Significant, somehow, their going separate ways—strange and a little troubling.

--------

Before Roberta could complete her planning, spring had arrived in all its glory—and the translation of the Gaelic letter had come.

Whatever the four of them might have imagined could in no way have prepared them for its contents. It was to open doors and close them. It was to change their lives and the lives of those around them in both East New Hope and West . . . in Washington, D.C. . . . and throughout the rest of the world. Not that it could be recorded in history books because written down, it might hamper future operations.

Great-grandmother Glamora's letter had been relatively brief. Translated from Celtic, it rambled on and on—showing signs that those who attempted transcribing the words into English had trouble with the near-obsolete language. The newer version had no punctuation. Words were misspelled. Phrases were often repeated. Confusing though the jumbled words were, the message was even more so.

Courtney read the meaningless words, pausing to punctuate, then reread them, before handing the translation to Efraim with a shake of her head. "What do you make of it? Only one word stands out: *key*. The rest is a hopeless maze of names. Surely this was meant for earlier generations?"

"Eat sompin', you chil'ens a-gonna plum tucker yuh sweet se'ves out. Dis heah worryin's no good a'tall," Mandy scolded. "Nevah wuz ah one whut thunk fastin' was—well, not whatevah 'tis de good rabbi claims—"

Courtney's mind was still on the letter. It was Clint who thanked Mandy and took the plate of cinnamon rolls from her capable hands. "What we need is some fresh coffee. Any beans ground?"

"Groun' 'n biled—come wid me." Mandy, smiling broadly, led the way into the kitchen.

Courtney, something turning over and over in her mind, sat stone-still in the ladder-back chair across from the rolltop desk where Efraim, with Roberta looking over his shoulder, frowned with concentration.

None of this made sense, she thought, reaching beneath the table to touch the release hinge of the secret drawer. Efraim's reason for sending for her had been to see that she had the furniture—or did he suspect even then that it contained a secret yet to be unlocked? Her mind took a step backwards. She remembered an inquisitive look from Old Alfie as he pointed to the desk. What was it he wanted to know? Something in his watery eyes had asked a question—or did they warn her?

"What is this word?" Roberta broke the silence, pointing a forefinger at the letter.

"Castle," Efraim said quietly. "I remember our father's saying there was one in the family—or some cold, drafty place that passed as such. So that must be what the key opens. See how the letter reads? And—look here—our ancestor wanted to have the youngest daughter of Gabriel Glamora's daughter to inherit the so-called castle. Complicated, but that boils down to Blessing, Courtney. Just as our father's mother wished *his* daughter to have the furniture. Surely she must have had enough of the men's dueling so—" Efraim began reading silent then, face darkening from the look of near-amusement of just moments before.

In the silence that followed, the only sound was a whine of the wind in the pines and the steady *drip-drip* of rain off the eaves. The sounds were mournful music in Courtney's ears—a dirge, although she could not have explained why. Lost in thought, she was unaware of Clint's setting the coffee service on a low table before them.

Efraim, his face still dark, handed the letter wordlessly to Clint, and it was Roberta who poured the coffee which went untasted. They sat motionless, all buried in their separate thoughts (Courtney thinking that one castle in the family was a shock, but *this* was ridiculous, and seeing visions of courtyards, men in velvet knee-pants and ladies with diamonds as big as wild hazelnuts at their ears). All except Courtney took turns at rereading in search of something they may have missed or, worse, read into the strange and frightening letter. Courtney's shock was too great for comment—too great even for her to be sure she was hearing the fragmented conversation correctly.

"Some of it fits," Efraim was saying, "only I had no idea it was so far-reaching. Could it be possible? Yes, I guess it could—"

"It is such an old letter, Efraim," Roberta said. "Names could have changed, and many immigrants had their names changed legally so as to sound 'American.' Surely, you put no stock in similarities—"

"There are ways of checking. And yes, I do believe—make that *understand*—that even in that dark, long-ago time there was a ground swell about creating a *pure* race, exterminating all human beings except the *intelligente*—those without blemish."

Roberta's face blanched. "You mean persecution of the Jews?"

Clint spoke then. "That is part of it. According to our information, however, a century of rivalry in Prussia, the powers wanting anarchy, the Reich seeking power by overthrow of the government—"

"Reich—overthrow of *which* government?...Reich means—what?" Courtney asked tonelessly.

"Courtney, darling, drink your coffee. You are so pale—" Clint's tone was pleading. "We have known part of this and the truth is that some of it is at the local level and still in existence just as the Civil War goes on and on, even here—as well as hatred of the Indians and prejudice against the Jews—"

Nobody was finishing sentences, and nobody had

answered her question. "Reich?" Again she whispered the word.

"The word is not transferable," Efraim answered. "There is no such word in English, making it a sort of mystic realm or empire, but not quite. Just say it is a cruel and inhuman power. And here is the list of local, blind followers...."

# CHAPTER 33

# The Ugly Necessity
# of Suspicion

❦

Summer came and went. Jonda, more beautiful than ever at 16, came home for a brief visit. She brought news that a noted school in Seattle heard her in concert and offered a scholarship. Nobody could doubt her talent and complete dedication, but there was no room for romance. Courtney accepted in her heart that John had indeed been the love of Jonda's life. Jordan had elected to remain for a summer session since he was producing a religious Christmas pageant, one which he had written himself— and would Mother and Dad believe that it was all so demanding that there could be no trip home, no matter how brief?

The children must go their own ways, Clint had said, and she had repeated the words to Roberta. The fact that Courtney fully believed them did not ease the ache in her heart. "I guess I would hold them forever, Lord," she confessed in her prayers. To others, she said nothing.

Kenney spent most of his time with Donolar, she supposed, learning everything there was to know about bees, butterflies, and roses. Donolar reserved his Indian history and legends—as well as his literary quotations—for Blessing and Yada, who were inseparable at home, although Kenney confided that his younger sister had eyes only for Tad at school. Perhaps the boy would help fill the void when Roberta took Yada away. For yes, she continued to insist that the ten-year-old should accompany her. If Courtney was certain that Blessing should remain here, Roberta and Yada would look in on the truth or myth of the Glamora-castle story.

Courtney had never been more certain of anything.

Roberta had not insisted. "I understand. After all, your young Kennedy will finish school here this year, leaving you only one fledgling, like us. And the timing is poor in view of the situation here—"

Roberta chatted on, perhaps filling her in on more recent developments. If so, Courtney failed to hear. Roberta's words had pricked her heart. How could she have forgotten that Kenney was 12 and that he indeed would complete all that the Kennedy School had to offer? If only one could clip the wings of time the way Mandy scissored the wing feathers of her wandering rooster to keep him from "flyin' de coop."

---

School opened. With the children under the careful eye of Miss Lizzie, Courtney felt free to accept Roberta's invitation to come along to West New Hope for a few necessities she had been unable to locate. And yes, it would give them an opportunity to listen in here and there. Clint was busy at the mine while Efraim worked between the bank and his East New Hope branch of the law offices. All of them kept mum about the letter's contents, even in the presence of the children. So a breather would be nice.

A warning wind twirled colored leaves about the buggy, almost covering the back trail, a shortcut the men had developed from an old cow trail. Shorter, yes, and safer, too, as it kept Courtney and Roberta from the dark caverns of the forest. The sky was unbelievably bright. But something—the threat of winter in the wind's voice, perhaps—caused Courtney to shiver in spite of the heavy sweater she had worn. The feeling grew as, at Roberta's suggestion, they went to the newspaper office first.

Editor Jennings, white hair neatly combed but eyes showing fatigue, met them with hands extended in shy friendliness. He blew a bit of dust from the only two chairs in the office, motioned them to be seated, and set fire to the crisscrossed kindling in the old potbellied stove.

"Getting cold already. Pull up a bit closer if you're chilled. These things give a choice of being too hot or too cold," he grinned.

Roberta picked up a newspaper and scanned the headlines, then nodded with approval. "At first I was concerned, but now I am glad that you are making a big deal of this—tossing out fishing lines for information, while hiding the bait."

Roberta's tone was casual, but Courtney felt that she was doing some fishing on her own. She was studying Willie closely, almost as if she were bracing for a blow. "Any further leads, Willie?"

The editor scratched his head, almost in bewilderment. "I don't know, some hunches maybe. Let's see," he shuffled papers about on his desk, bewilderment increasing. "Now, that's strange. They were here just minutes ago, and now there's no sign of them. Who has been in here? Nobody—that is, nobody who would arouse suspicion. Just the postmaster and a couple of stragglers wanting to advertise land—"

"What papers, Willie?" Courtney spoke for the first time. "Were they similar to the propaganda you found before?"

His answer caused her to move closer to the stove. "Stronger—more threatening—dangerous—*dynamite!*"

His apprentice, wearing a black rubber apron, entered from the small printing room, seemingly unaware of Courtney and Roberta's presence. "Mr. Jennings, take a look before I finish setting the type—"

"We have guests, boy. Greet 'em properly."

The boy turned. He was older than Courtney would have thought at their first encounter. And, for a single moment, she thought his surprise was feigned. His direct gaze, however, almost dispelled a cloud of doubt she seemed to feel hanging over her about almost everyone.

The three of them exchanged greetings and the young man turned to go. "Goodbye—and please tell Mr. Clint and Mr. Efraim that I appreciate my training. Prepares me for moving on, you know."

"I thought you liked it here," Roberta said in surprise.

"Oh, I do!" he said with surprising passion. "I like the city . . . Washington . . . my country . . . but is that enough in this troubled world? I want into the feverish activity of a big office—for doing greater work, you understand?"

"No, I am afraid I do *not* understand," Courtney said slowly.

"Oh, the energy and enthusiasm of the young," Willie said with a somewhat embarrassed laugh. "Wanting to conquer the world—"

*Conquer the world.* Courtney felt cold again, but when she turned, the young man was gone.

On their way out, Roberta greeted a Mrs. Winslow, an overweight lady—a fact which even careful corseting and her dressmaker failed to conceal. Her manner was pleasant as she extended a plump hand, made heavier by an array of rings. Even so, Courtney found herself studying the high sweep of blue-toned hair (done with bluing—such as Mandy used in the rinse water—by some careful hairdresser) and the discreetly applied makeup and wondering if her behavior was not as discreetly acquired. Winslow . . . *Winslow* . . . the name was familiar.

Oh yes, the wife of the new manager of the bank. Clint and Efraim deliberated before taking him into their employ. The man's record was as clean as a new slate, but wasn't he a shade too dressy, a little flashy, actually. "Mort Winslow would look more at home on a platform handing out leaflets than at the neighborhood gatherings." They had said more about the possibility of his intimidating farmers, miners, and lumbermen seeking loans. The diamond stickpin . . .

But Courtney's mind kept going back to one phrase. *Handing out leaflets.* Those words had stuck.

"It is nice to meet you, Mrs. Desmond," Helene Winslow said twice. "I understand that you ladies have organized a—well, sort of protest group. Nice—yes, very nice. We must think of the future, not concentrate on the past—move ahead, the way you are doing."

Protest? Courtney hoped that Roberta would protest the label and was surprised when she failed to do so. Instead, she was inviting the banker's wife to feel welcome. Was that really wise?

Of course it was! Courtney told herself that she must overcome being so suspicious of everybody. It was a disgusting habit, perhaps unchristian. And yet, she sighed in resignation, this was the course they had agreed upon. How else could they solve the problem—so ripe for trouble—without being watchful? She must put personal feelings aside.

What was Mrs. Winslow saying? That she was delighted over the editor's taking on an apprentice and that Jeptha Heinz was just the lad? Jeptha Something Roberta had spoken of was by name Jeptha Heinz. "Of course, there are those who think that he digs into matters that are of no concern and question why he did all the night work at the printing office. Of course, he is wise," Mrs. Winslow dabbed at her nose daintily with a lace handkerchief, "to track down the source of this pernicious material. You knew, of course?"

"Of course," Roberta said with a *But how did you know?* question in her voice.

Goodbyes were strained and Courtney was relieved and happy to see several women approaching whom they knew very well. Their dark calico dresses, practical capes, and open, scrubbed-clean faces were a pitiful contrast to Helene Winslow, who summed up the women coolly and then went inside.

"Somethin' ain't right here—like it was 'bout to bust,"

Widder Brown whispered hoarsely. "And me—I'd like hit t'be them beer barrels—"

"Not yet!" Roberta protested. "Just keep up the good work."

They finished shopping quickly. Courtney purchased only red hair ribbons for Blessing who had demanded braids in place of curls.

# CHAPTER 34

# The Burning Question

❦

Widder Brown was to become a legend among the valley women. Hadn't she warned them that something was " 'bout to bust"? Her prediction became a reality with uncanny suddenness.

Without fanfare, Roberta and Yada left and Efraim accepted Courtney and Clint's invitation to move from Oakwood Knoll to Welcome Acres for the duration of his family's European quest. It was wise to say little about Roberta's plans, she and Efraim decided. Why enlarge the bedding ground of speculation as long as Courtney would carry on both with the women's organization and Efraim's welfare.

Blessing moped, losing interest even in her beloved art. "Darling, Yada will be home before you know it. And you need other friends."

"I have other friends, Mother," Blessing, who was less gregarious than the other children, assured her. "It isn't that—"

Courtney laid down the pencil with which she was making notes for her next column. "Want to talk about it?"

Blessing answered without hesitation. "I just wonder if I explained as much to Yada as I should have. Maybe I could have said more about Jesus—what Brother Jim calls the way of salvation. I think Rabbi Epstern has told him more about the Torah and Uncle Donny has explained more about Indian beliefs than I have said about

God's gift of love. I wonder if Yada knows I belong to Him?"

"*Belong* to him?"

"To Jesus." Blessing's great eyes looked out over Donolar's bright chrysanthemum bed. "I guess Uncle Donny is right—flowers say it best. He says the petals preach sermons all their own. Do you understand?"

Courtney was astonished at her daughter's wisdom. Yes, Courtney understood—and more. There was a joy that flooded her being which went past understanding. Love in every sense of the word—God's Word!

She reached out her arms and Blessing, once more a little child seeking reassurance, walked into them. "I drew a picture," she said against Courtney's shoulder. "A picture of clouds, which are dust beneath God's feet. And we stand in that dust—but only we cannot see Him until Jesus clears the way. That is why we have whirlwinds, Uncle Donny says. I will send it to Yada—and tell him—about love—"

Courtney looked down at her precious child, another gift from the Creator. Tender reverence filled the room in that moment alone with God—as little Blessing slept.

And that is how Clint found them . . . mother and child . . . his madonna.

———————————

That very night tragedy struck. Someday, Courtney hoped with all her heart, the horrible scenes and what they led to would fade. But she would never forget the beautiful moments before them, as if to lure her mind from all possibility of danger: Donolar's arrangement of white mums, like a snowdrift, ringed by sweet-scented pine . . . the shaft of late sunlight on the sloping roof below the dining room turning the centerpiece gold, then bronze . . . the one twilight star winking through the ceiling-to-floor window, then another and another in the darkening sky as Clint lighted the candles. Were those ageless stars keeping watch as the moments ticked away? Did they hear Clint's prayer of thanksgiving, Mandy's mellow voice struggling with a simple psalm, then Kenney and Blessing's prayer for Auntie Ro and Yada's safety? Did the stars care what happened in the planet Earth in its circled orb around them?

There had been no opportunity to repeat details of happenings in West New Hope to Clint and Efraim. In the busy days that followed, Courtney's memory of the events diminished and became so diminutive that it was easy to decide the incidents were of no consequence. Now talk radiated from the children like the spokes on a shining wheel. They were excited about this and that so normally, so happily, while Clint and Courtney exchanged loving glances of pride. *Home*—what a beautiful word!

Then, without warning, the dining room was filled with light, bringing back a memory too horrible to recall. *Fire!*

Outside there were voices. Loud. Frightening. Then the rush of hurried feet. The children led the push to the window.

There on the lawn was—*oh dear God, no!*—a burning cross!

Courtney squeezed her eyes shut, closing out sight of the tongues of flame licking their lips in frenzied glee at taste of the burning wood. She was unable to close out sight of the memories they triggered: burning of Cousin Bella's beloved Mansion-in-the-Wild . . . the fiery door of her own dreams. Neither could she shut out reality. Even behind closed eyelids she saw the hungry flames, felt the acrid taste of smoke, and sensed the torch of hatred against them. *Who . . . why?* Her heart felt carved in stone. Fixed. Permanent. Incapable of beating.

Opening her eyes, she saw that the men had extinguished the fire. Little puffs of smoke, visible in the light of a nearby lantern, wafted skyward, sending smoke signals to ring a full harvest moon.

"Mother, look!" Kenney all but screamed, a message Blessing repeated. Only then was Courtney aware that instinctively she had drawn the children to her although she was incapable of thinking.

Indians were closing in from all directions, a sight which brought Donolar rushing back into the house, babbling for the first time since Courtney could recall. "Enemies—friends—who knows—but the butterflies?" Donolar's voice trailed off in a tangle of quotations.

For the first time, Courtney made no effort to comfort her brother. She had stiffened, listening. At first, there was only the sound of her own breathing. Then there was a strange chanting as the younger men linked hands, stamping out the still-red coals with their bare feet.

"See fire—smoke signals—we come. Friends. Stamp out fire's magic—kill Wicked Power. Ai-*eee*!"

And as suddenly as they had appeared, the Indians were gone—the wrong direction! They were—why, they were leaping with what surely must be war cries toward Oakwood Knoll!

Bedlam followed. Courtney, cautioning the children to stay close, rushed downstairs. The men were gone, leaving only Grandma Old, supported by two very young maidens. The old woman reached out a gnarled hand to offer a honeycake. A token of appreciation for coals— good omen, she said.

Courtney was to recall the gesture of love and asked God's blessings on the dear old lady in her evening prayers. Courtney thanked Him also for Donolar's recovery—his loosened tongue which thanked Grandma Old properly. Her own eyes were focused on the ragged flames leaping and fluttering in the moon-drenched dark surrounding Efraim and Roberta's home. Threads of brightness spread through the brushwood, then seemed to explode in a burst of sparks. Would Oakwood Knoll be next? It was hard to think with the children chattering excitedly. What was Donolar saying?

"See, Kenney? Indians have conquered. Fire is their captive—see the pots? They have slain Red Dragon and are taking live coals to rekindle Pure fire. They choose carefully and their hands are fire-scarred from sifting the embers. We must thank the Almighty that the enemy does not know His ways. They prefer darkness because their deeds are evil. Our red friends fear darkness, but God provides for all His children. He sent the Indians a moony night, the only time of Pure Fire. It is Great Spirit's sign for them."

Sure enough, before the wondering eyes of Courtney and the two children, the triumphant braves were filing past, their fire pots trailing mares' tails of smoke behind.

Now, mingled with the sick-sweet smell of wetted-down embers, was the homey smell of coffee . . . normalcy. Praise the Lord for Mandy, and, yes, for the minute-sized German housekeeper whose generously large voice could persuade a helpless world to sit up and take notice that bread was the staff of life—even honeycake.

But the night had not ended. Welcome Acres was surrounded suddenly with men, women, and children, all talking at once. Children with other children; men carrying weapons (Courtney noting with shock) and muttering about the Constitution's giving the right to bear arms; and the women knotting together as a some-what militant group, a step beyond what Roberta had in mind when organizing them. What—?

"We saw 'em Miz Desmon' . . . but no way o'recognizin' none . . . wearin' sheets, they was . . . sure as shootin', with holes cut fer eyes."

The jumbled words became more jumbled in Court-ney's shocked ears. "Who, ladies? What has happened?" she asked in a shockingly calm voice.

" 'Y them what burnt th' cross in front o'th' church . . . sure did, 'n we washed it away . . . scart them ghosty men, too . . . cowards they wuz . . . coverin' faces 'n high-tailin' it . . . but pore Tobias . . . pore Tobias—"

"What about Rabbi Epstern—is he all right?" Courtney gasped.

The women nodded like a flock of birds pecking away
in a grain field. "They burnt one uv them strange stars—
you know, with six points—at his door," Cara Laughten
said quietly. "We women took care whilst th' men put out
th' fire at th' church 'n shot up in th' air to skeer 'em—"

"Tobias?" Courtney inhaled a breath and held it.

"Ole Toby's awright, Miz Courtney," Widder Brown
said. "Down by th' river bank a-praying his heart out,
stayed on his prayer bones while 'twas t'others that went
fire fightin'. Guess we'se all a-gonna hafta fight—I tole
youse sumpin's 'bout t' bust—so we's boun' on fightin'."

"That is precisely what they—whoever they are—
want—" Courtney began but was interrupted by half a
dozen women who shrilled, "So we fight fire with fire,
that's what we do!"

Courtney was relieved when Brother Jim and Miss
Lizzie appeared, both with sooty faces. Brother Jim
threw open the front door to admit Clint and Efraim,
whose faces showed such fatigue that it broke Courtney's
heart. With a little cry, she sprang forward to reach high
and draw their ash-covered heads in with her arms.
Hysteria was near the surface—hysteria which turned to
a foolish desire to laugh uncontrollably. Instead, she
kissed each in turn.

"Talk about sackcloth and ashes!"

Brother Jim took over. "Tobias is right! We all belong
on our knees," he said. "Let's seek the Lord's guidance in
apprehending and bringing to justice these weasels—
after we praise Him for sparing our lives. Is it well with
thee?"

"No!" the cry was unanimous.

"Then," he said triumphantly, "we pray about the
burnin' question!"

───────────────

Later Courtney tried in vain to recall who most of the

guests were. They speculated dangerously as to who might be responsible for the fires.

"Why," she asked Clint after they read *The Gazette*, "did Willie decide to include feature articles about Roberta and Yada's trip—the two castles—and all the details? Is it wise?"

Clint shook his head.

# CHAPTER 35

# At Home and Abroad

❧

Courtney and Clint talked at length after the burning episode. Questions were piling up, they agreed. It was best, Clint said, to play the situation down a bit now— talk less and listen more. Efraim, however, held out for more exposure. Things must be brought out into the open. Letting them fester would give the enemy the advantage.

Efraim did not argue, but it was plain to see that he was unconvinced that they should play down the recent events. There was restraint in his manner. There was a strangeness, a stiffness. And Courtney had a feeling that he had doubled his probing rather than slowing it down.

She was right, she knew, when Archie Sylvester rolled his wheelchair onto the post office porch in spite of the rough boards being slippery with the first frost. Waving a wasted hand, he drew Courtney's attention as she crossed the street to the dry goods store.

"Telegram," he said in his usual short manner. Casual, yes, but beneath the green visor, which she sometimes suspected he wore more to mask his curiosity than protect his eyes, he was watching her every move.

Courtney accepted the yellow envelope, thanked the postmaster, and was ready to take her leave when he volunteered that the message was for Efraim. Courtney nodded, not trusting her voice. Surely the man knew she could read. Her silence served to offend him.

"Hardly worth sending. Just one word: CONFIRMED."

With that, Mr. Sylvester skidded his wheels in negotiating a turn back into his dismal office.

Ignoring his rudeness, Courtney bypassed the dry goods store and hurried to join Clint. He was still in the hardware store pondering the size of nails he needed for fence repair. "Finished," he smiled.

She related the incident on the way home and was surprised when Clint said only, "I think I understand."

"Then explain to me," Courtney wanted to say. But a cold rain which dark clouds said could turn to a downpour began falling, compelling Clint to adjust the buggy top. And afterward the talk turned in other directions: conservation of the forests, his stand, and objections he faced . . . the one remaining Kennedy Mine—and should he close it? . . . then with a crease between his eyes, problems at the bank ("Oh, just things," he said and brushed that topic aside).

The wind, weary from play in the treetops, began complaining like a feverish child then swept down in a regular tantrum. Trees bent beneath the force. The temperature dropped, and unexpectedly the rain turned partially to snow.

"Possible blizzard," Clint said, urging the horse forward. "We would be smart to pick up the children at school."

But Miss Lizzie, the best weather forecaster in the valley, had dismissed school early and taken their children home. Mr. Haysacker sat alone in the shadows of the forthcoming storm. At the sight of Clint and Courtney, he leaped from his desk, grabbing for his cane and shuffling papers with his free hand. "I—I wasn't expecting company—"

Obviously. But why, Courtney wondered, did their appearance startle the teacher? What was the long sheet of paper that slipped from his hand to the floor as he sidled forward, his back toward the desk as if to conceal something?

She murmured something she hoped was an apology and turned to go. The teacher followed. Clint, she saw from the corner of her eye, scooped up the fallen paper but did not return it to the desk. How strange that Clint should fold it quickly and shove it into his pocket!

It disturbed her that Clint made no mention of the matter. She was equally disturbed at Efraim's reaction to the telegram—rather, his lack of reaction. He simply nodded, tossed the yellow sheet with its single-word message into the fire, and with only the slightest inclination of his head motioned Clint into the library.

The hour grew late. Mandy was waiting dinner. Would Courtney-hon get the menfolk to the table? Should they be disturbed? Courtney wondered, refusing to acknowledge the wee spark of resentment she felt when they were so secretive. She hesitated at the library door, hand lifted for knocking. But their low-pitched voices stopped her, rendering her almost incapable of motion.

"—and the list goes on and on," Efraim was saying. "According to the Secret Service, Haysacker and Hachsacker are one and the same—"

"That scares me." Clint's voice was as hard as the nails he had bought. "His teaching would put him in a position to poison the children's minds—overinterest in Jonda could have been a spying ploy—"

Clint's angry voice trailed off and Courtney was able to make out very little of her brother's reply except for disjointed phrases and a few familiar names. "...in deep...newspaper...knew there was a leak there... the boy's clean...bank...all a part of Alex Heston's framework...no, not the mastermind...get word to the government..."

"I concede that you were right, Efraim—no more stalling. And we must double our guard—watch out for Courtney, the children, *ourselves!*"

"First," Efraim's voice dropped even lower, "read the list—"

Courtney hoped the Lord would forgive her for what she was about to do. Was it possible to get forgiveness in advance? She hoped so as, for the first time in her life, she eased the massive door open a hairbreadth and eavesdropped in an effort to hear the names.

But Efraim dashed her hopes. "I made an error in saying a few names aloud. Chalk it off to anger, shock—whatever. The government could have my head for that! So commit the list to memory, Clint, as I have. Then burn it. It is best that we forget this meeting, behave normally, and above all, make no mention of names even when we are sure we are alone. Walls have ears, you know."

Flushing guiltily, Courtney fled to the bedroom. She, too, must play the game. Innocently, she was patting her hair in place when Clint rejoined her as Mandy gave the dinner bell an impatient clang.

"You look lovely—I love you in blue—" he said absently.

"Hyacinth," she corrected with a smile.

———————

A week later the mail brought a strange letter from Roberta. There was some delay, due to the unusual circumstances of the will, she explained. Both she and Yada were disappointed. On the other hand, the legal red tape gave her an opportunity to check out the contents of Great-grandmother Glamora's message. The letter contained much more than the first translation revealed. The exact location of "said castle." Some family history Efraim and Courtney would appreciate. And now this was strange, was it not? Roberta asked. A list of names of persons dedicated to some common cause—their reason for coming to America in the first place. Generations of hate . . . disregard for human life . . . power being their god.

Efraim read the letter aloud, carefully omitting the names and skipping to the bottom where Yada had written a message to Blessing.

> I will answer your letter when my mother is less hurried. Right now there is no time for much of anything. You see, I have enrolled in a class of ancient religious history, all Jewish, of course, as it is mostly law. It all makes me wonder. I have hung your drawing above my bed. It is nice to think that God is there, watching over me. Do you suppose He can see through the dust beneath his feet, Blessing? I miss school, and I miss you lots and lots. Do you draw pictures for other boys? I hope not for the Tadpole! Love, Yada.

Efraim and Clint laughed. Courtney did not. *Tadpole*, Tad Jennings. *The leak?*

# CHAPTER 36

# Come Home—*NOW!*

❧

In the days that followed, Courtney had trouble remembering exactly which topics to avoid in the presence of Clint and Efraim. There had been no further incidents of the frightening burnings, so it was safe to ask why they had happened. Neither of the men could answer, but cautioned her to be careful. Courtney assured them that she was ever watchful, particularly regarding the children's safety. Both looked at her with approval and called her "good girl" a bit too lightly. Courtney no longer felt resentful. They were doing a good job, although she wondered sometimes why responsibility fell on the shoulders of these two men in particular. She was proud of both.

The household ran smoothly. Courtney called the Women Involved together, more to help soothe their fears since the fiery incidents than to assign additional duties. They were fascinated with her sharing news of Mrs. Glamora, Jonda, and Jordan; and they ate heartily of Mandy's brown betty, delighting her with requests for the recipe.

When they had left, Mandy volunteered that she had visited with her friend Hannah again. "She talks a heap, but she's runnin' skeered and skeered me, too. Dat woman she dun sez dat hit's not safe fo' us colored foks heah no mo'—dem men in white sheets dun declared on bein' 'niggah haters.' Is dat a fak—er lack unto dem tales 'bout ghosts walkin' in graveyards?"

The question gave Courtney an opportunity to caution Mandy about the children's safety and to assure her that the men would protect her. Mandy looked relieved, but Courtney was certain that more was on her mind. "What is it, Mandy?"

"Hit troubles me—dem thangs Hannah sez de lady uv de house is boun' on sayin' 'bout Miz Rueben. She don' trust no Germans neithah 'n sez dey's bent on startin' war. Courtney-hon, I dun seen wat war's boun' on doin', but I reckon as how dis German woman we can tol'rate." Mandy's words were condescending. She was as loyal as they come, even to the housekeeper, although (Courtney thought with amusement) the two would never sign a peace treaty. It came as no surprise when the cook, as if afraid of softening, added: "Me, I don' put no stock in sech unkind words—dat Miz Rueben ain't smart 'nuffer warrin'."

"Thank you for sharing, Mandy. We trust you both. That is something to be thankful for. There is so much distrust—which is what all this idle talk is about. Just be watchful, and Mandy—I doubt if it is necessary to say this—but guard your words, even with your friend."

"Oh, Courtney-hon, may de good Lawd strike me down dead iffen I wuz t'b carryin' tales!" Dear Mandy. The world had need for more like her.

Kenney and Blessing strolled in for their afternoon snack at that moment. Kenney complained about Mr. Haysacker's lack of knowledge in biology, then wondered aloud why he kept asking for Jonda's address.

Careful to keep her voice steady, Courtney said, "Please Kenney, disregard such requests. It is impolite of him to ask for a young lady's address."

Kenney popped a molasses cookie into his mouth, taking an enormous bite. "Half-moon!" he said, holding up the remains. Then, as the other half disappeared, "Total eclipse!"

"Kenney," Courtney chided gently, holding back a smile.

Turning the conversation, at which he was a champion, Kenney said, "I tell him nothing. He's different from Miss Lizzie. *He* does all the telling. Miss Lizzie makes us search out the answers for ourselves."

Blessing nibbled at her cookie until her brother left the kitchen. Then, turning to Courtney, she said suddenly, "I wish Yada were home instead of at that school. He says he understands my faith in Jesus just as he said he understood my picture, but when he explained it, it was different than I meant. Yada thinks it's important to recite lots of Bible verses and all the laws, but," Blessing paused to wipe her mouth thoughtfully, "does he know that love is law, too? I should have said more, but the words are hard to say. I have to paint them."

Courtney's heart swelled with pride. "You are doing well, darling."

When Blessing spoke again, it was about Tad. Tad wrote "silver poems." Tad knew so much about writing. He carried her books. Well and good. But oddly, Blessing made no mention of his faith or his lack of it, or her concern one way or the other. Courtney wondered why.

---

Letters between the Desmonds and the Glamoras crossed the sea as Roberta and Yada stayed on. Roberta wrote at length of the elegance of the castle which, as far as lawyers could determine, would belong to herself and Courtney jointly. Furnished wrong, of course—it was modern instead of mellow. And the walls should be— well, a bit grim instead of draped with chintz. It was a disappointment, really. Roberta was homesick for the old, the tried, and the true in family and friends as well as decor. Yada appeared happy with his studies one day, depressed the next. "He is such a thoughtful one, you know, and loves perhaps too deeply for his own good."

Efraim longed for his family but confided to Courtney that in a way he was glad that they were far away—just until things settled a bit, of course, and he could be sure these poisoned minds did not see his son as a target.

And then came the letter from Roberta which changed his thinking.

> I found the castle which Great-grandmother Glamora told of—so yes, it exists. There is something awesome about it, so weathered and drafty-looking. I am uncertain as to whether I would have had the courage to enter the uninhabited place even were entry possible. There is a heavy iron fence around it, as if to guard its secrets, but the gate was open. What bluffed me were traces of chains which had locked it—and the tracks—fresh ones— leading to the door. I am convinced that the key fits the lock, but (can you see me shivering?) there was somebody inside—or else the house is haunted! Coward that I am, I can only hope that I was not spotted by some spy. Forgive me for going melodramatic . . .

At that point, Roberta's letter stopped. The remainder bore a later date. She was sorry, she said, but the lawyers had summoned her to see if the heirs would like to sell her father's property—and what did Efraim and Courtney think?

"I have no interest in what happens to those beastly castles," Efraim growled. "I think my wife and son should come home."

He picked up the letter and resumed reading aloud:

> I was unable to resist one more look-see at the Glamora castle. There is a magnetic pull to those strange turrets. But let me tell you that I had the scare of my life. The gate was chained, but would you believe that the key unlocked it? I slipped through the thistles grown up where

the hedge once was and did not see the guards—
*armed* guards—until they fired what must
have been a warning shot! You see, I made it as
far as one of the cobwebby windows. Can you
believe that the inside is an absolute garrison?
Troops . . . caches of artillery . . . everything set
up as if to conquer the world. Then the shot!
But that was not what panicked me. It was
recognition—I mean, one of the men called
me by name as I fled the scene like Goldilocks
when caught in the house of the three bears. It
is terrifying. What do you make of it and how
on earth did anyone here know me by name? I
think I will—

Efraim shredded the letter with shaking fingers without completing the rest of it. "I *know* what you will do!"
His voice was an absolute hiss, almost as if he were
talking to Roberta. Then, after throwing the shredded
letter into the fire and stirring the licking flames with
a poker to make sure that every word was destroyed,
Efraim turned to Courtney and Clint. "It all figures," he
said. "That is where orders are coming from—world-
wide, just as Washington suspected. I will cable today:
COME HOME—NOW!"

# CHAPTER 37

# Void—and Without Form

❦

Spring brought a blush of green to the hills, shy violets peeking from the shadowy cleavage of rock breasts to the body of the mountains, a million blossoms to the orchards—and the homecoming of Roberta and Yada.

Their arrival was unfortunately timed for Blessing. "Why did it have to be on the last-day-of-school picnic?"

"I think that's a good time," Kenney said. "This way Yada can see his old friends and take part in the relays. I want him when we choose sides because he runs like the wind!"

*Like the wind. Rose Wind, his mother.* Courtney felt a sense of apprehension. Was it wise for Yada to make an appearance?

Concern caused her to miss a part of the children's conversation. She came back to the present when Kenney, peeking inside one of the several large baskets of food Mandy and Mrs. Rueben were packing, spoke.

"Ummmm—yummy! Does this feast come before or after the duel?"

"Stop teasing about it," Blessing begged, her olive-dark eyes enlarged with something akin to fear.

Courtney had no idea what the talk was about, but she realized with a start how very grown-up her baby was. Those remarkable eyes—so serious until her rare laugh came. Then little firefly sparks lighted her lovely eyes and starry twinkles of joy softened her face, showing how very vulnerable she was. Such a perfect lady.

Mandy bustled in to shoo Kenney away from the

baskets into which she had packed black-crust bread, sweet rolls, Indian corn pudding, butter fresh from her new mold which shaped flowers in the top, and a variety of dried-fruit pies. Boiled eggs, baked beans, fried chicken, and the fresh-frosted cakes would top off the baskets at the last minute.

" 'Nuf t'feed de res'vation iffen a young'un ah knows gits hissef outa mah kitchen—afore ah switches 'is legs!"

Kenney impishly looked back over his shoulder in leaving. "They'll be there," he said wisely. "My dad's going to announce about some of the land grants that are going back to them. Think Indians like pickles?" He reached for the jar.

"Out witcha!"

Blessing seemed deaf to what was going on. Courtney decided her problem took priority over Kenney's surprise announcement. "Want to come into the library where we can talk, honey?"

Blessing shook her head. "It is something I must talk to God about."

"Yada?"

Again she nodded. "I have promised to eat dinner with Tad, and now I wonder what to do."

Mandy snorted. "Once uh promise iz give, hit's kept, dat's what!"

Courtney felt herself flinch. Just how much had she promised Roberta? She had forgotten in view of all that had happened since. Maybe Roberta had forgotten also. "Let God tell you," she murmured, wondering whether she meant her daughter or herself who needed answers.

---

Never had the valley seen a turnout such as the picnic brought. Problems seemed to have been folded away, at least for the day. The planned program went well. Miss Lizzie and her young charges took their bows while Mr. Haysacker stood back, applauding mindlessly, his ear cocked toward a man made faceless by the forward tilt of a wide-brimmed, black hat. Instinctively, Courtney let her eyes wander through the crowd until she caught sight thankfully of Blessing. With head held high, she stood between Tad and Yada. Roberta and Efraim were shaking hands with friends inconspicuously. But where was Clint?

Then she caught sight of him elbowing his way forward to the improvised platform. Of course! As mayor, Clint would express his appreciation for the program, congratulate those who had completed studies offered here and—and then, with a thudding heart, she remembered what Kenney had said. He would announce the grants!

The drumming of her heart grew louder, muffling his every word. She only knew that Clint's eyes were bright and about him there was a look of exhilaration as he paid tribute to his brother-in-law who had worked so hard in Washington to achieve this. But there was more work to do. Victory was not theirs until—

*Until there was peace.* Surely that would have completed Clint's sentence. But Roberta, having worked her way to Courtney's side, was whispering in her ear as Efraim, wiping beads of perspiration from his forehead, mounted the platform to stand beside his brother-in-law.

"What's she up to?" Roberta rolled her eyes discreetly toward Helene Winslow, garbed in a tight-fitting red-white-and-blue vertical-striped dress. Designed to make her look thinner, the dress made the banker's wife look more as if she were draped in a too-tight flag. The result was so ludicrous that Courtney had to smother a smile, at the same time wondering along with her sister-in-law why Helene Winslow bothered with such a "low-brow" gathering. "I could choke her with my bare hands . . . boil her in oil slowly . . . maybe we're too civilized . . . ought to flog her through the crowd as they did evildoers a century or so ago in England. . . ."

Courtney's ears were tuned to Efraim's brisk speech. "Let us stop judging others. What we see on the surface only masks the truth. If only we could look inside the heart, as the Lord alone can do, we would find the real truth. What we see on the surface of our fellowman only blinds us to truth." Efraim paused for Brother Jim's booming "Amen!" and its many echoes, then proceeded: "Be patient. Our legal system, like our democratic form of government, works. It only falters when individuals corrupt it—"

Courtney's eyes were studying Helene Winslow. What *was* she doing here? The crowd had broken into applause, giving an opportunity to whisper the question to Roberta.

"What makes you suspect Mrs. Winslow?"

"Womanly instinct—*look!*"

Helene Winslow opened her bag, withdrew a folded sheet of paper, and handed it to somebody whose face was lost behind the man with the wide-brimmed hat. Quickly, Courtney stood on tiptoe and managed to see— of all people—Jeptha, Willie's apprentice.

"It could be just a bit of social chitchat," Courtney offered.

"Or a list such as our men have memorized."

"You knew?"

"I am a lawyer, Courtney. It is my business to snoop."

"I wish we had a copy of that list, but—"

"We do!" Roberta said. She strained forward to watch Jeptha with a crooked little smile with just a hint of smugness in it. "Right here in my shoe! Hey, what do you mean that little pimple could be innocent? If he were, would he run like a scared rabbit? Watch our children—"

And Roberta was gone. The world was whirling madly. There was a feel in the air of impending storm, although the sky continued faultless. Courtney strained her eyes for sight of the children and found them.

But in the process she lost sight of Roberta. Women who witnessed the scene later reported that Miz Glamora descended on that reformed newspaperman's helper like the seven plagues of Egypt, wrestling him to the ground like unto what a man would, grabbed something important-like from his hand so fast that he squeaked like a mouse. "An' he fairly flew in 'is gitaway," Widder Brown clinched it, "feet never once touchin' th' groun'!"

Courtney herself took no note. The world was still whirling too fast. Else, how could Mr. Haysacker (*Hachsacher*) be at her side looking down with a flirtatious smile? *Flirtatious*—how dare him? And yet his eyes were as cold as marbles.

"I suppose that by your husband's actions he thinks he can change things?"

"He intends to try!" Courtney said with outward dignity, her throat dry.

"Lucky man, Clint Desmond. With a loyal woman like you at his side, it's easy to be a Napoleon. He knows diamonds from paste." The teacher reached out and touched her hand. Did he think flattery would garner information? What was he searching for?

Courtney jerked her hand away. "You are being impertinent, sir," she said coldly. "For your information, my husband has no desire to become a Napoleon. And I choose to make no reply to your personal remarks. Please remember your position here and let there be no repeats of such behavior, Mr. Haysacker."

The man leaned forward with a near leer. "You may call me—"

"Mr. Hachsacher?" Courtney asked angrily and regretted it immediately.

The man's face turned ugly, the angry eyes narrowing, a coiled rattler ready to strike. As Courtney hurried away, she realized that she was being followed. Glancing ahead, she saw a growing knot of men gathering near the platform where Clint and Efraim were shaking hands with well-wishers. They were armed! There was no time to cry out. There was a roll of drums . . . shouting . . . chanting. Indians! The earth was void and without form. . . .

# CHAPTER 38

# Roundup

❦

It was strange, Courtney realized later, how very few knew that a deadly crisis had been prevented or rather, postponed. Few had seen the Women Involved group recover the paper from Jeptha. And few had seen the danger building as, one by one, the enemy joined a rapidly growing number at the platform. Nobody at all had witnessed the ugly scene of the man calling himself Haysacker in his hateful and uninvited attempt at familiarity, she was quite sure. That was before Courtney or the others—except for Clint and Efraim—knew that the place was surrounded by officers of the law, men who had sworn to risk their very lives to protect the innocent, except—

The Indians were not a part of the plan! Chief of the Lost Tribe, arms crossed, came afoot with a half-dozen braves, painted according to ancient custom, riding beside him in syncopated gait.

"We come in peace," the chief said, his stone face never once relaxing. "Bring peace pipe!"

When he stepped aside, Grandma Old, dismissing the two maidens at her side, stumbled clumsily forward. Beneath the sagging skin withered by age, the planes of her face showed earlier beauty. Today she *was* young, Courtney thought tenderly: flushed . . . bright of eye . . . and carrying a garland of rare star lilies as bright as their name, as brilliant as the dark eyes of the old, old woman. At first, she babbled. Then slowly the words came. Nobody, she said, except the Lost Tribe knew hiding place of star lily. It waited for royal daughter's son. Great Spirit had promised peace. Great Spirit had sent it through royal daughter's gift. *Yada!*

Yada, composed as always, showed no surprise. He walked forward and dropped to his knees before her. Grandma Old strained forward, her aching joints refusing to bend. "I grow clumsy with age," she scolded herself, as the wreath fell to the ground.

Yada, like the gentleman Roberta and Efraim had brought him up to be, gathered up the wreckage. Now the beautiful lilies would fade and die. His young mouth quivered as he returned the crushed flowers to his respected Grandma Old. One knowing the Indian ways as Yada had learned them would understand his emotions, Courtney realized. He did not want anything to die, not even a flower. Yesterday perhaps it would have made little difference, but yesterday was gone.

Today the gnarled hands were honoring him in the only way they knew how. Peace. In some strange way he did *not* understand God had made use of him in expressing appreciation for which they had no words.

Courtney was so entranced with the ceremony that she hardly heard further words, if there were any. She became conscious of the real world around her at the sound of Brother Jim's booming voice. The celebration called for a prayer meeting...letting "the heavens declare the glory of God"...and what more fitting "tabernacle for the sun" than Welcome Acres? Suddenly, Courtney—practical again—felt the beauty of the ritual dissolve and banish previous fears. There were a million things that only she, Mandy, and Mrs. Rueben could do at Welcome Acres.

Ordinarily, it would have surprised her that the front door was unlocked. In the rush of the day, the detail went unnoticed except as a convenience. "Take care of the kitchen, Mandy...we will need extra chairs, Mrs. Rueben...and I will attend the rest." With those hurried words, Courtney kicked the door closed with the heel of her kid boot then, by force of habit, turned to lock it. No need for the bolt, too, she thought, as she rushed from fireplace to fireplace lighting fires. Donolar, who was too caught up in the ceremony for her to interrupt him, could arrange flowers. She should have located Roberta . . . left word for Clint as to her whereabouts . . . nobody knew. No matter. All would arrive soon. No time for hindsight.

For once, she wished that Mrs. Rueben were less concerned about the sun fading the carpets. Must the drapes always be drawn? She groped in the darkness, feeling for the pull cords.

And then she stopped. Something had alerted her, although there had been no sound. Only then did she recall that the door had been unlocked. A prowler? How silly—everybody was at the program. Maybe, she thought with a momentary smile, Miss Lizzie had arranged a welcoming committee, knowing that her husband—

She was about to call out when, moving ahead a step, she bumped into an overturned chair. Somehow she knew instinctively that the room had been ransacked. Hardly daring to move, she waited. Mandy and Mrs. Rueben had entered through the back door. If there was trouble there, they would sound an alarm. Any moment they would be here—

The feeling which had alerted her became a sound. A long, drawn-out protest of the front doorknob . . . a click. The lock was being forced cautiously, so silently that except for the slight squeak nobody could have heard. The door was opening now, Courtney knew by a slender strand of light which quickly disappeared. And, although she dared not turn, there was a draft of fresh air swirling about her feet.

The intruder—one, two, how many?—groped forward in her direction.

Everything happened at once then. There was a muffled shuffle of footsteps—footsteps that led upstairs. Then more footsteps all around her, it seemed. The crash she heard was followed by a howl of rage. Men appeared from everywhere, made visible when Mrs. Rueben began opening the drapes. Who spoke first, Mandy or the man she had seen wearing the black, wide-brimmed hat? Seconds later, both talked at once.

"Ah dun busted 'im wid mah kitch'n stool—'n ah'll set right heah in de middle uv 'is belly, officer suh!"

*Officer sir?* The faceless man was an officer? But how did Mandy know, and how did he get here? A million questions to ask.

"Thank you for your help, Mandy," the faceless man was saying as he wiped blood from the fallen intruder's brow. "Just a scratch—"

The next sound was Courtney's own voice. "Watch out!" she screamed as a crouching figure sprang from behind the overturned chair and aimed a weapon at the officer.

"Drop it!" The steady voice came from behind her. It had a familiar ring, but Courtney's mind was too dulled to attempt identification.

The gun fell from the second intruder's hand. "There's more uv us!"

"I know—found two outside and there's another behind that table who is in for trouble unless he comes out with his hands high!" the familiar voice growled. *Willie! Willie Jennings.* And on the side of the law, thank goodness. Never mind his apprentice for now.

"What can I do to help, Willie?" Courtney asked boldly as the slinking figure rose sheepishly from beneath the table—more afraid, she suspected, than waiting to pounce on a victim. "And who are these men?"

"Dis 'un ah knows," Mandy said from her perch in his middle. "Mistah High-'Mighty hissef, de bankah wid dat fancy wife whut lafs at me!"

*Mort Winslow?* How many more surprises could a day hold? Plenty, she was to learn. Willie was answering her question. "You can help, Mrs. Desmond, by fetching a rope. Go ahead—tie his hands. The roundup has begun!"

# CHAPTER 39

# No "Mourning After"

❦

By the time Clint and Efraim reached home, the "accused"—seven of them in all—were securely tied and lined up with what could hardly be called dignity. Four (two still unidentified) law enforcement officers were dividing their time between the lineup and the ladies who "gallantly assisted."

"Name, please," the man with the black hat said in address to the banker. "State your business—*and* what you were doing here!"

Mort Winslow, no longer arrogant, whined. "I need to see my lawyer—and a doctor about this hammer blow—may be a fatal injury—"

"A towel to staunch the blood, Mrs. Rueben. The fatal blow is a scratch. *Name*, or—" with a knowing look, "aren't you sure?"

A man in uniform was checking names on two lists. "Morton Winslow, *alias* Morton Thurlow, *alias* Winslow Nadeau, *alias* Morton Salt—you've got to be kidding! What've you got to do with this—?"

"Wait a minute here—looks like this Mr. *Somebody* is in a separate racket. That's their undoing, you know—fighting amongst themselves, get greedy—" the man wearing the gray uniform and a tin star said.

"My wife," the banker whimpered. "she—she has needs."

"Which only somebody else's money can buy? You mouse! Robbing the widows and orphans because of a greedy woman. Look at this!"

He held up a sheaf of papers. "Embezzlement...
extortion..."

Something clicked in Courtney's mind. This was no
first-time offense. One misstep would result in letting
him slip through their fingers. "May I suggest identification? You understand why."

"I understand. Thank you, Mrs. Desmond." Pushing
his hat back to reveal a level glance of gray eyes, the man
she had seen talking with Haysacker nodded, as he
pulled a badge from his vest pocket. "Thomas J. Quattlebaum, member of the United States Department of
Justice, *pro tempore*—that is, until the Attorney General
assesses the wisdom of a permanent investigative force.
This is a federal case in view of the cross-country kidnapping charge—"

*Kidnapping! Oh, dear God, please—*

"Soooo, Mr. Nobody, what were you looking for?"
Mr. Quattlebaum demanded. "And are these your ac-
complices? Make it easier on yourself!"

"Nobody—that is, except my wife. She-uh-mentioned
jewelry—and a key—said Haysacker knew—and would
help. But he's not who he says and—thought the key
unlocked a vault—his share going to a cause—"

"We know about him!" Willie Jennings broke in. "And
we know about my so-called apprentice who had been
grinding out the un-American pamphlets to poison the
minds of our children."

*The children!*

Once more Courtney's mind fled the scene in search of
her family. Some of this made sense. Some did not. All
that mattered was the safety of her loved ones. The
questioning went on. Mandy had taken the stand. "Yes-
suh-eee! Ah dun 'xactly wat y'all said, yore honah—Ah
up 'n tole dat Hannah-frien' uv mine 'bout dem stones 'n
de key—knowin' y'all wuz a-gonna sub'stute flour-paste
'uns—tole 'er twuz sekret-lak—dat allus gits 'er tongue
a-waggin' 'n, yep! ah dun tole Mistah Clint 'n Mistah
Efraim us'n 'ud be—dat funny wud—"

"Decoys," Willie supplied. "Good girl, Mandy."

Mandy smiled so broadly she all but dislocated her jaw. "Dey's *heah*! Mistah Clint 'n all de res', ah'm a-trustin'—"

Courtney rushed outdoors, eyes devouring the sight of Donolar helping Blessing from the buggy, with Kenney, Yada, and Tad following solemnly behind . . . Efraim and Roberta swinging hands, deep in conversation . . . Brother Jim . . . Miss Lizzie . . . Tobias. But Clint?

And then she was in his arms. Laughing. Crying. She had been brave long enough. Liberated or not, it was time for her husband to take charge, which he did after a rib-cracking hug and a soft-spoken term of endearment.

---

There never was such a prayer meeting as that, valley folk were to tell the next generation. The Lord's ears must still be ringing with their praise. No contritions. No petitions. Just plain old-fashioned shoutin' out the glory like that black woman talked about. Contributed a lot, that Mandy did—took away a peck of false thinking about color. Why, in the eyes of the Lord, she was as white as snow. Come to think on it, the Almighty might just be color-blind as she claimed. And who would have dreamed that funny, tongue-tied little German knew so much about socialism and—what was that phrase, *communism*, was it? Something dangerous anyway, having to do with destroying freedom. Only natural, they speculated, since Mrs. Rueben came from away across the ocean— too far for that silly thinking to be any problem in such a peaceful valley as this, except for the feebleminded, and hadn't they all been rounded up? The only "common storehouse" that Karl Marx and his buddies could create here was a jail!

Of course Editor Willie Jennings knew a heap about such things, even something called a *Communist Manifesto*, and words like *bourgeoisie* (that Mrs. Rueben helped him pronounce). But where did that countrified Jepthro fit in? Must be smarter than he looked, putting out all those leaflets for innocent children. Good for Willie—watching out like he did. Now *there* was a real hero. Why, Willie would make two of that Marx. Do away with religion, would they? Let 'em try! Like Brother Jim and Rabbi Epstern said, the Lord probably would blow fury like fire from His nostrils at their denials of His existence.

Of course, brave as their men were, the women pointed out that all that male brawn was less powerful than the wit of their mates. Now if it hadn't been for Women Involved—well, history would have been different. Yes, little children, it *was* a little like *Ali Baba and the Forty Thieves*, with every single member being a Morgiana the slave girl, slipping around whispering messages to the men in the oil jars. Only this was no fairy tale, their suspecting that odd-acting Mr. Haysacker (or whatever his German name was). Who knew how he outfoxed the school board when he never held so much as a teaching certificate? That smart Mrs. Glamora was right, as you can see—allowed to vote next year like you'll be. Maybe we women shouted out the glory a little louder than the men that night, looking ahead like we did to our children's future. God had plans for us.

"Yep," Widder Brown was to add, " 'twas some prayer meetin' with both them devout men a-prayin' like they was a-tryin' to outdo one 'nother. Course, Tobias talked in tongues, but he was one smart man—yep, one smart man—like I'm a-gonna explain. . . ."

---

Dawn came, but there was no "mourning after" feeling, emotionally or from lack of sleep. Once valley folk resolved all mysteries (their thinking remaining well within the parameter representing their world), the nightlong parley turned to more peaceful matters. Over staggering stacks of sourdough pancakes swimming in Mandy's carmelized-sugar syrup and countless cups of Mrs. Rueben's pride, "der coffee vich der spoon v-loat maybe," they gloried in the ceremony which returned certain lands to the Indians. Wasn't it enough to melt the heart of a strong man watching Yada link the two races? Did ever one see such a look of—what was it: pride, joy, sadness mixed in. Hoping the Lord would forgive if it sounded disrespectful, but wasn't it a touch of trans-figuration? Never had they beheld such a look of sancti-fication, surrender, on earth as it was in heaven. Could it be that . . . well (over still more pancakes), better not speculate what Tobias knew.

Best they be getting home. They filed out, still singing praises.

———————————

Donolar had gone to Innisfree. The children, pre-ferring privacy in their emerging independence, had retired to their rooms—Yada, considering Welcome Acres one of his two homes, stretching out on the giant black leather couch in the library to sort out his feelings. Neither he nor the adults below heard Blessing's soft weeping.

Downstairs, their parents—too tightly wound for sleep—began the conversation anew. "If only it could end here," Efraim said, as he absently stirred still an-other cup of Mrs. Rueben's brew. "If only the valley folk were right but—well, ask your questions. I am braced."

"You suspected Archie Sylvester all along, and I never knew why. How could he have organized those blind sheep into the Cross-and-Star-of-David burning?" Clint mused, more to himself than to his brother-in-law.

"Oh, it was easy to hypnotize a bunch of losers and rebels with different causes into a hate-group. It's amaz-ing how brave cowards are with their faces hidden. The sheets offered a shield. Archie himself washed his hands like Pilate, you know, his wheelchair being his mask. But," Efraim sampled his coffee, grimaced, and pushed it aside, "his position gave him access to all messages—and, dangerously, they flowed overseas by secret code. Time for confessions—still to be kept in the family."

Roberta's laugh was strained. "You are working with the government."

"Forgive me, darling, for not telling you. Can you understand?"

"Easily—if *you* can! I, too, am involved—part of my mission in Europe—"

# CHAPTER 40

# Waiting for Doors to Open

❦

What a sunrise! The whole world looked newly created as the brilliant sun topped the zigzagging mountain range to pave a sapphire-blue morning sky with streets of gold. Trees took shape as towering castles of dark clouds toppled, like evil in the presence of good. If only her own heart could feel as tranquil, Courtney thought, as she watched in wonder. If only her nagging concerns would topple like the clouds, burying her questions, doubts, misgivings.

"Better pile in, little one," Clint said gently as he joined her at the window. "Yesterday—or is yesterday just an extension of today?—is gone. Why darling, you are trembling. To bed with you!"

Courtney shook her head. "Sleep would be impossible. Oh Clint, I feel so helpless, so left out. *Useless*—that is the word. Everybody knew except me—even Mandy and Mrs. Rueben. I had no chance to help."

Clint's intake of breath registered genuine surprise. "I never thought of it that way, sweetheart. If I hurt you—" his voice broke as he reached out to draw her close. "Played no part? Why, you were the heroine! You did what nobody else could have done. You looked after us all, kept everything running so *normally*, and cared for the most precious commodities in this valley: our children! And all the while you inspired the women, writing your encouraging columns, keeping us all on even keel, reminding us of God's love and protection—"

"Why wasn't I told?" Courtney interrupted in a small voice.

"For your own protection, and as a part of our shield. As it was, you carried on so naturally that nobody saw you as a threat, while suspicion stalked the rest of us. You were so sensitive that you figured out most everything all by yourself, anyway. And you were so courageous when the showdown came unexpectedly—"

Courtney felt a little ashamed. Life was not a rehearsal. Clint's voice was so tired and drained that she felt he might be falling asleep on her shoulder. With victory in sight, the battle had lost most of its savor because of her selfish demand for recognition. Reaching up, she placed a finger on his lips, then stroked the lines of concern from his forehead.

"Forgive me, my darling. I guess I needed reassurance—there is still so much I fail to understand. Why all this struggle for power?"

"One of life's mysteries," Clint said tiredly. "It dates back to biblical times, so the pattern is as old as time itself. Maybe it will always flourish. But it is up to us as God's chosen ones to fight evils which would destroy civilization. These little men who see themselves as leaders are in reality puppets. They keep conspiracies alive by organizing students groups and petty little hate-groups—anything to make the nonthinkers believe that American people are aggressive, have no friends outside the New World—you know the story, Courtney, how ferment begins and spreads. While those at the top—"

"Who?" Courtney asked as she had asked so many times before.

Clint turned palms up. "Those who fear Christians and Jews alike. Once upon a time Christians were food for the lions, you know—and now, as always, the Jews are without a home. *Who* remains to be seen."

Courtney felt a desperate tightening in her throat. "Oh Clint, can't we just do our bit *here*? Attend the needs of our family and—?"

"These *are* their needs, my darling. We are nearing the terminal. Then, yes, matters will be out of our hands. Do you think the Lord would have us wash our hands? We must confess our shortcomings instead of claiming to be the 'pure,' hiding our infirm or putting them up for public ridicule. Doesn't God tell us to confess openly, then try to do better with His help? If we quit now," Clint paused realizing that his rage was pointless, a waste of energy, unless he was willing to make good his idealistic thinking. "Quite a sermon," he grinned, "but do you understand?"

"Yes, my eloquent husband," Courtney said modestly, "and I love you for it!"

---

The next week was busy. Courtney strove to bring back a certain peace and harmony in Welcome Acres, arranging her schedule so that she could spend margins of each day with the children. She listened to their separate versions of all that had happened around them and tried to come up with answers at the level of their understanding. It was hard to explain matters that she herself was unable to comprehend as her mind dug deeper than the minds of Mandy, Mrs. Rueben, and the women of the valley. Roberta thanked her warmly, admitting that she had feelings of guilt at her frequent absences because of her continued involvement. Courtney reassured her that Yada was like her own.

The words brought tears to her sister-in-law's eyes. "Oh Courtney, what would I do without you? I have learned so much from you. You are so natural, so unselfish, so giving, and—uncomplicated."

"Leave off the halo, dear Ro," Courtney said. "Come to think of it, you make me sound like a cross between a martyr and Old Reliable."

Roberta embraced her even as she glanced at her watch. "You are Mrs. Wonderful! And Courtney, I meant it when I said you had taught me some valuable lessons. Watching Yada at the ceremony, I realized how wrong I was in trying to take over his life. As Blessing once said, 'Yada is Yada.' It was unfair of me to ask that you help me bring the two of them together. I—I now know that God created them, our Yada and Blessing, as they are—and they are in His hands."

"I taught you all that?" Courtney was wide-eyed.

"And more, like how to give myself in love—I had never experienced real love from my father, and you understood. How to love my child so much that I stopped clinging and let go. How to love God enough to do everything in His Name. Even how to love these enemies we are struggling against. And how to extend Christian love to unbelievers."

"Oh, Roberta! You humble me completely." Tears were near the surface, but Courtney felt an urge from a Higher Source to say something left unsaid. *What, Lord?*

"I guess," Courtney finally said softly, "what I am trying to say is that we can not force love. We just have to be submissive, waiting for a door to open, ready to step inside when gently love beckons."

" 'Gently love beckons,' " Roberta repeated reverently. Then, briskly, "What are you trying to do—send me to my meeting sobbing my heart out?"

---

Courtney found herself studying people carefully. Someone here, probably the least suspected, was capable of arousing public opinion enough to keep the cauldron of hate boiling. The conspiracy could sway a local election, a national election and—perish the thought—keep poking at the dike of love until it broke, threatening the country, letting the floodgates open to wash the very foundation of faith away.

One moment she was sure that God would never allow that. The next, she knew that it was up to those who loved the Lord to *be* that foundation.

It was like waiting for another door to open. Strange that she would have said that to Roberta. Needed here was a key to that door—obviously a person. And then came the startling realization that they were overlooking something obvious. Somewhere, somehow, the strange events fit together. Where, after all, was the key that Roberta took—and why did she think of it now as entrance to that door?

# CHAPTER 41

# A Last Letter
# from Lance

❦

It was Blessing who brought Lance's letter to Courtney as she packed away starched ginghams Mandy had finished on Tuesday. Tuesday was ironing day—a cardinal rule, according to Mrs. Rueben's code. She and Mandy had established a more compatible relationship since both became heroines in their eyes and those of the other women. As co-conspirators, they must stick together. Therefore, the cook would help the housekeeper in exchange for Mrs. Rueben's assistance in the kitchen "iffen she cud brang 'ersef t'follow o'dahs," which she did.

"A letter for you, Mother," Blessing said listlessly, laying it on the library table and immediately turning for an exit.

"Thank you, darling—want to join me in a treat? I smell spice cookies and Mandy has skimmed the milk."

"Thank you, no. I am busy and—"

The sentence hung in midair. Courtney's heart went out to her beautiful child who was reaching the stage her older sister had gone through so recently. *Recently?* Well, it seemed so anyway.

This surely must be the hardest part of being a mother—standing by waiting for a door to open, knowing when to hold back until love beckoned, so mother and daughter could be reunited.

One near-tragic glance from the velvet-dark eyes and her jewel was gone. It was as if Blessing, since the ceremony, had knotted a velvet rope around her young heart, shutting out the world with a sign: DO NOT TOUCH.

Sighing, Courtney picked up Lance's letter, observing that it was thicker than usual. It began colorfully. He enjoyed the ever-changing seasons in his Alpine villa: the brilliant red rocks made redder still when rains washed clean the ribs of the mountains, the bitter-cold winds which piled high the snowdrifts like icing on a wedding cake, the unexpected warm days which signaled to the strange lily-like flowers like fallen stars, begging—as it were—for the earth to give up its dead. And summers—

Dear Lance. He saw everything with the eye of an artist. She must share the letter with Blessing, who could appreciate it, perhaps showing it to Tad.

Forcing her mind back to the letter, Courtney noted that the handwriting changed from Lance's headlong scrawl to a cramped style very uncharacteristic of him. She slowed her reading. The message lay ahead.

As you know, something evil is happening—something which only you can slow. Please, dear Courtney, do not allow yourself to feel used. You were the only one that all involved felt totally able to trust. Your father must have sensed your special qualities, communicated them to Grandmother Glamora. How wise they were, but how misled in naming Old Alfie as guardian of the key. Of course, nobody expected Gabriel Glamora's untimely death which tested the integrity of the caretaker. Sadly, Mr. Ashbury held onto the key, misusing his power. He would forward it here—nobody would suspect a decaying castle as an arsenal, enough ammo to blow up the world! Duplicates were made before returning the key, so all was in order when Efraim uncovered the suspicious-looking files in Washington. It must have cost your brother dearly to allow you to be involved; but, of course, you were guarded all the while. It must have come as a great shock (Roberta did tell you?) to learn that the innocent old man of our childhood would be involved in *fascio* (repressed peasants in the socialist unions of workers—blindly led to believe it a citizen's duty to render blind obedience . . . abolition of elections . . . eventual overthrow of the government . . . world power . . . racism . . . and a God-less universe). If all this sounds confusing, bear in mind, dear Courtney, that innocence is your charming weapon. Your guilelessness, your purity—yes, you truly are the madonna your husband has named you. I am ever re-minded, when looking at my painting of you, of the Scripture: "Be still and know that I am God." But I am digressing . . .

"Why all this?" you must wonder. A fulfill-ment of the Bible, I guess—evil in the high places. But, armed with truth, you can help create another frontier—one which makes use of the knowledge that faith *does* work . . . faith in the Almighty . . . our neighbor . . . and our country's survival. We win, not by violence (always the stupid man's tool!) but by peace—working out our problems by honest debate and mutual agreement, not by subtle insinua-tions that arouse hatred. All this you know, but—

Courtney let the remainder of the letter drop into her lap. She was seeing a new Lance. The Lance she had loved as a child and prayed for as an adult. The Lance who, although he did not put it into words, had felt God's call and answered. This her heart could accept—even rejoice over. It was her mind which refused to function.

Mr. Ashbury's betrayal...Efraim's strange way of getting at the truth...Roberta's silence. And there was more. The worst was yet to come.

Lance's letter went on to mention names both familiar and unfamiliar. He talked about those who were out for quick money, criminals, would-be assassins (like the Bellevues—Clint's half-brothers)—who saw themselves as leaders and were cowardly puppets. Yes, Old Alfie *was* at the top, working through European powers. And he talked about history's being what history had always been—evil leading down the path of destruction. And then the bomb came.

> I hope that all went well when all of you read of Roberta's father's involvement. She hoped you would understand and never make mention again once her letter spelled it all out. How sad that her father's days must end in prison here, rotting away, as it were. The papers showing his death under other circumstances were cover-ups, half-truths, *lies*, as her attorneys discovered. She probably told you that Arabella Kennedy knew all along...

The pages fluttered to the floor. What did it all mean? And why had Roberta kept the story from them? And then Courtney's head cleared. Of course—Efraim had read his wife's letter, grown agitated, and destroyed it. The message had gone up in flames. It really made no difference now who understood what—just as long as they knew. The remainder was dreadful, but hardly news.

> So, you must know that your mother unwittingly contributed to the conspiracy here—idly chatting away about goings-on there in the Northwest...answering questions...volunteering information to gain social status,

gossip being more precious than silver. . . . Be happy, my darling, guard that love. I am returning the key . . . knowing that you hold the one which opens the door to happiness. Some day I will paint you the rainbow with which you have enriched my life.

Gently, Courtney laid the letter aside. Lance had made her mistress of the Mansion. Cousin Bella's dream came together now.

# CHAPTER 42

# *Jehovah-Shalom!*

It took Courtney, Clint, Roberta, and Efraim, a full week to finish their accounts—sometimes laughing, sometimes crying. Paragraph after paragraph, page after page, they went over every detail—culprit after culprit captured, details cleared up, evidence piling up. As for the conspiracy here, it was over...last chapter...end of story.

Exhausted but exhilarated, they agreed that the important thing was that their love for one another had never faltered. There had been no doubts between them. Now they all understood God's ways more fully.

Efraim, expanding his chest, as they toasted their toes before a blazing fire in the upstairs library fireplace, said with masculine pride: "I feel that I could move Mt. Hood over the Oregon line and into Washington!"

"That takes a lot of faith," Roberta reminded him.

"I've got it!" he said with conviction.

An earlier wind had died down. The sky had cleared. As the fire burned low, a thin sickle moon was visible, snared as it was in the branches of the apple tree which had grown tall since its planting when Welcome Acres was completed. Clint slipped his arm around Courtney as Efraim led Roberta to the window for a better view.

It was then that voices, easily recognizable as Brother Jim and Tobias', floated up the stairs from the downstairs parlor.

"Do you suppose anyone will ever know the part we played?" Tobias asked.

"Does it matter?" Brother Jim answered. "What counts is that our heavenly Father is well-pleased."

"Ah, how well Satan picks his tools and trains them to be followers. No arguments such as you and I enjoy, good brother."

One could envision Brother Jim nodding in agreement. "That would appear to be the weakness in their reach for power."

"But in a man's weakness he is made strong—agreed?"

Brother Jim's voice filled the downstairs. "Right, pilgrim! Right, according to the New Testament which fulfills the Old!"

Silence. Then: "Anger, distrust, violence—all transgressions against God's laws are indications that self-control has failed to work. The same goes for government, as I would hope our brethren have learned. It is easier to explode a cannon than to form an opinion," Tobias said in a voice that went with a long face.

"And easier to spew out venomous words than bridle the tongue."

The rabbi responded with a soft moaning in Hebrew. "I mourn for those not versed in the law," he concluded.

"As do I—as do I—" Brother Jim retorted. "But law, like the Sabbath, is for man—else none of us would taste eternity. Without law, granted we would be lost both ways, but there is no way to keep it without the help of love, the door which only Jesus can open."

Again the silence. And again, it was broken by Tobias. "Building up, not tearing down made this country great, tamed the wilderness, and tamed the hearts—"

Tobias Epstern's voice trailed off but did not stop. Courtney unashamedly strained her ears to hear more. The two men, devoutly dedicated to God (so narrowly and yet so vitally separated), were speaking of recent events. And as they so often did, they were addressing their religious views. And yet, she was certain that they had gone from the abstract to the concrete even before she heard mention of Blessing's name, and then Yada's.

"Yada knows that the pen is mightier than the sword," Tobias' voice droned on in higher-pitched volume. "He has mastered the spirit of the Good Book, Brother Jim. The lad knows that the words herein (there was a rustle of pages) can conquer in battle—either that raging within himself or any conflict within the flock. He is a still-water-runs-deep person, a born thinker—as is the Desmond young lady. Thank you for your patience and support. Little Blessing needed to know the background before deciding, just as Yada did. They know that truth goes beyond tradition and is more than the ritualistic lighting of candles on the menorah for Hanukkah or setting up the nativity scene at Christmas. It is enlightenment within the heart."

"Amen, dear friend, *amen!* Out of the mouths of babes—as those blessed children have seen it!" Brother Jim's voice sounded as if he were dancing. Then, as if to himself, he speculated: "As I suspect, you are seeing the inner light."

Tobias made no reply.

*What could it mean?* One thing was certain. The conversation revolved around the two pairs of parents in the upper room. God surely would bring a revelation, Courtney felt, as—without a word—she stepped forward, knelt at the hearth, and pressed her cheek to the warmed-brick altar. Instantly Clint was at her side, and then Roberta and Efraim. Hands clasped, their lips moved in silent prayer. Some groanings were too deep for utterance.

---

The memory was to be borne back on memory's wings two years later when Rabbi Tobias Epstern stood on the brow of a little hill, looking over his shoulder to call "*Jehovah*-Shalom!"

*The Lord bring peace.* Yes, the peace that passes all understanding. But much was to happen before that farewell. Tobias' mission was not finished.

# CHAPTER 43

# Without Warning

❦

Why, Courtney wondered later, did one pray—only to be surprised when the answer came? "Thy will be done." Over and over she had said the words, as she went about the business of running the great house, "Welcome Acres," in much the same manner Arabella Lovelace had managed Mansion-in-the-Wild. Cousin Bella, too, must have prayed often; but, Courtney realized with a pang of guilt, the woman's indomitable spirit was as invincible as the rugged western frontier. With surprising simplicity, Courtney prayed and then folded the matter away like last week's line-dried laundry. If garments were to become unfolded and soiled without use, why bother? God would provide in His way, in His time. In short, she *believed*. There were no surprises.

"Well, I am working on it, Lord," Courtney said as she inspected the dining room the night of Kenney's party. "Certainly, You have provided me with enough examples!"

Tonight's reason for celebration was another of those examples. Despite the many prayers she had sent up for guidance on Kenney's higher education, Courtney was to be surprised (startled actually) when, without warning, Miss Lizzie received notice that her services would be needed without interruption when the public *high school* opened in the fall—right between East and West (knitting Old Town and New Town together). The name, appropriately, would be New Hope High—and Kennedy Desmond would be a member of the first class! An added blessing was the inclusion of a special science department. So tonight indeed was special—so special that Jonda and Jordan, busy as they were, would interrupt their tours and be home with the "family." That included the immediate family, plus Brother Jim and Miss Lizzie, Tobias Epstern, Roberta, Efraim, and Yada, of course, and (at Blessing's request) Editor William Jennings and his son, Tad. Courtney wondered briefly why and then went into action, letting excitement take over in her heart, praising God for His guidance of Kenney.

Now she stood admiring Donolar's centerpiece, glad that he had chosen daffodils instead of the apple blossoms. The golden trumpets flooded the dark room with sunshine. Although it was spring, some of the late-April days insisted on wearing a gloomy face. Pushing the heavy brocade drapes aside, Courtney took a moment to drink in the glory of the climbing red roses Donolar had wound around the white fence surrounding his Isle of Innisfree. At the last moment he planned a surprise, he said—something, she suspected, to do with roses.

She was right. But his surprise came after another, far larger surprise, making the head wreaths his creative fingers had woven anticlimactic.

Greetings were emotional, with the twins dominating the scene briefly. There was so much for them to tell. As Mandy tried to hurry the diners to the festive dining room before the chicken pies and wild mustard got cold, everybody knotted around the prodigals to demand reports. The golden twins, animated with happiness, graciously answered questions...yes, it was true, the two of them *were* to begin work together as a brother-sister team. Travel? Yes. Concerts? Yes. And (surprise, surprise!) an engagement off Broadway in New York! *But* (tactfully) they were famished, and only Mandy's cooking would fill the bill. There followed a flurry of candlelighting, Brother Jim's fervent prayer, and mountains of food. Courtney's cup overflowed as, with a heartful of gratitude and pride, she leaned back to feast her eyes on her loved ones as talk flowed around her.

The spirit of learning was alive and doing well, they said. Maybe Jonda and Jordan would wish to consider starting a music department in Willamette University, oldest university in the West, you know—yes, still growing, and Kenney planned to enroll once he finished at New Hope. Books had been important here from the beginning, according to Widder Brown.

Brother Jim chuckled. "She vows—and I'd say the Widder's as truthful as they come—that her first husband's parents called his 13 family members together for a solemn discussion as to which they ought to spend the first winter's wheat money and the good lady of the house's egg money on—a new roof or a set of books, including the Bible. Decided on the books, of course, and read 'em in the rain!"

"All the others—schools, that is—were founded by churches," Clint offered. "Aunt Bella's ancestors brought the educational method from the East. Nobody wanted government help on account of taxation."

Tobias listened intently before asking which churches took on the responsibility.

"Let's see—" Brother Jim yanked an ear in concentration, "Methodists—or was it Congregationalists and Presbyterians?—after the friars brought the missions. Then Episcopalians and Baptists fit in there somewhere after those 12 sisters of the Order of the Holy Names of Jesus and Mary came down from Canada—and the Friends—"

The rabbi shook his head. "Hard to understand—" he began.

"It's called freedom of religion," Donolar broke in quietly.

"Guaranteed by the Constitution," Kenney cinched it.

Talk turned to the other hard-won freedoms, which shaped the conversation for a babble of reporting voices, details the twins were hearing for the first time regarding recent local struggles to preserve those freedoms.

Then, exhausted from talk, the group *oh'd* and *ah'd* over Mandy's seven-layer curd cake and green apple pies.

It was proper, Courtney knew, for the hostess to continue eating until her guests completed their meal, but would Brother Jim ever reach that point? Roberta patted a yawn, but Brother Jim took no notice. Instead, between forkfuls of pie which floated like an island in a sea of Jersey cream, he began another topic, one Courtney had planned to reserve for the Big Moment.

The new school—and Kenney's graduating at the top of his class!

Talker that he was, Kenney was good for two hours. When at last he slackened his speed, Clint took advantage and suggested the library for coffee. It was then that Courtney realized Donolar's surprise did not materialize. Was there something she had missed?

Pulling her chair from the table, Clint leaned down. "You will feel better after coffee, sweetheart," he whispered in her ear.

Dear Clint. Dear wonderful husband. Courtney gave him an appreciative smile and busied herself making all comfortable around a sleep-inducing fire.

Then, without warning, all thought of sleep was gone!

Brother Jim whispered something to Tobias who, in turn, whispered the message in Yada's ear. The boy nodded solemnly. Small details, but Courtney was to remember them later—even Efraim's picking up the nut bowl that Mrs. Rueben set on the hearth, cracking a walnut, and pressing half the rich meat between Roberta's lips. And Donolar had disappeared. Where—

Brother Jim cleared his throat. "Yada has an announcement," he said.

Yada stood soldierly-tall and without hesitation said, "I have decided to become a minister," he said, "and—" he turned to Clint, "I wish to ask for your blessing."

"My *what*—my *who*? You mean—?"

"Yada means both, Daddy," Blessing said, threading her hand through Yada's.

# CHAPTER 44

# Two Crowns of Roses

❦

Courtney had no clear memory of what happened next. All was bedlam. Roberta choked on her walnut meat. Efraim dropped the walnut dish, sending the nuts bouncing all directions. And everybody talked at once. Tobias' deep bass voice rose above the others, but Courtney failed to hear a word he said.

Why, these two were children—just children—and they were asking consideration on such momentous matters? The world spun off its axis and she felt that surely she was about to be ill.

Certainly, she had no clear memory of Donolar's reappearance, although he must have placed the crowns of red rosebuds on the heads of both Blessing and Yada. At least Blessing was wearing hers when she came into her parents' bedroom what seemed like an eternity later—and, admittedly, with more poise than her mother possessed. Yada, walking straight-shouldered between Efraim and Roberta, wore poise which matched. Somewhere a clock struck. Then came the sound of laughter. Otherwise, she would have been certain that it was a dream as she closed the door behind her daughter and, stalling for time, saw it change shapes, then right itself to proper proportions only to change from dark walnut to a rainbow of colors. . . .

When the colors dissolved, Courtney saw that Blessing had seated herself at Clint's feet. Her legs, longer than Courtney had realized, were crossed childishly, but there was a disarming maturity about the sober, upturned face.

"Are you stern with me, Daddy?"

Clint looked down at her tenderly. "Not stern, darling—just surprised and—"

"Embarrassed?"

Courtney's heart went out to them both. A child begging to be understood. And a father who *did* understand and yet was struggling with words to say what must be said.

Blessing said them for him. "I know you think we are too young. We know that, too. But Daddy, we have always been so open, so able to talk, and I—I insisted that you and Mother, Uncle Efraim and Auntie Ro must know. It will be a long, long time, but if families arranged marriages like they once did, tell me—would you have looked farther than your *own* family?"

Clint met the great, pleading eyes squarely. "Truthfully, no. But Blessing, that is hardly the question. It is a matter of timing. How can you ask our permission for something you yourself may have outgrown in, say ten years? Even five."

"How can one fall out of love? I have always loved Yada."

"What about Tad?" Courtney asked lamely.

"Tad will always be my friend. But I love Yada."

"Odd," Courtney mused aloud, "I would have supposed it to be the other way around." Then something within her bristled. This talk was preposterous. Somehow in her sweet manner, this extraordinary child had placed both her parents on the defensive. And, yes, mention of an *arrangement* opened an old wound. "Parents do *not* arrange marriages."

"I know," Blessing whispered with surprising reverence. "God does."

———————————

Brother Jim and Tobias stayed tactfully out of the way

in the months to come. Did they expect suggestion of a sunrise duel, or were they allowing time for objective thinking and family caucuses?

Caucuses they got. Courtney and Clint grew closer together than ever before, once they were in control of their emotions. After all, deep down they should have expected this. What were the children asking that was new? At least it was what they had prayed for—indirectly.

"Actually," Clint said, "God has answered our prayers without our help! Yada's decision to enter the Christian ministry is proof that he listened for God's voice more carefully than we adults did. He has had exposure to the entire Bible and put the law of love above all others." His voice took on excitement. "The boy could fill any pulpit where he is needed, bringing to it an intelligence born of faith—and yet, he knows the ways of the Indians and their beliefs. Possibilities are endless. I can foresee gradual conversion through gentle persuasion...Jewish Christians...pagan Christians—are there such?"

Courtney felt a revival within herself. "And such a man would have need of a devoutly Christian wife," she said slowly, just before Clint pulled her to him. Another door had opened to let tenderness in.

It was easy to talk with Roberta and Efraim after that. There must be ground rules, of course. Doors closed, and doors left open.

"But it all makes sense, once Blessing is of age, Yada is out of seminary—and have you forgiven me, Courtney?" Roberta asked haltingly.

"Forgive you, Ro?"

"Oh Courtney, my dear, dear Courtney. Please never entertain the idea that I instigated this—that I held you to that silly half-promise about our children. I tried to run the lives of Efraim and Yada—"

It was good to hear Efraim laugh again. "Have you ever known my wife to fail at *anything*?"

# CHAPTER 45

# Love with Honor

❧

Summer came in wearing golden robes—the kind that promise a season of abundance, and long, languid evenings filled with katydid songs. Brother Jim and Rabbi Epstern rejoined the group to express conviction that Blessing and Yada knew exactly what they were doing.

"Their hearts belong to God and they will remain steadfast to His laws," Tobias said, his voice mixing pride with humility. "Right, good brother?"

"Amen to that!" Brother Jim replied. "There will be no bending of the Holy Word. 'Love with honor' is how Yada says it."

Courtney's brown eyes met Roberta's amber-spoked ones. There were tears in both. *Love with honor. How beautiful....*

There was only one further mention of the matter.

"Miss Lizzie, you know a lot about children. Why would Blessing have complained because Yada was so polite—so proper? I would think his manners would please her," Courtney said uncertainly.

The teacher laughed. "His manners pleased Blessing, too. Just one of the many reasons for hero-worshiping him from the beginning. But, you see, pulling hair ribbons, untying sashes, and poking young ladies with pencils are most boys' ways of showing admiration. Yada never teased, and she found that alarming. Her reaction was to turn to Tad." Miss Lizzie paused to laugh and wipe her pinch-on eyeglasses, "It was her way of re-belling. It worked. Remember Yada calling him 'Tad-pole'?"

---

Fall made good the promises of summer. Mandy and Mrs. Rueben canned enough for a nine-month blizzard. Instead, the winter was mild. Azaleas and rhododen-drons, handsome with white, pink, and rose-purple blossoms, painted the hills—and became the Washing-ton state flower. Mandy moved the baby chicks outdoors a month early in spite of Mrs. Rueben's dire predictions that it was a false spring. Courtney, marveling at the miracle of renewal, allowed the children to remove their long underwear and changed to shorter sleeves herself as she grubbed happily in the petunia beds. But the greatest miracle, admittedly, had been Blessing and Yada's devo-tion to their studies. The world seemed to have returned to its rightful course.

The good weather held. On one of the bright, sunny days of leafy May, Roberta came to bring news of the castle. It had sold.

"The lawyers deposited the money (she named a siz-able amount) to a trust fund, to be divided equally among Yada, Kenney, the twins, and Blessing." Roberta tapped her front teeth with the end of her pencil, scrib-bled some figures on a pad, and looked at Courtney in amazement. "What with the trust left Yada from his natural mother's estate, Efraim and I have a rich son. This Tobias would consider God's favor, but it can rain on both the just and unjust. Oh Courtney, I am glad that our children know where their *real* treasures are—that their castle is in the sky!"

A ray of sunshine crept into the library window, preening before the wide mirror above the rolltop desk, to send a shower of rainbow hues dazzling across the carpet. How like the children: dancing with vitality, filled with affection and trust, heads in the clouds but feet firmly planted on the ground, reaching for sunbeams to create a more beautiful world for others until they, like the sun's reflection, returned to their Source. Yes, they were rich indeed. Very rich!

"What about the other castle, Ro? The garrison—"

"Confiscated by the government. Does it matter?"

"Not in the least. The past is gone. But what a glorious future!"

---

The next two years were to see fulfillment of virtually all the valley folk had prayed for. The serpent of prejudice appeared to have crawled away. Revelers sought more fertile ground—an environment where saloons and painted women were in good supply. Gold-hungry stragglers straggled elsewhere as, one-by-one, mines shut down and Washington became the agricultural state that nature intended. A gaunt, hollow-cheeked man who gave very little impression of being alive, came from the nation's capital, sat immobile through a council meeting, and gave blanket approval to Mayor Clint Desmond's proposal that a good stand of timber be allowed to remain. This meant placing some restrictions on homesteading, which meant that a petition was needed. Enough signatures were garnered and they, rather than the witless man's efforts, won favor in the eyes of Congress, all but guaranteeing his re-election. But more importantly, it guaranteed the preservation of the state's natural resources for future generations.

Bumper crops propelled Washington to its rightful status in the Union. Soaring wheat profits, combined with the newspaper, the bank, and the one remaining Kennedy mine, elevated the Desmonds and Glamoras' rank to undisputed leaders at the dawn of a more restful new era. Roberta and Efraim had fewer clients in the changed atmosphere, which gave them more time for community service and church work. The age of violence past, Brother Jim found less need to get himself all lathered up in the pulpit. Instead, he softened voice and word, little knowing that one day he would be quoted widely, considered great for his time.

The frontier man who knew the sinking sands of struggles and hardship (one newspaper wrote) taught the pioneers that there was a foundation beneath the shifting ground of despair. That foundation was God's gift of love, His Son who was beaten, spat upon, and crucified not because of His wrongdoing, but because of mankind's. So let the storms come! Watch other foundations shake, rattle, and collapse. God's foundation would stand where there was faith and love—*if* love moved one toward tolerance, acceptance, and respect. More than fondness, sentiment, or passion, love was caring and forgiving, yanking others by the hair if need be to bring them from the caves of darkness into the sunlight as God has rescued him. There must be HONOR WITH LOVE. . . .

# CHAPTER 46

# Through the Shining Door

❦

Time moved too swiftly. This Courtney thought as Blessing and Yada finished at Kennedy School—and again as Kenney completed New Hope High and prepared to enter Willamette University. It seemed like only moments later that Blessing and Yada were graduating from high school.

Dressing for Blessing and Yada's graduation, Courtney examined her face in the mirror. It seemed only yesterday that she and Clint had laughed at her horrified discovery of a single gray hair. The single hair (which Clint refused to let her pull) became a pencil-slim streak which widened with the years. In the glow of the lamplight, it was Cousin Bella's face she saw, a faint smile of pleasure playing at the corner of her usually stern face. The illusion passed and Blessing's floated into its place. So alike, all of them, tying the generations together.

"Why so sober, darling?" Clint, fumbling with his tie, inquired.

"Here, let me help," Courtney replied, laying down her hairbrush. "I was thinking that the time has come for me to pile my hair on top—"

"Never! You are my madonna as you are," he said softly, removing her fingers from his tie to kiss the tips.

She enjoyed the moment, then returned to the tie. "Clint—"

"Yes, my love?"

"Where do they go—the years? It is as if some invisible umpire were making the calls. We respond, make the plays, and the game is over."

Clint's reply was indirect, but beautiful. "Not the game, darling—time. We ask, 'Where do the used-up years go?' forgetting that life is not made up of measured years or months or days, but moments like this, spent with our mates, our families, friends, and our Lord. These are the treasures laid up in heaven. Time is God's gift to us. *How* we spend it is our gift to Him."

Time, then, was a giver, not a taker. Time was taking their children away, but it would bring them back.

Time continued to bring changes to the valley as well. Women Involved increased in membership, and members raised their voices an octave. They accepted offices in the church. They marched into offices of the sheriff and the marshal and demanded that the so-called "vigilance committee" be disarmed. Decent, God-fearing folks worked days and slept nights. They did not drape themselves in sheets and prowl around like ghosts escaped from a cemetery looking for recruits. Vigilantes, that's what they were—taking law into their own hands which was a heap different from citizens' rights to bear arms like they had learned from studying the Constitution. Officials agreed among themselves that it was healthier to face the outsiders than irate women swinging brooms. Afterward they conceded that it looked right nice on their record to have made a last-second rescue of what appeared to be a lost cause. These women were more quick-witted than previously thought.

Caught up in a state of euphoria, the women made use of their power. Mrs. Rueben, emerging from her language-barrier cocoon, said she felt as strong as "der Limburger, Liederkrantz, and Bratwurst vat was sent from der ole country." Not to be outdone, Mandy said the triumph caused her insides to rejoice "lack unto dat ah feels w'en de lid comes off'n a stubborn jar uv dill pickles." Cara Laughten, less timid now, felt "as stout as fresh-groun' coffee!" And so they tackled a bigger job.

The Board of Education hired two new teachers, both men, and got into a (supposedly) private squabble as to which of them should serve as principal. "Private" the meeting was not! Word reached the listening ears of Women Involved. They attended the meeting en masse and demanded that Miss Lizzie be promoted. She was more qualified, and didn't they claim to have shed the evil skin of prejudice? It was Roberta's art of gentle persuasion, borrowed from her courtroom victories, which cinched the matter.

"You men are a powerful body," she said sweetly, "and we know that you take your duties seriously. You are shaping the frontier—possibly pulling ahead of areas of this great country with longer histories. Now," Roberta leaned down to meet each eye in a head-on collision and lowered her voice as she had done as Portia in *The Merchant of Venice*, "would it not be satisfying for you to be the *first* august body to make such a momentous decision—giving proper status to a *woman*?"

The chairman sighed. "Men, I may regret this mightily, but I move . . ."

"All in favor say 'Aye!' " someone interrupted. And Miss Lizzie was in. Only later, did the ladies recall that they failed to consult *her*.

---

In the year that followed Miss Lizzie's appointment, Jonda and Jordan wrote frequently. Their letters, always spirit-lifting and filled with love, brought news of Jordan's having a Christian play published and Jonda's progress with an original Christmas opera entitled "Ophir"—news which pleased Tobias. Eyes closed, he drummed his fingers together and all but sang out: "A region mentioned in the Good Book as a source of gold in 1 Kings. We talked. She remembered."

Jonda remembered other matters as well. She made frequent mention of Blessing and Yada, asking for details on their plans. When would Yada complete seminary? *And when—?* Courtney always laid aside Jonda's letter at that point. *Give me time, Lord*, she prayed.

And then time was up. On borrowed wings, the years had slipped away. Yada graduated and was ordained ... Blessing received a degree which prepared her to teach art, with emphasis on great works in Christian art. *And now they wished to be married.*

"They have fulfilled all their promises to us," Clint told her gently. Courtney could only nod mutely. Blessing, her baby, would be leaving in only a short time ... and be gone perhaps for a long, long time, maybe thousands of miles. It was going to be painful, letting go. Clint's eyes were tranquil and reassuring like the blue vault of sky arching overhead. "It will be a wrench to have her go, my darling, but we are not losing her. Wherever the Lord takes her, she will be with us. We have brought up our children to be free thinkers—but how can they be, unless we grant them their independence?"

How wise Clint was. What a wonderful husband and father. He was trying to help her realize that Blessing did not belong to them—not even to Yada. She belonged to God who in His infinite wisdom had allowed her to bless their lives with earthly love as a foretaste of the everlasting glory of love to come. Until then, Blessing was to serve His purpose. And she, Courtney, must let her precious butterfly go as Roberta had surrendered her Yada—else they would return to the dark caves against which Brother Jim had cautioned. Love must keep her from making that journey out of the sunlight of His love. And meantime, all she wanted for Blessing was happiness. Happiness such as she herself had known. For a poignant moment, Courtney remembered her own wedding—the moment when Clint slipped the heirloom pearl on her finger with a look of consternation and delight.

Her heart turned an unexpected cartwheel. "Ours has been a perfect marriage, my darling—and yes, it is what I want for our child."

---

Does a mother ever remember her daughter's wedding? Blessing had wanted a home wedding. Weddings made a house a home, she said. And now, with June sunlight pouring through the living room windows, adding liquid gold to the yellow roses massed on an improvised altar, Courtney's heart could only record a rainbow seemingly arched above the tender scene. Cara adjusted Jonda's full-skirted turquoise satin maid-of-honor dress which matched her periwinkle eyes, gently scolding her own two giggling bridesmaid-daughters for stepping on the hems of their pale yellow dresses and then tying their crushed-velvet sashes which matched the maid-of-honor's gown. Misty-eyed, but steady of hand, Jonda adjusted the cap veil over Blessing's raven hair without envy.

"Oh, Blessing, sweet Blessing, you are a beautiful bride."

"And you will be too—someday," a radiant Blessing was saying. "Love will come—"

Jonda's beautiful face, so like Vanessa's, did not change expression. "It has, dear little sister—a long time ago—and like all love, it has inspired me to greater things. Be happy for me."

From downstairs, Miss Lizzie's fingers touched the ivory keys and soft strains of organ music floated up. Below stood the white-faced groomsmen—Jordan, Kenney, and Tad—with yellow rosebuds on their lapels. Brother Jim and a black-robed clergyman (*Tobias?*) floated in a sea of faces...a million surely....

Roberta squeezed Courtney's hand as they descended the stairs (Roberta in yellow that lit up her eyes, and

Courtney in pale blue that turned her hair blue-black). "I could laugh, cry, sing, dance—shout!" Roberta whispered.

Dear Roberta: beloved sister-in-law, friend, and mother-of-the-groom.

"Dearly beloved ..." and Clint was surrendering their daughter to a tall, breathtakingly handsome stranger. Yada: *To Know ... To Believe ...*

A radiance seemed to fill the room as Mr. and Mrs. Yada Glamora turned to greet those gathered in the name of love....

Such a beautiful wedding, valley women would tell their grandchildren. Who would have thought in the old days that a Protestant minister and a Jewish rabbi could breathe the benediction over a couple with such loving fellowship? A few things were peculiar-like—Latin was it, or Hebrew language that the rabbi used?—and the groom able to answer as if he understood. Then surely there was some significance to the toast followed by the groom's stomping right down on the stemmed water glass, hoping to shatter it—which he did. And it was odd how those two men broke bread together, dipping it in wine (berry juice beyond a doubt). It looked like the Lord's Supper, except that Jewish people don't celebrate with communion, do they? Still and all, Tobias was different, maybe a little unorthodox. Some said it was in remembrance of the Passover—could be. More bread, all fancy (Mandy refused to give out her recipe—said it was an Epstern family secret), was passed around so everybody could break off a little pinch—yes, strange, but sweet and touching. Nobody—guests, that is—ever knew who the old, old hunchback was, but the bride and groom sure made a fuss over her—bowed down to kiss her leathery skin as the old crone put a little flower in each of their hands and went into a kind of trance. She said something about listening for soft spring songs and the contented sighs that brought blessings from Rose Wind. It softened the heart somehow, just watching.

Oh, and there was one big laugh that broke the solemn ceremony. The bride should have known not to turn backwards to toss her bouquet. Those roses her Uncle Donny prepared came with such force, that they hit Tobias right in the face, they did! And so sudden-like that, taken aback, he up and caught the bouquet to protect himself. Oh, how the people laughed...a *man* catching the bridal bouquet! So *he* was to be married next? Even he laughed until he cried, and then he was right jolly during that sumptuous wedding feast.

---

"Did all go well?" Courtney asked Clint during a moment's respite in the receiving line.

"Beautifully," Clint said from the corner of his mouth as he pumped yet another hand. The crowd was thinning his eye noted, as he glanced at the two's and three's still huddling in small groups on the lawn by the hitching posts. Then his gaze settled on his wife, so girlishly trim in her blue gown, her dark hair shining in the mellow glow of lamplight, the uptilted brows arched fetchingly above the brown-velvet eyes, and cheeks rosy with hours of excitement.

Courtney met his gaze and saw what she wanted to see: appreciation, approval, and exultation—eyes smiling along with his lips. "Yes, beautifully—the way you have managed this house, brought up our family, and especially my heart!" his voice rang with sincerity.

Unaccountably her heart commenced to sing. Where once there had been doubts that she could carry on tradition, there was now complete assurance that God would see her through no matter what lay ahead. No longer would life flicker like a candle in the breeze. It would glow steady and warm with love and anticipation.

"I wish Cousin Bella could know," she said softly.

"She always knew. Let's get out of here!"

Giggling like runaway children, the two of them stepped onto the side balcony over which a full-faced silver moon sailed. "Soon Welcome Acres will be jam-packed with grandchildren, and that will complete my aunt's dream. Until then," he said, taking her tenderly into his arms, "I want you all to myself once more. Just honor my graying temples and be my bride again."

---

All the children were gone—as was summer. The blazing heat of August gave way to chrysanthemum-filled autumn and what Mandy called "blanket-pullin' nights." And now Tobias was going, too.

His work was finished here, the gentle man said. He had basked in the warmth of God's favor and seen all his prayers of supplication answered. Rose Wind had been versed in the law according to his commitment, and he had carried out her dying wish that her son have the same knowledge. Both had chosen a way no longer foreign to him. If they were right, surely God in His lovingkindness would reveal the proper path of righteousness for himself. At least he had a message that others should hear while there was time. He was weary of praying against enemies, more inclined to pray *for* them.

There had been an unhappy period when he had had to testify in court against the transgressors who would have thrown the Christians to the lions without his help. He had no real compunction about putting away the murderers, but was happily surprised to note that some of the blind followers had suspended sentences and another chance. And as for the weaklings, what did it matter? Stripped of their vanity, robbed of the evil imag-inings of power, they were as grass that withereth....

Courtney and Clint wanted to have a farewell party at Welcome Acres, inviting the valley folk who had grown so fond of Tobias. But he declined in favor of a "family dinner" (strictly *kosher*, he grinned). So here they sat inhaling fragrances from Donolar's Autumn Glory roses mingled with Mandy's chicken and dumplings, Indian corn pudding, and deep-dish apple pie. All those present and accounted for: Desmonds, Glamoras, Brother Jim, and Miss Lizzie were wondering privately how the pious-to-a-fault rabbi would react to Mrs. Rueben's passing the loaf (for which Mandy vowed "dat woman" had stolen the recipe) to be tasted in farewell gesture.

After words of appreciation and praise, the group fell strangely silent. It was the end of an era. A special part of them would be gone. Only Brother Jim seemed unaware of an awkwardness. Something was on his mind, where nothing ever remained without vocal release.

"Well, my friend, have you given thought to your obligation?"

Tobias blotted his beard with his crisp linen napkin, folded it as if he would be returning, then crumpled it as a sign of departure. "I have—and, while it is true that I am a lonely old man, I must be sure that my actions are not self-serving."

"Self-serving! Why, the Good Book spells it out plain as day in divers laws and ordinances. Need I remind you concerning widows? That, yes, I will quote: '. . . the wife of the dead shall not marry without unto a stranger; her husband's brother shall take her to him to wife.' Can this sister-in-law of yours cook?"

Courtney suppressed a smile, pressing her own napkin firmly to her mouth, then letting it drop in surprise at Tobias' answer. "Lydia? She is the best of them all—barring Mandy here. In fact, that quality alone won my youthful heart, but—as you know, 'He who hesitates is lost'."

"Amen, my friend, *amen*! Try and remember that!"

"Good brother, I remember—taught as I was by my brother's boldness which made my Lydia his wife. And now that she is alone, I must go to comfort her, ease her loneliness—"

Brother Jim and Tobias fell onto one another's shoulders and sobbed emotionally. And then the rabbi, carrying a battered suitcase tied together with a rope, trudged up the hill with nary a backward glance. At the top he stopped, squared his shoulders, and waved a white handkerchief. *The white flag of surrender!*

Before Courtney's startled eyes, the white door of her dreams—behind which was the heavenly being—swung open. It closed behind Tobias, leaving a rainbow around her heart. A twilight-soft peace descended.

Brother Jim blew his nose. "He's no longer the leper of the colony in anyone's eyes," he said in awe.

"He never was in the eyes of God," Clint answered.

# *Devotionals by June Masters Bacher*

## QUIET MOMENTS FOR WOMEN

Though written for women, this devotional will benefit the entire family. Mrs. Bacher's down-to-earth, often humorous experiences have a daily message of God's love for you!

## THE QUIET HEART

In this all-new devotional by June Masters Bacher, each daily devotional begins with a suggested Scripture reading, and through anecdotes, poetry, and prayer inspires each reader to see life with a fresh perspective. A day-by-day "friend" that encourages a quiet heart so you can come to know God and learn how much richer knowing Him makes each day.

## MYSTERY/ROMANCE NOVELS

Echoes From the Past, *Bacher*
Mist Over Morro Bay, *Page/Fell*
Secret of the East Wind, *Page/Fell*
Storm Clouds Over Paradise, *Page/Fell*
Beyond the Windswept Sea, *Page/Fell*
The Legacy of Lillian Parker, *Holden*
The Compton Connection, *Holden*
The Caribbean Conspiracy, *Holden*
The Gift, *Hensley/Miller*

## PIONEER ROMANCE NOVELS

Sweetbriar, *Wilbee*
The Sweetbriar Bride, *Wilbee*
Sweetbriar Spring, *Wilbee*
The Tender Summer, *Johnson*

## BIBLICAL NOVELS

Esther, *Traylor*
Joseph, *Traylor*

**Available at your
local Christian bookstore**

Dear Reader:

We would appreciate hearing from you regarding this Harvest House fiction book. It will enable us to continue to give you the best in Christian publishing.

1. What most influenced you to purchase *Gently Love Beckons*?
   - [ ] Author
   - [ ] Subject matter
   - [ ] Backcover copy
   - [ ] Recommendations
   - [ ] Cover/Title
   - [ ] _____

2. Where did you purchase this book?
   - [ ] Christian bookstore
   - [ ] General bookstore
   - [ ] Department store
   - [ ] Grocery store
   - [ ] Other

3. Your overall rating of this book:
   - [ ] Excellent  [ ] Very good  [ ] Good  [ ] Fair  [ ] Poor

4. How likely would you be to purchase other books by this author?
   - [ ] Very likely
   - [ ] Somewhat likely
   - [ ] Not very likely
   - [ ] Not at all

5. What types of books most interest you?
   (check all that apply)
   - [ ] Women's Books
   - [ ] Marriage Books
   - [ ] Current Issues
   - [ ] Self Help/Psychology
   - [ ] Bible Studies
   - [ ] Fiction
   - [ ] Biographies
   - [ ] Children's Books
   - [ ] Youth Books
   - [ ] Other _____

6. Please check the box next to your age group.
   - [ ] Under 18
   - [ ] 18-24
   - [ ] 25-34
   - [ ] 35-44
   - [ ] 45-54
   - [ ] 55 and over

**Mail to:** Editorial Director
Harvest House Publishers
1075 Arrowsmith
Eugene, OR 97402

Name _____

Address _____

City _____ State _____ Zip _____

**Thank you for helping us to help you in future publications!**